MW00627282

VI KEELAND

ISBN-10: 1-959827-25-1
ISBN-13: 978-1-959827-25-2

The Rivals
Edited by: Jessica Royer Ocken
Proofreading by: Elaine York, Julie Deaton
Cover Model: Tobias Cameroon
Photographer: Walter Chin
Cover designer: Sommer Stein, Perfect Pear Creative
www.perfectpearcreative.com
Formatting: Elaine York, Allusion Graphics, LLC
www.allusiongraphics.com

THE RIVALS
SINCE 1962

"Love me or hate me, both are in my favor.
If you love me, I'll always be in your heart...
If you hate me, I'll always be in your mind."

-Unknown

CHAPTER 1

Sophia

"Wait!"

The agent pulled the nylon belt across from one pole to the other and clicked it into place, blocking passage to the gate. She looked up and frowned, finding me barreling toward her with my wheelie bag dragging behind me. I'd run all the way from Terminal A to Terminal C and now huffed5 like a two-pack-a-day smoker.

"I'm sorry I'm late. But can I please board?"

"Last call was ten minutes ago."

"My first flight was late, and I had to run all the way from the international terminal. Please, I need to be in New York in the morning, and this is the last flight."

She didn't look sympathetic, and I felt desperate.

"Listen," I said. "My boyfriend dumped me last month. I just flew back from London to start a new job tomorrow morning—a job working for my dad, whom I don't get along with *at all*. He thinks I'm not qualified, and he's probably right, but I really needed to get the hell out of London." I shook my head. "Please let me get on that flight. I can't show up late on my first day."

The woman's face softened. "I've worked my way up to manager in less than two years with this airline, yet every time I see my father, he asks if I've met a man yet, not how my career is going. Let me make sure they didn't close the aircraft door."

I breathed a sigh of relief as she walked over to the desk and made a call. She came back and unlatched the belt barrier. "Give me your boarding pass."

"You're the best! Thank you so much."

She scanned the e-pass on my phone and handed it back to me with a wink. "Go prove your father wrong."

I rushed down the jetway and boarded. My seat was 3B, but the overhead compartment was already full. The onboard flight attendant approached, looking very unhappy.

"Do you know if there's room anywhere else?" I asked.

"Everything is full now. I'll have to ask them to gate-check it."

I glanced around. The seated passengers all had eyes on me as if I was personally holding up the plane. *Oh. Maybe I am.* Sighing, I forced a smile. "That would be great. Thank you."

The flight attendant took my bag, and I looked at the empty aisle seat. I could've sworn I'd booked a window. Double-checking my boarding pass and the seat numbers on the overhead, I leaned down to speak to my seatmate.

"Ummm...excuse me. I think you might be in my seat."

The man had his face buried in a *Wall Street Journal*, and he lowered the newspaper. His lips pursed as if he had the right to be annoyed when he was sitting in *my* seat. It took a few seconds for my eyes to make their way up to the rest of his face. But when I did, my jaw dropped—and the seat thief's lips curved into a smug grin.

I blinked a few times, hoping maybe I'd seen a mirage.

Nope.

Still there.

Ugh.

I shook my head. "You've *got* to be kidding me."

"Good to see you, Fifi."

No. *Just no.* The last few weeks had been shitty enough. This couldn't be happening.

Weston Lockwood.

Of all the planes, and all the damn people in the world, how on Earth could I be seated next to *him*? This had to be some sort of cruel joke.

I looked around for an empty seat. But of course, there were none. The flight attendant who hadn't been happy to take my bag appeared at my side, looking even more agitated now.

"Is there a problem? We're waiting for you to take your seat so we can push away from the gate."

"Yes. I can't sit here. Is there another seat somewhere?"

She planted her hands on her hips. "It's the only open seat on the plane. You really need to sit down now, miss."

"But..."

"I'm going to need to call security if you don't take your seat."

I looked down at Weston, and the asshole had the audacity to smile.

"Get up." I glared at him. "I at least want the window seat I'm supposed to have."

Weston looked at the flight attendant and flashed a megawatt smile. "She's had a thing for me since middle school. This is her way of showing it." He winked as he stood and held out his hand. "Please, take my seat."

I squinted so hard my eyes were nearly slits. "Just get out of my way." I tried to skirt around him without making body contact and slid into my window seat. Huffing, I jammed my purse under the chair in front of me and buckled my belt.

The flight attendant immediately started her pre-flight safety announcements, and the plane began to back away from the gate.

My asshole seatmate leaned over to me. "You're looking good, Feef. How long's it been now?"

I sighed. "Obviously not long enough, since you're sitting next to me at the moment."

Weston grinned. "Still pretending you're not interested, huh?"

I rolled my eyes. "Still delusional, I see."

Unfortunately, when my eyes slid down from the back of my head, I got a close-up look at the man I'd spent my entire life despising. It figured the jerk only got better looking. Weston Lockwood had been a hot teenage boy. That was impossible to deny. But the man sitting next to me was downright gorgeous. Masculine square jaw, Romanesque blade of a nose, and big, blue bedroom eyes the color of an Alaskan glacier. His skin was a rugged tan, and the corner of his eyes had little crinkles that—Lord knows why—I found sexy as hell. His full lips were surrounded by what looked like day-old stubble, and his dark hair could probably use a cut. But instead of looking messy, Weston Lockwood's style screamed *fuck you* to the corporate world of buzzer-tight, neat trims. Basically, he wasn't my usual type. Yet looking at the jerk made me wonder what had ever attracted me to my usual type to begin with.

Too bad he was a jerk. *And a Lockwood*. Though those two statements were actually redundant, since just *being* a Lockwood automatically meant you were a jerk.

I forced my gaze to the seat in front of me, yet felt Weston's eyes on my face. Eventually, it became impossible to ignore, so I huffed and turned back to him.

"Are you going to stare at me the entire flight?"

His lip twitched. "I might. It's not a bad view."

I shook my head. "Knock yourself out. I have work to do." Reaching underneath the seat in front of me, I grabbed for my bag. My plan had been to read up on The Countess hotel during the flight. But I quickly realized my laptop wasn't in my bag. I'd tucked it into the front compartment of my carry-on suitcase, because I'd assumed that bag would be in the overhead compartment. *Great.* Now my laptop was gate-checked. What were the chances it would be in one piece when I got it back—if it was even still in my bag at all when I retrieved it? And what the hell was I going to do to keep myself occupied on this flight? Not to mention, the meeting with The Countess lawyers was tomorrow morning, and I wasn't the least bit prepared. Now I was going to have to stay up most of the night to study the materials when I finally got to the hotel.

Awesome.

Just freaking awesome.

Rather than freak out, which would be my typical M.O., I decided I might as well get some much-needed sleep since I wouldn't be getting it tonight. So I closed my eyes and tried to rest as the plane took off. But thoughts of the man next to me kept me from relaxing.

God, I disliked him.

My entire family loathed his entire family.

As far back as I could remember, we'd been the Hatfields and McCoys. Our families' feud dated back to our grandfathers. Though, for most of my childhood, we'd also traveled in the same social circles. Weston and I attended the same private schools, often saw each other at fundraisers and social events, and even had mutual friends. Our family's homes on the Upper West Side were only a few blocks from each other. But just like our fathers and grandfathers, we kept as much distance as possible.

Well, except for that *one time.*

That one terrible, ginormous mistake of a night.

For the most part, I pretended it had never happened.

For the most part...

Except for every once in a while...

Every once in a blue moon...

When I thought about it.

It wasn't often.

But when I did...

Forget it. I took a deep, cleansing breath, pushing *those* memories out of my head.

That was the absolute last thing I should be thinking of right now.

But why the hell was he sitting next to me, anyway?

Last I'd heard, Weston lived out in Vegas. He ran his family's southwest-area hotels—not that I'd been keeping tabs on him or anything.

So what were the chances I'd run into him on my way to New York? I hadn't been to the east coast in at least six years now. Yet we wound up sitting next to each other, on the same flight, at the same time.

Oh!

Shit.

My eyes flashed open.

He couldn't be.

Please, Lord. Please don't let it be that.

I turned to Weston. "Wait a minute. Why are you going to New York?"

He grinned. "Take a guess."

Still not wanting to believe it, I held on to hope. "To...visit family?"

He shook his head, maintaining his arrogant smirk.

"Sightseeing?"

"Nope."

I closed my eyes, and my shoulders slumped. "Your family sent you to manage The Countess, didn't they?"

Weston waited until I opened my eyes before delivering the blow. "Seems like we're going to be seeing more of each other than just this short flight."

CHAPTER 2

Sophia

"Going the wrong way, Fifi."

I stepped off the elevator on the fourth floor, only to be greeted by Mr. Wonderful himself.

"Go away, Lockwood."

He stepped into the elevator I'd just exited, but reached forward and stopped the door from closing. Shrugging, he said, "Suit yourself. But there's no one in conference room four twenty."

I turned back. "Why not?"

"They moved the meetings to the hotel's attorney's office—downtown, in the Flatiron Building."

I huffed. "Are you kidding me? No one contacted me. Why did they move it?"

"Don't know. Guess we'll find out when we get there." Weston let go of the button on the panel and stepped back. "I'm leaving. You coming or what? They're not delaying the start time, and traffic's gonna be a bitch."

I looked back over my shoulder in the direction of the conference room. No one else was around. Sighing, I stepped into the elevator. Weston was behind me at the rear of the car, but the minute the door closed, he took a step forward.

"What are you doing?"

"Nothing."

"Well, move back. Don't stand so close."

Weston snickered, but didn't budge one bit. I hated that I noticed how good he smelled—a combination of a freshly chopped oak tree and something clean, maybe with a little leather thrown into the mix. The damn doors couldn't open fast enough. The moment they did, I darted out. I took off into the lobby and ran for the front door without looking back.

Forty minutes later, after an attempted cab ride that didn't make it more than half a block in ten minutes, followed by two hot-as-hell subway rides, the second of which smelled delightfully of freshly baked urine, I rushed into the lobby of the Flatiron Building.

"Can you tell me what floor Barton and Fields is on, please?" I asked the reception desk.

"Fifth floor." He pointed to a long line. "But one of the elevators is out today."

I was already late and didn't have time to wait. Sighing, I asked the security guard, "Where are the stairs?"

After climbing five very long flights of stairs in four-inch heels while carrying a leather bag full of files and my purse, I approached the double glass doors to The Countess hotel's law firm. The receptionist was helping someone, and two other people were ahead of me in line, so I checked the time on my phone. I really hoped they didn't start the meeting on time after moving it without notice. Then again, how could they? It had probably taken Weston just as long to get down here. When it was finally my turn, I approached the receptionist.

"Hi. My name is Sophia Sterling. I have a meeting with Elizabeth Barton."

The receptionist shook her head. "Ms. Barton is uptown for a meeting this morning. What time is your appointment?"

"Actually, our meeting was originally scheduled uptown at The Countess, but it was moved here."

The woman's brows drew down. "I saw her leaving as I walked in this morning. But let me double-check. Maybe she came back while I was getting coffee." She punched a few keys on her keyboard and listened through her headset for a minute before removing it. "She's not answering. Let me run back and check her office and the conference room."

A few minutes later, a woman in a suit walked out from the back with the receptionist. "Hi. I'm Serena, Ms. Barton's paralegal. Your meeting is uptown at The Countess today. In room four twenty."

"No. I was just there. That's where it was originally scheduled, but it was moved here."

She shook her head. "I'm sorry. Whoever told you that gave you the wrong information. I just called Elizabeth on her cell and confirmed. The 9AM meeting started almost an hour ago."

I felt heat rise from the bottom of my feet up to the top of my hair. *I'm going to fucking kill Weston.*

"I'm so sorry I'm late," I announced as I entered.

The woman sitting at the head of the conference table—who I assumed was Elizabeth Barton, The Countess's chief counsel—looked at her watch. Her face was stern. "Perhaps someone who was on time would be kind enough to fill you in on what you've missed." She stood. "Why don't we take a ten-minute break, and I'll answer whatever questions you have when we reconvene."

Weston smiled. "I'll be happy to fill Ms. Sterling in."

The attorney thanked him. She and two other men I'd never seen before walked out, leaving me alone with Weston. It took everything in my power not to blow my top—at least until she was out the door. Weston got up like he, too, was going to take a break and walk out of here unscathed.

Not a chance in hell.

I stood in front of the door so he couldn't get out.

"You *asshole!*"

He buttoned his jacket with a smug smile. "Didn't they teach you anything at Wharton? All's fair in love and war, Fifi."

"Stop calling me that!"

Weston picked imaginary lint off the arm of his overpriced suit. "Would you like me to fill you in on what you missed?"

"Of course I would, asshole. Because it's your fault I wasn't here."

"No problem." He folded his hands and looked at his nails. "Over dinner."

"I am *not* having dinner with you."

"No?"

"No!"

He shrugged. "Suit yourself. I was trying to be a gentleman. But if you prefer to go straight to my suite, I'm good with that, too."

I cackled. "You're out of your mind."

He leaned forward. Because I was blocking his way, I had nowhere to go. And I wasn't about to give him the satisfaction of flinching. So I stood my ground while the idiot *who still smelled delicious* brought his lips to my ear. "I know you remember how good we were together. Best *hate fuck* I ever had."

I spoke through gritted teeth. "I'm sure you've never had any other kind. Because no one in their right mind would like you."

He pulled his head back and winked at me. "Hold on to that anger. We'll make good use of it soon."

By eight o'clock that evening, I really needed a drink. This had been the never-ending day.

"Can I order food here, or do I need to get a table?" I asked the bartender at the hotel restaurant.

"You can order at the bar. Let me get you a menu."

He disappeared, and I settled onto a stool. Pulling a notepad out of my gigantic purse, I started to scribble down everything my father had said in the last twenty minutes. I used the word *said* loosely. Because what he'd actually done was scream at me from the minute I'd answered the phone. Not even a hello—he'd just started to rant, yelling question after question. Had I *done this yet* or *done that yet*, but never taking so much as a breath so I might actually get a few words in and answer.

My father *hated* that Grandfather had assigned me to look after The Countess. I'm sure he would have preferred my half-brother, Spencer, do it. Not because Spencer was competent in any way—make enough donations to an Ivy League school and they miraculously let anyone in—but because Spencer was his puppet.

So when my cell phone flashed Scarlett's name, I put my pen down for a much-needed break.

"Isn't it, like, one in the morning there?" I asked.

"Sure is, and I'm bloody knackered."

I smiled. My best friend Scarlett was just *so* British, and I loved every *knickers*, *knackered*, and *knob* that came out of her mouth.

"You have no idea how much I needed to hear your terrible accent right now."

"Terrible? I speak the Queen's English, my dear. You speak *Queens* English. Like, as in that dreadful borough stuck between Manhattan and Tall Island."

"It's *Long* Island. Not Tall Island."

"Whatever."

I laughed. "How are you doing?"

"Well, we hired a new woman at work, and I thought she might be a possible replacement for you as my only friend. But then we went to a movie last weekend, and she wore *leggings* with the outline of her thong showing through."

I shook my head with a smile. "Oh boy. Not good." Scarlett worked in fashion and made Anna Wintour look tolerant of a style faux pas. "Let's face it. I'm just irreplaceable."

"You are. So have you grown bored with New York and decided to return home to London yet?"

I chuckled. "It has been a trying twenty-six hours since I departed."

"How's the new job?"

"Well, on day one, I was late for a meeting with the hotel's attorney because the representative of the family that now owns the other part of the hotel sent me on a wild goose chase."

"And this is the family of the man who *fifty years ago* was boinking the woman who owned the hotel, at the same time your grandfather was boinking her?"

I laughed. "Yes." While it was a bit more complicated than that, Scarlett wasn't wrong. Fifty years ago my grandfather, August Sterling, opened a hotel with his two best friends—Oliver Lockwood and Grace Copeland. The story goes that my grandfather fell in love with Grace, and they became engaged to wed on New Year's Eve. The day of the wedding, Grace stood at the altar and told my grandfather she couldn't marry him, confessing she was *also* in love with Oliver Lockwood. She loved both men, and refused to marry either, because marriage was an act of dedicating your heart to one man, and hers was not available for only one.

The men fought over her for years, but ultimately, neither could steal half of her heart away from the other, and the three eventually went their separate ways. My grandfather and Oliver Lockwood became bitter rivals, spending their lives building hotel empires and trying to best each other, while Grace concentrated her efforts on building one luxury hotel, rather than a chain. All three were enormously successful in their own right. The Sterling and Lockwood families grew into the two biggest hotel owners in the United States. And though Grace only ever owned one hotel, the first that the three of them had started together, The Countess, with its sprawling views of Central Park, grew to become one of the most valuable single hotels in the world. It rivaled the Four Seasons and The Plaza.

Three weeks ago, when Grace died after a long battle with cancer, my family was shocked to find out she'd left forty-nine percent of The Countess to my grandfather and forty-nine percent to Oliver Lockwood. The other two percent went to a charity, one that was currently auctioning off their new ownership to the highest-bidding family—which would in turn give one of us a very important fifty-one percent controlling interest.

Grace Copeland had never married, and I saw her final act as a beautiful Greek tragedy—though, I guess to outsiders it seemed crazy to leave a hotel worth hundreds of millions of dollars to two men you hadn't spoken to in fifty years.

"Your family is nuts," Scarlett said. "You know that, right?"

I laughed. "I absolutely do."

We talked for a little while about her last date and where she was thinking of going for holiday, and then she sighed.

"I actually called to tell you some news. Where are you right now?"

"In a hotel. Or rather in The Countess, the hotel my family now owns part of. Why?"

"Is there alcohol in your room?"

My brows knitted. "I'm sure there is. But I'm not in my room; I'm at the bar downstairs. Why?"

"Because you're going to need it after I tell you this."

"Tell me what?"

"It's about Liam."

Liam was my ex. A playwright from West London. We'd broken up a month ago. Even though I knew it was for the best, it still caused an ache in my chest to hear his name.

"What about him?"

"I saw him today."

"Okay..."

"With his tongue down Marielle's throat."

"Marielle? Marielle who?"

"Pretty certain we both know only one."

You've got to be joking. "You mean *my cousin* Marielle?"

"The one and only. Such a twat."

I felt bile rise in my throat. How could she? We'd grown pretty close while I lived in London.

"That's not the worst part."

"What's worse?"

"I asked a mutual friend how long they've been shagging, and she told me close to six months."

I felt like I might be physically sick. Three or four months ago, when things had started to go south with Liam, I'd found a red Burberry trench coat in the back seat of his car. He'd said it was his sister's. At the time, I didn't have reason to suspect anything. But Marielle definitely had a red trench.

I must've been quiet for a while.

"Are you still there?" Scarlett asked.

I blew out a deep breath. "Yeah, I'm here."

"I'm sorry, love. I thought you should know so you aren't nice to that slag."

I'd been meaning to call my cousin, too. Now I was glad I'd gotten so busy.

"Thank you for telling me."

"You know I always have your back."

I smiled sadly. "I do know that. Thanks, Scarlett."

"But I have some good news, too."

I didn't think anything could perk me up after what she'd just told me. "What's that?"

"I fired one of my senior editors. I found out she'd been avoiding covering certain designers based on their race."

"And that's your good news?"

"Well, not really. The good news is that she had a ton of things on her schedule, and I'm going to have to work a gazillion hours to cover them."

"I'm thinking you don't get the meaning of good news, Scarlett."

"Did I mention that one of the gazillion things I'll have to cover is a fashion show in New York in two weeks?"

I smiled. "You're coming to New York!"

"That's right. So book me a room at that grossly overpriced hotel your granddaddy's dick now owns half of. I'll email you the dates."

After we hung up, the bartender brought me a menu. "I'll take a vodka cranberry, please."

"You got it."

When he came back to take my order, on autopilot I ordered a salad. But before he could walk away, I stopped him. "Wait! Can I change that, please?"

"Sure. What can I get you?"

Fuck the calories. "I'll have a cheeseburger. With bacon, if you have it. And a side order of coleslaw. And French fries."

He smiled. "Bad day?"

I nodded. "Keep the drinks coming, too."

The vodka cranberry went down smooth. As I sat at the bar, looking at the notes my father had spewed at me and thinking about my cousin Marielle screwing Liam behind my back, I started to get angry. My immediate reaction had been to feel hurt when Scarlett told me, but somewhere between the first vodka and the second I ordered, that shifted to pissed off.

My father can go to hell.

I work for my grandfather. No different than he does.

And Marielle has bad hair extensions and a nasally, high-pitched voice.

Fuck her, too.

And Liam? *Fuck him the most.* I'd wasted a year and a half of my life on that cardigan-wearing Arthur Miller wannabe. You know what? His plays weren't even that good. They were pretentious, just like him.

I gulped a quarter of my second vodka in one swallow. At least things couldn't get much worse. I suppose that was the bright side.

Though I'd thought that a few seconds too soon.

They absolutely could get worse.

And they did.

When Weston Lockwood sidled up and planted his ass on the bar stool next to mine.

"Well, hello, Fifi."

"So how have the last twelve years been treating you?"

Weston ordered a seltzer with lemon and sat looking at me, even though I stared straight ahead, completely ignoring his presence.

"Go away, Lockwood."

"Mine have been pretty good. Thanks for asking. After high school, I went to Harvard, though I'm sure you know that. Got an MBA from Columbia and then went to work for the family business. I'm a vice president now."

"Gee, should I be impressed that nepotism got you a fancy title?"

He smiled. "Nah. Plenty of other things to be impressed with. You remember what I look like naked, don't you, Feef? I've filled in nicely since eighteen. Whenever you're ready, we can go back to my room, and I'll treat you to a little looksee."

I turned and scowled. "I think you left out something important that happened over the last twelve years. You obviously had a severe head injury that left you living in a fantasy world and unable to read emotions on other humans."

The asshole wouldn't stop smiling. "Those who protest the hardest are usually trying to mask their true feelings."

I let out a groan of frustration.

The bartender walked over and set down the food I'd ordered. "Anything else I can get you?"

"Bug repellent for the cockroaches around here."

He looked around. "Bugs? Where?"

I waved him off. "Sorry. No. No bugs. I was just being funny."

Weston looked at the bartender sympathetically. "We're going to work on funny. She's not quite there yet."

The bartender seemed a bit confused, but left anyway. When I reached for the ketchup, Weston stole a French fry from my plate.

"Don't touch my food." I leveled him with a glare.

"That's an awful lot of food. You sure you want to eat all that?"

"What's that supposed to mean?"

"Nothing. Just looks like a lot of meat for your little frame." He grinned. "Then again, if I remember correctly, you like a lot of meat. You did twelve years ago, anyway."

I rolled my eyes. Lifting my cheeseburger, I sank my teeth in, suddenly completely starving. The jackass next to me seemed to find my chewing riveting.

I covered my lips with my napkin and spoke with a full mouth. "Stop watching me eat."

Not surprisingly, he didn't. Over the next half hour, I finished off my food and guzzled another drink. Weston kept trying to make small talk, but I continued to shoot him down. Then my bladder was full, and I didn't want to try to balance my oversized purse, laptop, and planner while I hovered over a public toilet. So I reluctantly asked the pain in the ass to keep an eye on my stuff.

"I'd love to keep an eye on your *stuff*."

I rolled my eyes yet again. As I stood, I wobbled a little. Apparently the alcohol had given me more of a buzz than I thought.

"Hey, be careful there." Weston grabbed my arm and held on tight. His hand was warm and strong and—*oh my God, I'm definitely tipsy thinking this*.

I tugged my elbow from his grip. "I slipped on my heel. I'm fine. Just watch my things."

In the bathroom, I relieved myself and washed my hands. Catching a look at my reflection, I noticed I had mascara smeared under my eye. So I wiped it off and ran my fingers through my hair—out of habit, not because I gave a shit what I looked like for Weston Lockwood.

When I returned to the bar, my nemesis was at least preoccupied with something other than me for a change. I took my seat and noticed my drink had been refreshed.

"Sugar waxing, huh?" Weston said without looking over at me. "How is that different from regular waxing?"

My face wrinkled. "Huh?"

He tapped his finger at whatever he was looking at on the bar in front of him. "Is the sugar edible? Like, after you get all buffed out, you're ready for some action? Or are there chemicals mixed in?"

I leaned in and squinted at what he was reading. My eyes widened.

"Give me that! You're such an asshole!"

The jerk had taken my daily planner, which had been sitting on the bar to my left, and helped himself. I grabbed for the book, and Weston held up his hands in surrender.

"No wonder you're so cranky. Your period is due in a few days. Have you ever tried Midol? Those commercials crack me up."

I shoved my planner into my bag and waved for the bartender as I yelled, "Can I please get my check?"

The bartender came over. "You want to sign it to your room?"

I lifted the strap of my bulky bag to my shoulder and stood. "Actually, no. Sign it to this *asshole's* room." I thumbed toward Weston. "And give yourself a hundred-dollar tip from me."

The bartender looked at Weston, then shrugged. "No problem."

With a huff, I took off toward the elevator bank, not waiting or giving a shit if Mr. Wonderful wasn't happy about paying the bill. Impatiently, I jabbed my finger against the button to call the elevator a half-dozen times. Whatever the alcohol had done to ease my anger, it now came roaring back with a vengeance. I felt like throwing something.

First at Liam.

Then at my father.

And twice at that asshole Weston.

Thankfully, the elevator doors slid open before I took my anger out on some unsuspecting hotel guest. I hit the button for the eighth floor and wondered if the minibar would have some wine.

"What the hell?" I pressed the button on the panel a second time. It illuminated, yet the car continued to sit there. So I jabbed my finger at it a third time. Finally, the doors started to glide closed. Just as they were about to shut completely, a shoe blocked them from closing.

A wingtip shoe.

Weston's smiling face was there to greet me when the doors bounced open.

My blood was near boiling. "So help me, Lockwood, if you try to get in this car, I can't be responsible for what happens to you. I'm not in the mood anymore."

He entered the elevator anyway. "Come on, Fifi. What's wrong? I'm just playing around. You're taking things way too seriously."

I counted to ten in my head, but it didn't help. *Fuck it.* He wanted to get a rise out of me? He was going to get one. The doors slid shut again, and I turned and backed him into a corner. Seeing my face, he at least had the decency to look a little nervous.

"You wanna know what's wrong? I'll tell you what's wrong! My father thinks I'm inept because I don't have an appendage dangling between my legs. The man I spent the last eighteen months with was cheating on me with one of my cousins. *Again*. I hate New York City. I despise the Lockwood family. And you think you can get away with anything you want just because you have a big dick." I jabbed my finger into his chest and punctuated each staccato word with another stab.

"I'm

Tired.

Of.

Men.

My father.

Liam.

You.

Every single fucking one of you. So leave me the hell alone!"

Frazzled, I turned back around and waited for the door to open, only to realize we hadn't started to move yet. Great. Just fucking great. I jabbed the button a few more times, closed my eyes, and took deep, cleansing breaths as we started to move. Halfway through breath three, I felt the heat of Weston's body behind me. He had to have moved closer. I continued to try to ignore him.

But the fucker *still* smelled good.

How the hell could that be? Whose cologne lasted for—what had it been now?—twelve hours? After the gauntlet run he'd sent me on across town this morning, I probably smelled like BO. It pissed me off that the *asshole* smelled...*fucking delicious*.

He moved closer, and I felt his breath tickle my neck.

"So," he whispered in a gravelly voice. "You think my dick's big."

I turned and scowled at him. While this morning he'd been clean-shaven, he now had a five o'clock shadow all along his chiseled jaw. It gave him a sinister look. The suit that hugged his broad shoulders probably cost more than Liam's entire sweater wardrobe. Weston Lockwood was everything I hated in a man—wealthy, good looking, cocky, arrogant, and fearless. Liam would hate him. My father already hated him. And at the moment, those were actually Weston's strong points.

While I struggled with my body reacting to his scent and how much I liked the stubble on his face, Weston slowly reached out and put a hand on my hip. At first, I assumed he thought he needed to steady me, as he had when I'd wobbled in the bar. Had I wobbled again? I didn't think I had. But I must've.

Though when his hand glided from my hip around to my ass, there was no misunderstanding his intention. He was *not* trying to help me stay on my feet. In my head, my immediate reaction was to scream at him, but somehow my throat felt too clogged to speak.

I made the mistake of looking up from his jaw into his blue eyes. Heat flickered, turning them almost gray, and his eyes dropped to my lips.

No.

Just no.

This was not happening.

Not again.

My heart thundered in my chest, and the blood in my ears roared so loudly I almost didn't hear the ding of the elevator announcing that we'd arrived at my floor. Thankfully it snapped me out of whatever moment of insanity I'd slipped into.

"I...I need to go."

It took all of my focus to put one foot in front of the other, but I managed to walk down the hall and make it to my room.

Though...

I wasn't alone.

Again, Weston was behind me. *Close. Too close.* I fumbled in my bag, trying to find my room key when a hand snaked around my waist and rubbed along the top of my skirt. I knew I needed to nip this shit in the bud, but my body reacted insanely to his touch. My breathing grew shallow.

Weston's hand traveled up my stomach and stopped at the underwire of my bra. I swallowed, knowing I needed to say something before it was too late.

"I despise you," I hissed.

Weston responded by cupping my left breast and squeezing hard.

"I despise you, and that thing you call a dick that is trying to flatter me with a half-ass, lame erection pushing against my ass right now."

He leaned closer and reached around to cup my other breast. "Feeling's mutual, *Fifi.* But I know you remember that thing I call a dick is a fuck of a lot bigger than the little playwright had tucked between his legs—the little playwright whose inadequate dick is probably buried inside your cousin right about now."

I clenched my jaw. *Fucking Liam.* "At least he didn't have diseases. You probably have every STD in the book from whoring around Las Vegas."

Weston responded by pushing his hips into my ass. His hot erection felt like a steel pipe trying to burst through his pants.

But, God, it felt good.

So hard.

So warm.

Twelve years ago came flooding back. Weston was hung like a horse, and even at eighteen, he'd known exactly what to do with it.

"Let's go inside," he growled. "I want to fuck you so hard that you have trouble sitting in our meetings tomorrow."

I closed my eyes. A battle waged within me. I knew it would be a colossal mistake to get involved with Weston, especially with the war raging between our families. But damn...my body was on fire.

It wasn't like we had to be friends.

Or like each other, for that matter.

I could just use him this once.

Get my rocks off and go back to keeping my distance tomorrow.

I shouldn't.

I definitely shouldn't.

Weston pinched my nipple, and a spark shot through me.

Fuck it.

Fuck Liam.

Fuck my father.

Fuck Weston. Literally.

"Ground rules," I rasped. "Don't kiss me. And only from behind. You don't come until after I do, or so help me God, I'll snap that thing between your legs right from your body. And you use a goddamned condom, because I don't want whatever you're currently on antibiotics for."

Weston nipped at my ear.

"Ouch!"

"Shut up. And I have some rules, too."

"Rules? What rules do you have?"

"Don't expect me to stay after. You come. I come. I leave. In that order. You don't talk, unless you're telling me how good my cock feels inside of you. And those pointy-as-fuck shoes you're wearing stay on. Oh, and if I make you come more than once, tomorrow you wear your hair *up*."

I was so aroused I couldn't even stop to think about what I was agreeing to. I just wanted it...wanted him. *Now*.

"Fine," I bit out. "Now get inside, and let's get this over with already."

Weston took the key out of my hand and opened the door. He guided me in, not very gently, and pushed me against the wall. We were barely inside, and my cheek was already pressed against the wallpaper.

"Take my cock out," he growled.

I hated being told what to do, especially by him.

"Am I supposed to be Houdini? I'll need to turn around to do that."

Weston's chest had been leaning firmly against my back, and he released some of the pressure, taking a half step back so I could turn around. I wrapped my hand around his thick, bulging erection through his pants and squeezed. *Hard*.

Weston hissed.

"Take your own cock out," I growled.

A wicked smile spread across his face. He reached down, unbuckled his pants, and yanked down his zipper. Then he grabbed my wrist and slid my hand into his boxers.

Oh God.

The smooth skin was so hot and hard. And *thick*. I'd never been so turned on in my life. Though I wasn't about to let him know that. Reining in the emotions sparking through me, I locked my eyes with his and gave him a rough jerk up and down.

Weston's eyes gleamed. He ran his tongue over his bottom lip and spoke with a strained voice. "We'll call it even for sticking me with the tab for your dinner and drinks."

My brows drew together. I wasn't sure what he was talking about until he grabbed my silk blouse with two hands and yanked. It ripped open, the fabric tore, and more than one button pinged against a wall somewhere.

"It's a four-hundred-dollar shirt, asshole."

"I guess I'll have to buy you more dinners then."

His big hands groped at my chest. He used his thumbs to push down the lacy fabric of my bra, and my breasts eagerly spilled over.

Weston pinched one nipple hard and studied my reaction. A jolt of pain shot through me, yet I refused to give him what he was looking for.

"Is that supposed to hurt?" I mocked.

He growled and dipped forward to suck my nipple into his mouth. One hand grabbed the hem of my skirt and bunched the fabric, yanking it up to my waist. "Are you wet for me, Fifi?"

If he actually wanted me to answer, he didn't give me any time. Before I could formulate a sufficiently sarcastic response, his fingers lifted the edge of my panties. They slipped beneath the fabric, and he stroked me up and down once, then unexpectedly plunged inside of me.

I gasped, and a look of primal satisfaction crossed Weston's face. The bastard had gotten what he wanted—to make me lose control and react. It somehow gave him the unspoken upper hand, and we both knew it.

"So wet." He pumped in and out of me once, then a second time. "You've been soaked since the plane, haven't you, you little tease?"

My body was so on edge, I thought it entirely possible that I could come just from his hand, which had never worked for me before. Not with Liam anyway.

Liam.

That bastard.

Fuck him, too.

My anger level rose in unison with my arousal. Unable to focus on anything other than the way Weston's hand was making me feel, I completely forgot that my hand was still wrapped around his erection.

I squeezed. "Get the goddamn condom out already."

Weston's teeth clenched. He dug into his pocket and managed to pull a condom out of his wallet with one hand. Lifting the wrapper to his teeth, he tore it open.

"Turn around so I don't have to look at you."

He withdrew his hand from between my legs and spun me to face the wall again.

I looked back over my shoulder. "This better be worth it."

He sheathed himself and spit the wrapper to the floor. "Bend." He pressed down on my back, folding me in half at the waist. "Hold on to that wall with two hands or your head's going to be banging against it."

He hiked up the back of my skirt, and his arm wrapped around my stomach as he hoisted me up to my toes. My hands were splayed against the wall, palms sweating with the anticipation, when a loud crack echoed through the room. I heard the sound before I felt the sting on my ass.

"What the—"

Before I could finish my sentence, Weston thrust inside of me. The sudden, rough motion knocked the air from my lungs. He'd buried himself to the root, and I had to force my legs wider to ease the twinge of discomfort it caused. I could feel Weston's hips, pressed against my ass, begin to shake.

"So tight," he grunted. "So fucking tight."

His hand shifted from my back to my hip, and his fingers dug into my skin. "Now be a good little girl and tell me it feels good, Fifi."

I bit my lip and struggled to control my breaths. It was the best thing I'd felt in ages, even with just that one simple thrust. But there was no way I was admitting that. "It doesn't. You know, screwing usually involves an in-and-out motion, not just standing there."

"Is that the way you want to play it?"

I leaned forward, pulling three quarters of the way off of him and then slammed back, sucking him in fully again. It caused the most exquisite pain to shoot through me. "Shut up and move," I told him.

Weston growled and grabbed a handful of my hair. Giving it a good, firm tug, he held on as he rocked into me once and then stopped. "Jesus, your ass jiggles a lot. I should make you do all the work so I can stand here and watch the show."

"*Lockwood!*"

"Yes, ma'am." He chuckled.

Though he finally shut the hell up and got to work. It was hard and fast, desperate and angry, yet it felt so damn good. I don't think I'd ever gotten revved up so quickly—certainly not in the last year and a half of Mr. Rogers *making love* to me.

That thought, the thought of *Liam,* channeled all my anger toward the man currently pummeling my insides. Even though Weston was already pounding into me, I started to move with him, meeting every thrust, blow by blow. When he slid one hand around to massage my clit, I lost it.

Orgasms were something I usually had to work for. Like driving a car around the track for the Indy 500, I hoped I made it before my partner ran out of gas. But not today. Today my orgasm was more like a crash before I'd even made it through the first lap. It hit me with an intensity I hadn't expected, and my body quaked as I let out a loud moan.

"*Fuck.*" Weston sped up his thrusts. "I can feel you squeezing my cock." He pumped once, twice, and on the third time let out a ferocious roar and plunged to a new depth. My body enveloped him so tightly I could feel the pulsations as he unloaded inside of me, even through the condom.

We stood that way for a long time, both of us panting and attempting to control our breaths. Tears prickled at the corners of my eyes. I'd been so pent up with anger and frustration the last month, and suddenly it felt like the cork had popped off, and it was all about to come flooding out. *Jesus. Great timing.* No way was I going to let Weston see the flood I felt approaching. So I swallowed the lump in my throat and did what luckily came natural to me whenever I was around him. I acted like an asshole.

"Are we done? If so, you can leave now."

"Not until you tell me how much you loved me inside of you."

I tried to stand, but Weston spread his fingers between my shoulder blades and held me down.

"Let me up!"

"Say it. Say how much you love my cock."

"I'll do nothing of the sort. Now let me go before I scream bloody murder and hotel security comes running."

"Sweetheart, you spent the last ten minutes screaming. If you haven't noticed, no one seems to give a shit." Yet he pulled out and helped me upright.

It would have been better if he'd pulled out and left me standing there for the cold air to replace his warmth. But instead, after he made sure I had my balance, he tugged down my skirt. "You good? I need to get rid of this condom in your bathroom."

I nodded and avoided eye contact. It was bad enough my emotions were hitting me hard. The last thing I needed was niceties from Weston Lockwood.

He went into the bathroom, and I used the moments alone to pull myself together. My hair was disheveled, and my breasts overflowed from my pushed-down bra. I fixed both and grabbed a bottle of water from the minibar while I waited for Weston to come out of the bathroom. I didn't have to wait long.

Trying to avoid whatever awkward goodbye would ensue, I stood near the windows on the opposite side of the room, gazing out at nothing in particular. I hoped he'd just wave and slither out.

Then again, a Lockwood never did what a Sterling wanted.

Weston walked up behind me. He took the water bottle out of my hand and drank from it, then wound a lock of my hair around his pointer finger. "I like your hair like this. It's longer than you wore it in high school. And it's wavy now. Did you used to make it straight?"

I looked at him like he was nuts. "Yes. I used to straighten it. And thanks for the reminder it's time for a haircut. I think I'll chop it all off."

"What color would you say it is? Chestnut?"

The confusion lines in my forehead deepened. "I have no idea."

He grinned. "You know your eyes turn from green to almost gray when you're angry."

"Did someone teach you your colors today in nursery school or something?"

Weston brought the water bottle back to his lips and sucked the rest of it down. He handed it to me empty. "Ready for round two?"

I continued to stare straight ahead. "There won't be a round two. Not tonight or ever. Get out, Lockwood."

Even though I'd been trying not to look at him, I caught his mouth curving into a smile in the window reflection.

"Care to wager on that?" he asked.

"Don't flatter yourself. I needed a release. You were here. At best you were adequate. This isn't going to become a habit."

"Adequate? For that remark, I'm going to make you beg next time."

I rolled my eyes. "Get out. This was a gigantic mistake."

"A mistake? Oh yeah, I forgot you like scrawny dudes who are into literature and shit. Would it help if I brushed up on some poetry and recited it while we banged next time?"

"Out!"

Weston shook his head. "Okay...but like Shakespeare said, *It's better to have fucked and lost, than never to have fucked at all.*"

I almost let a smile slip out. "I don't think that's exactly what he said. But close."

He shrugged. "Guy was a bore anyway."

"*Goodnight*, Weston."

"Such a shame. Using your own fingers to the memory of what I felt like won't be half as much fun as round two."

"You have delusions of grandeur."

"'Night, Feef. Great to see you again."

"The feeling *isn't* mutual."

Weston walked to the door. It creaked as he opened it, and I watched in the window reflection as he turned around and looked back at me for a few heartbeats. Then he was gone.

I shut my eyes and shook my head.

When I opened them, the last thirty minutes or so really hit me.

Holy crap. What the hell did I just do?

CHAPTER 3

Sophia

I'd totally screwed up.

And I needed to fix it. *Fast*.

Before anyone else found out, and before I put what I was here to do in any sort of jeopardy.

Weston walked into the conference room the next morning at exactly eight forty-five. Our meeting was to start at nine o'clock. He grinned like a Cheshire cat upon finding me already inside.

"Good morning," he said. "Beautiful day today."

I took a deep breath. "Sit."

He thumbed toward the door. "Should I lock it? Or do you want to keep things a little on edge—chance getting caught? I bet you'd like that, wouldn't you? Someone walking in while your skirt was hiked up and my—"

I cut him off. "Shut the hell up and sit down, Lockwood!"

He smiled. "Yes, ma'am."

The jerk thought we were role-playing. But I was anything but playing. As far as I was concerned, my job was on the line. I waited until he sat and then took the seat across from him on the opposite side of the conference table.

Folding my hands, I said, "Last night never happened."

A smug smile spread across his annoyingly handsome face. "Oh, but it did."

"Let me rephrase. We're going to pretend like nothing happened."

"Why would I do that when I can close my eyes at any time and relive the moment?" He leaned back in his chair and shut his eyes. "Oh yeah, this is one I plan to watch over and over again. That sound you made when you came all over my cock? I couldn't forget if I tried."

"Lockwood!" I barked.

His eyes flashed open.

I got up from my chair and leaned over the table. It was a big table, so I couldn't exactly reach him, but it made it easier to keep him focused.

"Listen to me. Last night was a mistake—one the size of Texas. It should never have happened. Aside from how much I dislike you, and how much my family and your family loathe each other, I'm here to do a job. And my job is very important to me. So I can't have you lurking around, making inappropriate comments for the staff to overhear."

Weston didn't break eye contact, but I could see the wheels in his thick head spinning. He rubbed his thumb against his lip and sat up in his chair. "Okay. We can pretend last night never happened."

I squinted. That was way too easy. "What's the catch?"

"Why do you think there's a catch?"

"Because you're a Lockwood, and a narcissistic asshole who thinks women are toys put on this earth for you to play with. So what's the catch?"

He adjusted the knot of his tie. "I have three conditions."

I shook my head. "Of course you do."

He held up his pointer. "Number one. I want you to call me Weston, not Lockwood."

"What? That's ridiculous. Why does it matter what the hell I call you?"

"It's what everyone calls my father."

"So?"

"If you'd prefer, you can call me *Mr.* Lockwood. I might actually enjoy hearing you call me that more." He shook his head. "But not Lockwood. It's confusing to the staff."

I guess he sort of had a point. Though there had to be more to it than that. Weston wasn't about to waste one of his three genie rubs to appease employees, that was for damn sure. But I could live with the request.

"Fine. What else?"

Weston lifted a hand and cupped it around his ear. "What else, what?"

I shook my head. "You said you had three conditions. What are the other two?"

He tsked. "You were missing something at the end of your sentence. You said, 'Fine. What else?' But what you should've said was, 'Fine, what else, *Weston*?'"

Ugh. It had sounded like such an easy thing to do. It wasn't like I always called him Lockwood; sometimes I used *asshole.* So it should be easy enough. Hell, I should be able call the asshole *Your Highness* and not flinch, yet calling him Weston now after he'd *told me to* just felt obedient.

"Fine," I gritted out between my teeth.

Again he cupped his hand to his ear. "Fine...what?"

"Fine, *Weston,*" I said with my jaw clenched.

He flaunted a gloating smile. "That's it. Good job, Fifi."

I squinted. "I have to call you Weston, and you're going to continue to call me Fifi?"

Ignoring me, he folded his hands on the table. "Number two. You'll wear your hair up at least twice a week."

"What??" I scoffed. "You're insane." Then I remembered last night he'd tried to get me to agree to a bet where I'd wear my hair up if he could give me two orgasms. I'd kicked him out after one, though. "Why do you give a shit how I wear my hair?"

He neatened a few files stacked on the table in front of him. "Do we have an agreement on number two or not?"

I thought about it. Honestly, did I give a shit if he had some nefarious reason for wanting me to call him Weston and wear my hair up? It wouldn't kill me, and he could certainly request much worse. "What's number three?"

"You'll have dinner with me once a week."

My entire face scrunched up in disdain. "I'm not going out with you!"

"Think of it as a business meeting. We're running a hotel together. I'm sure there will be plenty of things we'll need to discuss."

He had a point, yet the thought of sitting across from him and sharing a meal really made me feel unsettled.

"Lunch," I said.

He shook his head. "My conditions are not negotiable. Take it or leave it."

I growled. "If I agree to your ridiculous conditions, you have to keep your end of the bargain. You will *not* mention what happened last night—not to one of your stupid friends, not to a staff member, certainly not to any of your obnoxious family. My momentary lapse in sanity will be forever locked away in your birdbrain, never to be spoken of again."

Weston held out his hand. I hesitated for so many reasons. Though in the end, I was going to have to work with him for a while, and it was my idea to put everything behind us so we could move forward as professionals. And professionals *did* shake hands. So while every bone in my body told me to avoid him at all costs, I nevertheless placed my hand in his.

Like in a sappy romance movie, the jolt that ran through my body made every hair on my arm jump to attention. And my luck, the idiot had to notice.

He took in the goose bumps prickling on my skin and smirked. "Dinner at seven tomorrow evening. I'll let you know where."

Thankfully, our nine o'clock appointment knocked and put an end to our private discussion. The hotel's general manager opened the door. He walked to my side of the table first. "I'm Louis Canter."

"Sophia Sterling. It's very nice to meet you." We shook.

Louis then reached out to Weston, and the two men shook while Weston introduced himself.

"Thank you for coming," I said. "I know you usually work from eleven to seven, so I appreciate you arriving early so we can spend a little time before your busy day starts."

"No problem."

"I read that you're the longest-running employee at The Countess. Is that right?"

He nodded. "It is. Started when I was fifteen, doing odd jobs for Ms. Copeland and both your grandfathers. Pretty sure I've held just about every position there is to have here over the years."

I smiled and motioned to the chair at the head of the table, the one between Weston and me. "That's incredible. We're very lucky to have someone with so much knowledge and experience. Please, have a seat. We just wanted to discuss the transition and listen to any concerns you might have."

"Actually." Weston stood. "Something's come up, and I need to step out. I probably won't be back until this evening."

I blinked a few times. "What are you talking about? When did something come up?"

Weston spoke to the general manager. "I apologize, Louis. I'll catch up with you tomorrow. I'm confident you and Ms. Sterling will be able to handle anything that needs to be handled for the time being. Sophia can fill me in tomorrow evening on what I've missed."

Seriously? We had a half-dozen meetings scheduled with key employees today, the entire purpose of which was to assure people their jobs were safe, and everything would continue to run smoothly. Everyone knew the Sterlings and the Lockwoods despised each other, which made them extra nervous. And he decides to ditch the meetings? What kind of a message would that send? One of the new owners doesn't even have time for you?

"Umm..." I stood. "Could I speak to you a moment before you go, Lockwoo—Weston?"

He flashed a gratified smile.

I nodded toward the conference room door. "Outside in the hall." I turned back to Louis. "Excuse me for just one minute, please."

"Take your time."

Once we were in the hall, I looked around to make sure no staff were in the vicinity. Planting my hands on my hips, I attempted to keep my voice down. "What the hell? We have a full day of meetings. What's so important that you're ditching?"

Like he'd done last night, Weston wrapped a lock of my hair around his finger and gave it a firm tug. "You can handle it, Fifi. You're a people pleaser. I'm sure you'll have all the staff feeling like the old bat kicking the bucket was a good thing by the time you're done."

I slapped his hand away from my hair. "I'm not your secretary. What you miss is your problem. Don't expect me to report back to you."

In response, the jerk winked. I freaking hated winkers. "Have a good day, beautiful."

"Don't call me that!"

And just like that, Weston Lockwood walked away.

The man made me nuts. Good riddance to the jerk.

I definitely didn't need him in the meetings.

I definitely was better off without him.

In fact, come to think of it, the only place the jerk was useful was in the bedroom.

And I wouldn't be making that mistake again.

That was for damn sure.

I settled back in for my meeting with Louis.

"So, as you know, the hotel is now owned by the Sterling and Lockwood families," I said. "Each family owns a forty-nine percent share, and two percent is owned by a local charity Ms. Copeland supported here in the City."

Louis smiled fondly. "Easy Feet."

I nodded. "That's right."

The charity Grace had left a two-percent stake to was an interesting one—run by one man with an annual budget of less than fifty-thousand dollars. The two-percent stake in The Countess was worth probably a hundred times that annual budget. No wonder the guy had been so anxious to sell his stake to one of us.

"Did Ms. Copeland have a personal reason for such a large donation to that charity? Not that it isn't a great organization, but it's pretty specific."

Louis leaned back into his chair and nodded. His eyes were warm as he spoke. "Leo Farley. He works in housekeeping."

The name didn't ring a bell. "An employee got her interested in the charity?"

"About six years ago, Leo was homeless. Long story, but he'd had a rough year. Lost his job, wife died, got evicted from his apartment, daughter committed suicide—all within the span of a few months. He sometimes slept in the alley around the corner, right next to the hotel's service entrance. Ms. Copeland went out for two walks a day, like clockwork at ten AM and three PM, just a few blocks each time. One afternoon, she ran into Otto Potter outside, and he was treating Leo's feet."

"Otto Potter is the guy who runs Easy Feet?"

Louis nodded. "That's right. He's a retired podiatrist. A lot of homeless people have trouble with their feet—untreated diabetes, walking around not wearing shoes, infections—all sorts of issues. He started Easy Feet to help the people here in the City who weren't walking on Easy *Street*. He and a few other volunteers go around and treat guys like Leo, right on the street."

"But Leo works here now?"

"Ms. Copeland took a liking to him. Once his feet got better, Leo started walking with her. Eventually she offered him a job. He's been employee of the month more times than any other employee. Works hard."

"Wow. That's a great story."

Louis smiled proudly. "Got plenty of 'em when it comes to Ms. Copeland. She was a real good person. Very loyal."

Considering what she'd left to the two men who'd once loved her, I'd say that was an understatement. It was good news for me, because loyal employers usually meant loyal employees, and I was hoping for smooth sailing while stuck here overseeing the hotel and protecting my family's interest.

Steering our conversation back to the reason for our meeting, I lifted a pen from on top of the notebook I'd brought. "So, tell me about the operations at The Countess. Is everything running smoothly? Are there any issues or concerns you'd like to point me to as I become familiar with how things run?"

Louis pointed to my pad. "Good thing you brought that notebook."

Uh-oh.

"First, there's the looming strike."

"Strike?"

"Ms. Copeland was generous and loyal, but she also kept the reins very tight when it came to managing things. I'm the hotel's manager. I oversee all the day-to-day operations, but she personally handled the business aspect of things. She was sick for a long time, and some of the things that needed handling didn't get handled."

I sighed and wrote down: *Strike*. "Okay, tell me all the details you know about the union issues."

Forty minutes later, I had six pages of notes on just the first problem.

"Anything else?" *Please say no.*

Louis frowned. "I'd say the next biggest problem is the double-booked weddings."

My brows rose. "Double-booked weddings?"

He nodded. "I'm sure you know, The Countess is one of the most in-demand venues for events."

"Yes, sure."

"Well, we have two ballrooms. The Grand Palace and The Imperial Salon. They book up to three years in advance."

"Okay..."

"About two years ago, we started to take reservations for The Sundeck. It's an exact replica of The Imperial Salon but also with a private rooftop sundeck."

"I didn't realize there was a rooftop sundeck."

He shook his head. "There isn't. That's part of the problem. Construction is barely even started up there, or in the new main ballroom space. And the weddings we booked two years ago are approaching pretty fast. The clients booked expecting to have an outdoor cocktail hour or service. We have the first one coming up in only three months. As you can imagine, the hotel serves some very influential families. The first event is for the niece of the mayor."

My eyes widened. *Shit.*

Things continued to go downhill from there. While from a visitor's perspective, the grand hotel appeared in tiptop shape, it had a laundry list of major issues that had been building over a long period of time. And now those issues were *my* issues. Over the next three-and-a-half hours, Louis unloaded problem after problem. We had so much to discuss that I had to reschedule the other appointments I'd made with senior managers this morning. By the time we finished our meeting, my head was spinning.

I stood at the door of the conference room. "Thank you so much for filling me in on everything today."

He smiled. "I guess it's a good thing there are two of you. There's a lot of work to do."

Weston Lockwood was the last thing on my mind, and Louis saw the confusion on my face.

"I was referring to Mr. Lockwood," he said, "meaning it must be nice to have someone in the trenches with you to handle all of this."

I smiled rather than tell him getting the Sterlings and Lockwoods to agree on anything might be the top problem for this hotel.

"Yes." I feigned the best smile I could muster. "It's nice to have someone I can count on." *To disappear, like he did today.*

"Let me know however I can help."

"Thank you, Louis."

After he left the conference room, I slouched in a chair, trying to organize my thoughts. I'd believed I was coming to New York to babysit a hotel while my family worked on buying out the minority owner. Apparently, I had my work cut out for me. While I sat feeling a bit shell-shocked, my cell started to buzz on the table.

I picked it up and sighed audibly.

There was only one man I wanted to avoid discussing everything I'd just learned with more than Weston Lockwood. So naturally, he had to call at this very moment. Taking a deep breath, I figured it was best to get the tirade over with. So I swiped to answer.

"Hi, Dad..."

CHAPTER 4

Sophia

"How the hell did this happen?"

My father started barking before we sat down at our table. He'd hung up on me five minutes after he'd called earlier today—the moment I'd mentioned a looming strike. I hadn't even had a chance to tell him about the rest of the issues. A half hour after he'd slammed the phone down in my ear, his secretary emailed to tell me my father would land at seven and dinner would be at Prime, one of the restaurants in The Countess. She didn't *ask* if I was available, rather she'd *told me* where we would be eating.

Not to mention, it had also been the first I'd heard that my father was even planning on coming to town tonight. And I definitely had no idea my half-brother, Spencer, would be accompanying him. Though in hindsight, I should have suspected as much on both counts.

"Well," I said. "Ms. Copeland was sick, and she let some things slide, thinking she would take care of them when she felt better. She obviously never had that opportunity."

The waiter came over to take our drink order. My father didn't give the poor man an opportunity to finish asking what we wanted before he rudely cut him off and barked "Scotch on the rocks—Glenlivet XXV Single Malt."

Because alcohol had to cost more than five-hundred dollars a bottle for him to find it worthy of consumption.

My puppet of a half-brother raised his hand. "Make that two."

No *please*.

No *thank you*.

And clearly neither of them had ever heard of *ladies first*.

I attempted to make up for their rudeness when it was my turn to order. "May I please have a glass of merlot? Whatever you have open is fine." I smiled. "Thank you very much."

If my father noticed my over-the-top abundance of manners, he didn't seem to care.

"Spencer can handle the union," he said. "He has experience dealing with Local 6."

Uh, no. "Thank you. But I can handle it on my own."

"I wasn't asking, Sophia," my father said sternly.

I'd let a lot of things slide with my father over the years, but this wasn't going to be one of them. Grandfather had given me the job of managing the hotel, and I planned to make him proud, on my own.

"With all due respect, Dad, I don't need Spencer's help. And if I do need some assistance, I'll reach out and ask for it."

My father's ears turned red. "You're in over your head."

"Grandfather has faith in me. Perhaps you can try having some, too."

Spencer joined in. "The guys who run the union are used to working with a man. Things can get pretty heated."

Did the jerk really just tell me the reason I needed help was because I was *a woman*? Now my ears pinked up.

Luckily, the waiter arrived with our drinks, allowing me a few seconds to calm down. As much as I wanted to explode, I wouldn't stoop to yelling or bullying to get my point across—that was my father's way. After the waiter passed out our beverages, I asked him to give us a few minutes since none of us had looked at the menu yet.

I gulped a healthy dose of wine and turned to give Spencer my full attention.

"I didn't realize union negotiation depended on the size of my dick. But don't worry, Spence, they used to stick us in the tub together when we were kids. I can assure you, mine is bigger than yours."

"Sophia!" my father interjected. "Act like a lady and watch your language."

As if being belittled by my father and half-brother wasn't bad enough, out of the corner of my eye, I saw Weston walk into the restaurant. Our eyes caught, and he did a quick sweep over my dinner companions before heading right for us. I downed the rest of my wine like it was a bottle of water.

"Mr. Sterling. How nice to see you." Weston put his hand on the back of my chair and graced our table with his most dazzling and annoying smile.

My father looked him up and down and snarled, "Jesus Christ, does anyone give a shit about this hotel? Here I was concerned that the Lockwood family would send someone to try to take my daughter for a ride. At least that's one thing I don't have to worry about if they sent you."

Weston's lip twitched, and his eyes flitted to me a moment. "Yes, you can sleep well at night knowing I'm not *taking your daughter for a ride.*"

Spencer leaned back in his chair. "I thought you were in Vegas."

"Moved back to New York nine months ago. You're slipping at keeping tabs on me, Spence."

I had to hide my smirk. My half-brother *loathed* being called *Spence*.

"If you're here," Spencer said, "then who's in Sin City keeping the strippers and casinos in business, Lockwood?"

Weston flashed a smug smile. "You mean like Aurora Gables? I hear she's got someone keeping her busy."

Spencer's smile wilted. *Interesting*. It sounded like Weston had done some homework and had gossip I needed to catch up on related to my perfect half-brother.

My half-brother's jaw remained clenched as he spoke. "What are you doing about the union issue?"

Weston glanced at me guiltily. "I met with them today. We're close to reaching an agreement."

My eyes widened. *That little shit.* He knew all about the union problem, yet he'd left me holed up, listening to the staff while he disappeared to take care of business. I'd underestimated him and assumed he was out screwing around. Meanwhile, he was two steps ahead of me, dealing with things we should've been working on together. Spencer and my father made me angry, but this? I was *furious.*

"You let a Lockwood go take care of business on his own?" my father snapped. "What the hell is wrong with you? Are you completely incompetent?"

Weston raised his hand. "Whoa. Hang on a minute. Take it down a notch, old man. There's no reason to raise your voice. Don't speak to Sophia like that."

"Don't you tell me how to talk to my daughter!"

Weston straightened his spine. "I'm not going to stand here and listen to you raise your voice to *any* woman. I don't give a shit if she's your daughter or not. Have a little respect."

My father stood and tossed his napkin to the table. "Mind your own damn business."

Things were spinning out of control, and I didn't like where we were headed. I stood, too. "Both of you, knock it off!" I pointed at my father. "I won't tolerate you raising your voice and calling me names." I turned to Weston and jabbed my finger into his chest. "And you—I don't need you coming to my defense. I can take care of myself."

Weston shook his head. "I forgot what a fun bunch you all are. I always knew the old man was a sadist. Didn't know you were a masochist, Fifi. Enjoy your damn meal." He turned and walked away.

My father and I were still standing, and I had no idea why, but I didn't want to be the first to take my seat.

"I've been here thirty-six hours," I said. "You need to give me some breathing room. If I need help, I'll reach out. We're all on the same side here, and I consider asking for assistance when needed a sign of a good leader, not a sign of weakness. Now, if you'd like to sit down and discuss the issues, perhaps provide some guidance from your years of experience, I'm happy to have that conversation. If not, I'll be ordering room service upstairs in my room."

My father grumbled something I couldn't make out under his breath, but nevertheless, he picked up his napkin and sat.

"Thank you," I said.

During the rest of our dinner, things were less heated, though the more I filled Dad in on the hotel's issues, the tougher it was for him to keep from bulldozing me into having Spencer join me in managing things. My half-brother did his usual nodding and repeating of things my father said, but he had nothing of real value to add.

I declined coffee and dessert, hoping not to prolong things any more than we had to, and luckily, they followed suit. We said goodnight in the hotel lobby, and on my way to the elevator, I was very tempted to stop in at the bar and have a shot or two. But I needed a clear head for my next meeting—the one Weston had no idea we were about to have.

"I knew you wouldn't be able to resist a second go 'round." Weston opened the door to his suite and hung on to the top of it.

I brushed past him and marched directly into his room. Turning around, I noticed for the first time that he had on nothing but an unbuttoned dress shirt and a pair of black boxer briefs. I motioned to his outfit. "What the hell are you doing?"

He looked down. "Ummm... Getting undressed."

I turned my head. "Well, put some damn clothes on!"

Surprisingly, he listened. He walked to where his slacks were draped over a chair and slipped them back on. He zipped up, but left the top button and his belt both open.

Turning to face him once he was decent, my eyes landed on a thin line of hair that ran from his unbuttoned pants up to his navel. I tried not to let it distract me, but that damn *happy trail*...well, it was sexy as hell. Which pissed me off even more.

Blinking a few times, I forced my eyes up to his face while my hands gripped my hips. "What the hell? You knew about the union issue and went to see them today? What kind of dumb game are you playing?"

Weston shrugged. "I didn't see my cell phone ringing after you apparently found out."

I scowled. "I only found out *today,* while you were already off holding a meeting!"

He inched closer. "Your father is a real asshole."

That was obvious. Everyone knew that, especially me. And I could spout off about him all I wanted, but no one else could—especially a Lockwood. "Don't talk about my father."

Weston's eyes widened, and his head pulled back. "Seriously? You're going to defend him after the way he spoke to you?"

"How he speaks to me is none of your damn business."

He smirked, but said nothing.

"What the hell are you smiling at?" I growled.

Weston tapped his finger to his front tooth. "You got a little piece of something stuck right here. Spinach or parsley, maybe? Did you have the oysters Rockefeller? They're really good, aren't they?"

"What? No! I didn't have oysters!" I reached up and rubbed at my tooth.

"It reminds me of when you were a kid. Remember that big gap you used to have between your front teeth? It would've taken something pretty big to get stuck in that thing. Why did you get rid of that anyway? I liked it."

I did have terrible teeth when we were kids. I'd spent countless hours in the orthodontist's chair over my five years of braces. Though I was surprised he would even remember that.

Weston caught me off guard when he leaned forward and scraped at my tooth, removing whatever had been stuck for me.

"Got it," he said, holding up his finger.

I have no idea why, but the simple gesture seemed so intimate, and it made me sort of warm. Thus, I countered that with as much frost as I could muster.

Smacking his hand away, I grumbled, "Keep your hands to yourself."

Weston took a step forward. "You sure about that?" He reached out and rested his hand on my hip. "You look like you could use blowing off some steam again."

I hated that my body immediately reacted to his touch. It pissed me off more than what he'd done or how he'd interfered with my father. "*Screw you.*"

He moved closer, and his fingers dug deeper into my hip. "We're finally on the same page."

"Why didn't you tell me you knew about the union issue?"

He leaned closer and inhaled deeply. "What perfume are you wearing?"

"Answer me, you asshole. Why didn't you mention the strike?"

"I'll tell you, but you're not going to like the truth."

"I don't like most things that come out of your mouth, but that's never stopped you from talking."

"The president of the union doesn't work well with women. If I'd told you there were issues, you would have insisted on coming, and the guy is a real piece of shit. He wouldn't have listened to a thing you said, and then the minute you weren't within earshot, he would have talked about your tits to me. Which would have pissed me the fuck off and made me punch him. It was best to avoid all that bullshit and just get it done."

"The way to deal with a sexist asshole isn't to give in to him. It's to address it head on, in a professional manner."

He seemed to consider what I'd said, then nodded. "Okay. My instinct was to protect you from the asshole, not subject you to his crap. But I get it."

The tension in my face softened. "Don't let it happen again."

The corner of his lip twitched. "Yes, ma'am."

He stared down at where his hand still sat on my hip, and my attention followed. Ever so slowly, his hand began to inch up.

Shit. An ache flourished inside me. I should've slapped his hand away and marched back out the door. But instead I stood there, watching as he caressed over my hip, traced along the dip of my waist, and smoothed up to my rib cage. When he reached the swell of my side boob, he looked up into my eyes.

I got the feeling he was giving me time to stop him—and I *really*, *really* wanted to. At least, my head did. My body...well, not so much. It had only been twenty-four hours since he'd touched me, and yet I felt so needy and desperate. The rise and fall of my chest sped up as I watched his hand lift from my side, graze over my silk shirt, and cup my breast and squeeze.

"God, I really despise you," I hissed as my eyes closed.

"Yeah, your nipples piercing through your shirt look like they hate me, too."

Weston dipped his hand inside the opening at the top of my blouse. He pushed down the lace of my bra and plucked one of my taut peaks. I hated that I let out a little mewl.

"You like it a little on the rough side, don't you?"

I kept my eyes shut. "Don't ruin the moment by talking."

The hand inside my shirt moved to my other breast, while his other hand gathered both of mine. Circling my wrists tightly, he leaned to my ear. "Maybe we should have a safe word."

Oh God. What the hell is wrong with me? Why does the idea of needing a safe word turn me on so much?

When I didn't respond, Weston nipped at my ear. "Pick a word, beautiful."

I opened my eyes. "*Asshole*."

His soft laugh vibrated against my skin. "I think you need a word that isn't already your pet name for me—one you don't say at least ten times a day when I'm around you."

"I don't need one. I'm not into kinky stuff."

Weston pulled his head back. "You despise me, and I'm about to tie your hands together behind your back so you can hate-fuck your day out of your system. Call it whatever you want, but you need a safe word, sweetheart."

He took his hand out of my blouse and reached for his pants, grabbing his belt buckle. With one firm tug, Weston yanked the leather through all the loops. The *whish* sound was one of the most erotic things I'd ever heard.

He released my wrists and lifted the belt to show it to me.

"Turn around. Clasp your hands together behind your back."

God, his voice was so raspy and thick. If sex had a sound, it would absolutely be this. Yet I hesitated to turn. It felt like a moment of truth. Was I really going to let a man I'd loathed for my entire life restrain my hands and do whatever the hell he wanted with me? Seeing the turbulence in my eyes, Weston cupped my cheek.

"I won't do anything you don't want me to."

"So if I don't want you to tie my hands?"

"Then I don't tie your hands." He looked back and forth between my eyes. "But you want me to, don't you? Stop thinking about what seems right or wrong and go with what you want, Soph."

It wasn't lost on me that he'd finally called me by my actual name. Taking a deep breath, I made the insane choice to throw caution to the wind. I held up a finger in warning. "Don't leave marks."

A wicked grin spread across Weston's face. Without another word, he guided me to turn around. Pulling my hands behind my back, he wrapped his belt around my wrists and cinched it snugly.

"Tug a bit," he said.

I did my best to pull my wrists free, but they didn't budge.

Weston walked me forward to a desk in front of the window. I'd assumed things would go the same way as the last time we were together—meaning I'd be bent over and he'd take me from behind. But again, I'd assumed incorrectly what Weston Lockwood was up to. He turned me around, gripped my waist with two hands, and lifted me onto the desk.

"Spread."

"We have rules," I panted. "Only from behind."

Weston gripped my knees. "That applies to when I fuck you. But I'm not ready for that yet."

I swallowed.

He edged open my legs. I didn't even try to fight him.

"Last chance. Safe word, Sophia?"

"Countess," I whispered.

He smiled. "Good choice."

He took a step back. With my legs spread and my hands bound behind my back, I felt incredibly vulnerable. Trying to feel more in control, I huffed, "Just get moving. Let's get it over with."

Weston bit his bottom lip, and I swear I felt it between my legs. There was something so damn sexy about the way he looked at me.

"You're going to look in my eyes while I finger you."

My jaw dropped open. This guy had some nerve.

Amused at my expression, Weston closed the distance between us again. One of his hands pushed between my open legs, and he not so gently shoved my panties to the side. Two fingers rubbed up and down my center, and then one plunged inside, just like he'd done last night. Yet somehow, I still hadn't been expecting it.

I gasped.

"So wet for me already."

He pumped his finger in and out, and my eyes fell closed.

"*Tsk tsk tsk.* Have you forgotten what I told you so soon? Eyes open, my little Fifi."

I started to say something, to tell him once again to stop calling me that, but then his finger glided in and out a few more times, and whatever thought I'd had disappeared faster than my inhibitions.

"Spread your legs wider so I can give you more. I love that you're so tight."

My head wanted to slam my legs closed, but my body craved the *more* he wanted to give me. Shamelessly, I opened my legs.

Weston smiled. He held my gaze as he slipped his finger out and pushed into me with two. I tensed for a minute, then relaxed as he continued to move in and out with methodical precision.

"One more..."

I'd been so lost in the moment, I wasn't sure what he was referring to until I felt a third finger enter me. I moaned, and my eyes shut again.

Weston waited a few seconds, and then whispered in my ear, "You're so beautiful when you're turned on. Such a shame you only want me to take you from behind. I bet the sight of you coming with my cock instead of my hand is absolutely phenomenal."

My breathing grew labored. His warm breath in my ear, along with the constant stroking inside of me had me so close already. Weston crooked his fingers and changed the angle of his pumps, and I knew it wouldn't be long before my orgasm.

He reached behind me and threaded his fingers into my hair. Yanking my head back, he sucked on my exposed neck.

"Ohhh...oh God."

He tugged harder on my hair, to the point that it hurt—but not enough to make him stop—and his thumb stretched to rub my clit.

"Eyes open when you come," he groaned as he pulled back to watch me. But I was so lost in the moment, I barely heard him. He repeated his words again, this time with a stern tone. "Eyes fucking open, Sophia."

My eyes flew open. On instinct, I went to grab for him, forgetting that my hands were bound behind me. The leather around my wrists had no play, and the more I pulled, the more it dug into my skin. Surprisingly, the feeling of being restrained didn't scare me, it actually seemed to turn me on. So I struggled a few more times in a vain attempt to get free, until I felt my body begin to climb over the edge. *Oh God.* With a guttural sound that was a cross between a moan and a yell, my orgasm ripped through me. Our eyes met, and the fire in Weston's eyes while he watched me orgasm kept me riveted in place. When the last of the ripples ended, I leaned forward and rested my head on his shoulder, allowing my eyes to shut.

It didn't take long for me to feel vulnerable again. I kept my eyes closed.

"Take it off," I whispered.

"You sure?"

I nodded.

Weston reached around and unfastened the buckle, freeing my hands.

I rubbed one of my wrists.

He looked down. They were red from friction burn, though it really didn't hurt.

"You want me to get you some ice?"

I shook my head. "I'm fine."

"Some cream or something?"

Him using that soft tone freaked me out almost as much as what I'd just let happen. I pressed my hand against his chest and nudged him to take a step back.

Righting my skirt, I snapped, "Don't be nice to me."

Weston's eyebrows jumped. "You want me to be a dick?" He thumbed behind him. "I'm sure there's some salt around here somewhere I could pour on. That will make it sting. Would that work for you?"

I narrowed my eyes and hopped off the desk. "You know what works for me? You not meeting with the union when I'm not present. We own equal amounts of this hotel, and you need my approval to ratify any agreements you make with them anyway."

"Really? Two minutes ago you were moaning, and now we're back to the union? Maybe we can put that on hold until after."

I brushed the wrinkles from my skirt. I hadn't planned on rushing out the door. Then again, I hadn't planned on what had just transpired either. But it hit me that I had the upper hand now—a way to make Weston feel as screwed over as he'd made me feel earlier. A slow, evil smile spread across my face, and I arched a brow. "After?"

He looked down at the substantial bulge in his pants and back up to me. "We're not done here."

"Is that so?" I walked toward the door. Opening it, I looked back over my shoulder. "I hope you feel every bit as screwed over as I did today. Sweet dreams, *Weston*."

CHAPTER 5

Weston

"So what's going on with you? I'm glad you didn't cancel our session again this week." Dr. Halpern crossed her legs and set her notepad on the table next to her.

It might've been the first time I didn't have to hide my ogling of her shapely calves. And that wasn't because she'd decided to wear pants for a change. She had the same long stems on display as she normally did.

I lay down on the proverbial patient couch like I always did, even though she'd told me it wasn't necessary and most patients sat up. Apparently, the shrink sitting in a chair across from the nutjob while he spilled his guts was more for the movies than real life. Though, if I had to come here, I figured I might as well get some rest out of it.

"Did I ever tell you about the time I had the croup?" I asked her. "I was probably four, and Caroline was six or so."

"I don't think you've mentioned it, no."

"My mother had given me the last of the ice cream, and my sister wasn't happy about it. Mom had set up a vaporizer in my room. So while I was enjoying my ice cream, Caroline went and peed in the vaporizer. When my mother went to put me back in bed, my room was a cloud of urine mist."

Out of the corner of my eye, I saw Dr. Halpern pick up her notepad and jot something down.

"You're taking notes about this? Is that because you're thinking of trying the gag on someone, or have you just found the root of all of my problems?"

Dr. Halpern set down her pad and pen. "I wrote down that you voluntarily spoke about your sister. Is there a reason you were thinking of Caroline today?"

I usually gave no real thought to anything the good doc asked, but today I did, for some reason. "Not that I'm aware of."

"Tell me about the last forty-eight hours. Even if parts of your day were mundane, I'd like to hear about them."

I shook my head. "You sure about that?"

Dr. Halpern folded her hands on her lap. "I am."

"Okay... Well..."

For the next twenty minutes or so, I walked her through my last two days, though I skipped over the encounters in private with Sophia, figuring those details weren't relevant to anything she needed to dissect. Yet she seemed to zone in on that part of my story anyway.

"So you and Sophia have some sort of history together."

"Our families do."

"When was the last time you saw Sophia before a few days ago?"

I smiled. "Prom night."

"She was your prom date?"

I shook my head. "No."

"But you saw her at prom?"

I thought back to twelve years ago. I could still see Sophia in her dress. It was red and clung to every curve. While most of the girls had looked nice, they'd also looked like they were going to prom. But not Soph. She'd looked elegant and stood out in a way that made me unable to take my eyes off her all night—even with my date telling me all the things she couldn't wait to do with me after the prom was over.

"Yeah. She didn't have such a great night."

"Why is that?"

"Her boyfriend was sleeping with her cousin. She found out when she overheard them having sex in the ladies' room stall."

"Oh my. That must've put a damper on her evening."

"Yeah, especially when I punched the dick in the nose." Remembering the face Dr. Halpern usually made when I cursed, I added, "Sorry. When I punched the loser in the face."

Dr. Halpern smiled. "Thank you. So you and Sophia were good friends, then?"

I smiled. "No, we hated each other."

"But you defended her honor."

I shrugged. "It was more that I didn't like her boyfriend."

"Why is that?"

I started to answer and then stopped. Why the hell were we talking about twelve years ago and whether or not I liked this guy? Turning to look at Dr. Halpern, I said, "Is there a point to all these questions? I think we've gone off track."

"What do you see as on track for today? Is there something specific you feel like talking about?"

I dragged a hand through my hair. "No offense, but if it were my choice, I wouldn't be here talking to you at all. So, no... There's nothing specific I want to discuss today."

She was quiet for a long time. "Let's continue. Were Sophia and Caroline friends?"

"Caroline didn't have a lot of friends. She was out of school so much and couldn't do most of the things normal kids did."

"Okay. So let's go back to Sophia and prom for a moment. For whatever reason, you felt the need to intervene in her relationship and got into an altercation with her boyfriend. Was Sophia upset about that?"

I shrugged. "As far as I know, she wasn't even aware it happened. She ran out right after she caught them messing around in the bathroom."

"And that was the last time you saw her?"

I smiled. "No. I was in a shit mood. All of my friends were getting drunk and acting like idiots, and I couldn't drink, so I left prom early. I ran into Sophia in the parking lot."

"Why couldn't you drink like your friends?"

"I had a procedure scheduled for the next morning. Caroline was sick again."

Dr. Halpern frowned. "Okay. So you ran into Sophia in the parking lot, and how was that?"

I smiled. "We argued. As usual. She thought I was there to gloat about what a jerk her boyfriend was. He didn't even chase after her. We'd both taken a limo to prom and gotten dropped off. I called my driver and had him come pick us up."

"Okay..."

I wasn't about to share that while Sophia was in the middle of bawling me out, I'd pressed my lips to hers, and the two of us wound up taking out our frustrations in a much more productive manner that night. "We... hung out for a while. I fell asleep at her house around the time the sun came up, and I woke up a half hour after I was supposed to be at the hospital. I got a cab and showed up in my wrinkled tux from the night before." I shook my head. "My mother made them do a blood alcohol test on me because she thought I'd put having fun over Caroline. She didn't believe me when I told her I didn't have a drop to drink."

Dr. Halpern picked up her pad and wrote for a full minute that time.

"Perhaps seeing Sophia reminded you of that time in your life—a time when you were helping your sister."

I guess that made sense. Though my sister had been the furthest thing from my mind last night, that was for damn sure. I shrugged. "Maybe."

We moved on from our trip down memory lane. When Dr. Halpern asked me how things were going at The Countess, I almost told her how I'd royally fucked up by sleeping with the enemy. But then I figured she might try to keep me here all afternoon to dissect the *real* reasons I'd done what I did.

Because no shrink accepts that sometimes you just can't handle how the cream buttons on a royal blue silk blouse make you insane. Or how the color of those buttons *exactly* matches the skin on her neck, and since you can't bite that neck like you really want to, you have to settle for listening to the little cream pearls ping against the tile floor.

Yeah, Dr. Halpern would definitely not understand that. Let's face it, if she did, she'd be out of business. Because in order for her to maintain this fancy midtown real estate, she needs to psychoanalyze the shit out of everything we do.

But the truth of the matter is, sometimes we just act on instinct like an animal. And Sophia damn Sterling has the uncanny ability to bring out the savage in me.

CHAPTER 6

Sophia

"You can have six rooms, if you want. Should I book it under your name? Will they be flying in with you or checking in on their own?"

Scarlett had sent me an email asking to book a second room for her upcoming trip. So I'd picked up the phone to respond since I was wide awake anyway.

"I'm not sure yet. But if you could book the room under Thomason, that would be brilliant."

"No problem."

"Isn't it the middle of the night there? It's just seven in the morning here, so it's, what...two in New York?"

I sighed. "Yeah. I couldn't fall asleep, so I figured I'd catch up on my emails."

"Jet lag?"

"Not really."

"Don't tell me you're losing sleep over that sloth, Liam."

"No, that's not it."

"So what's keeping you from getting the proper amount of beauty rest, then?"

I hadn't called my friend to unload my troubles. Well, maybe that wasn't so true, and unconsciously I'd hoped we'd get to chat. It had been four hours since I scurried out of Weston's room, yet my head was still spinning from what had happened.

"I...have a little problem."

"You *cannot* wear black pants with brown shoes, even if I'm no longer there to save you from yourself."

I laughed. "I wish it were that easy."

"Hang on a second." Scarlett covered the phone, but I heard her muzzled conversation.

"What is this?" she said curtly.

A man's voice answered. He sounded nervous. "Umm... It's...your coffee. From the new Cinnabon place you asked me to fetch it from."

"But what's inside? It weighs half a stone."

"Your cinnamon bun is inside."

"*What*?"

"You ordered a coffee with a cinnamon bun on top."

"I ordered a coffee with *cinnamon on top*. Who in their right mind thinks someone would want a cinnamon bun *inside* of a coffee?"

"Uh... Sorry. I'll go back."

"Yes, do that."

Scarlett came back on the phone. "Did you say *you* have a problem? Whatever it is, it can't be worse than the new assistant the temp agency sent over."

"I overheard. Sometimes I think you're too hard on people. But I promise you, that's not the case today."

She sighed. "So what kind of trouble have you gotten yourself into, love?"

"Well...you remember the family I told you about. The one that owns the competing hotel chains and now jointly owns The Countess with my family?"

"Sure. The Locks or something like that?"

"Right. The Lockwoods. Well, I don't think I ever mentioned that I'd accidentally slept with one of them—Weston. He and I are the same age."

"You *accidentally* slept with someone? Did you fall on his cock and it impaled you?"

I laughed. "No. I guess *accidentally* might not be the right word. It was more like I had a temporary lapse in sanity and slept with him. Anyway, it was a long time ago—the night of my high school prom, actually. I went with another guy and came home with Weston."

"You dirty dog. I didn't think you had it in you."

I smiled. "It's a long story. But I was acting out. My mother had died earlier in the year. I found out during the prom that my boyfriend was sleeping with someone; ironically, it was one of my cousins. That seems to be a thing with me. My father didn't show up for the gratuitous pre-prom pictures because it was also my half-brother Spencer's junior prom, and his was infinitely more important than my senior one. Anyway, I wound up leaving prom with Weston. He ditched his date, and it was a one-time thing. We hated each other, but the sex... Let's just say we were only eighteen, but it was mind-blowing."

"Ah. *Hate sex*. It's one of my favorites."

"Yeah, well, that's apparently my problem. It's one of mine, too."

"I'm not following."

"Weston, the guy from my prom, he's at The Countess. His family sent him, just like my family sent me. We're both here to manage things and figure out a valuation of the hotel so one of us can try to buy out the minority shareholder and take control of the property."

"And you're attracted to him, but you still don't get along?"

"Yes." I turned onto my side and sighed. "But I also accidentally slept with him again."

Scarlett screeched so loud I had to pull the phone from my ear. "That's fabulous."

"No, it's definitely not."

"Why not?"

"God, for so many reasons. Number one, I don't like him at all. He's arrogant and cocky and grates on my nerves by calling me this stupid name that he's called me since we were kids. And second, he's the enemy! Our families hate each other, and both of us are trying to outbid the other, just so we can get controlling interest and push the other family out."

"But yet you accidentally fell on his cock again?"

I smiled. "Yeah."

"It sounds...illicit. Maybe this is what you need after the doldrums of Liam Albertson the last year and a half."

"What *I need* is to keep away from Weston. I don't know what happens to me, but every time we have a fight, we end up clawing at each other."

"That sounds positively divine."

She wasn't entirely wrong. In the heat of the moment, it *was* positively divine. But the short, cheap thrill didn't last when the clouds of lust started to clear. And then I felt worse than ever. Plus, I was here to do a job, not fraternize with the enemy.

"Do they still sell chastity belts? I think I might need one."

"I think what you need is what you just got—to get laid by someone more exciting than Liam."

"Have you ever been attracted to someone you know is no good for you?"

"Do you not remember me telling you I slept with my forty-year-old psych professor my first year of college? He was divorced three times already, and his last wife had been a former student. It was the dumbest thing I ever did. But man, it was the best sex I ever had. The guy was like catnip. Every day I'd walk into class and say I wasn't going to do it again. Then he'd say, 'Miss Everson, could I see you after class a moment?' He'd say it in this tone like he'd caught me cheating, and he was going to scold me. And that was it. My ass went home with black dry erase marker all over it because he liked to pin me to the whiteboard."

"How did you eventually end it?"

"The semester ended, and I didn't sign up for Psych Two on purpose. As long as I didn't see him, I was fine."

I sighed. "Well, that's not going to work in my situation. We're both stuck here for the next month or so, at least."

"Well, fighting is what gets you hot and bothered about this guy, right?"

I felt disappointed in myself, but that was the truth. "Yeah. It's like I want to take my anger out on him physically."

"Okay, then. Just stop fighting with him."

I started to say that wouldn't work, but... *Huh*. It was a simple suggestion. Could it be that easy?

"I'm not sure the two of us can get along. We've never done anything but argue."

"Welp. Sounds like it's either make nice or you'll have another *accident*."

I guess it couldn't hurt to try. "Maybe I'll do that."

"Good. Then it's settled. You're going to get some shuteye for the next few hours, and I'm going to make the new temp cry by the end of the day."

I laughed. "That sounds about right."

"Off to sleep you go. Call me the next time you fall off the wagon and shag this Weston guy again."

"Hopefully, that won't be happening. I'll see you end of next week."

"Bye, love!"

Swiping my phone off, I plugged it into the charger on the nightstand before pulling up the covers.

Scarlett was right. It was simple, really. All I needed to do was be nice to Weston. That couldn't be too hard.

Or could it?

CHAPTER 7

Sophia

"Good morning, Weston." I flashed my most dazzling smile.

Apparently *dazzle* wasn't something Weston was used to seeing on me. His brows pulled down, and he studied me with suspicion. "Good morning?"

He was seated behind the desk in what had been Ms. Copeland's office. I'm sure he expected a fight over who got to use the big, corner office with the view of the park. But instead, I walked directly over to the round meeting table and kept my smile firmly in place.

"So, I'd like to fill you in on the other issues the general manager told me about yesterday. Maybe we could split up the list I've made and each be the point person for different things?"

"Uhh... Yeah, that makes sense."

Weston was definitely waiting for the other shoe to drop. Though I didn't have one. I'd given a lot of thought to the conversation Scarlett and I had early this morning and determined maybe she was on to something. Until the last few days, I'd considered myself pretty vanilla, but apparently some deep, dark part of me got off on arguing with this man. If Weston and I got along, I might have a better chance of not ending up with my panties around my ankles.

Weston got up from the desk and walked over to where I sat. This morning, I'd typed up a long list of the issues Louis and I had discussed. I slid three stapled pages over to the opposite side of the table and looked up at Weston.

"This is a list of things we should discuss. I prioritized them, but we should go over them all. I'm going to run downstairs and get some more coffee. Maybe you could read through what I've typed, and we can discuss it when I get back?" I stood from my chair.

The look on Weston's face was pretty comical. He was waiting for me to be difficult. *Not going to happen today, buddy.* I headed toward the door and then stopped and turned back. "Would you like me to pick you up some coffee? Maybe some fruit or a muffin, too?"

"Uhhh... Yeah, that would be great. I'll take a large black coffee and a blueberry muffin."

"No problem." This time I even managed to show my teeth with my over-the-top smile. Being sweet was almost like a new form of torture for Weston. *Who knew?* Maybe this wouldn't be so bad after all.

As I turned to walk out, he stopped me.

"Wait. You're not going to poison my coffee or something, are you?"

I laughed. "I'll be back in a few minutes."

My fake-cheery demeanor had seemed to sink in. On my way down to the coffee shop, I caught myself whistling. Not only did I enjoy making Weston feel off kilter, my neck really appreciated the lack of tension. I'd had a giant knot in it since I boarded the plane a few days ago.

When I returned to the office, Weston was still at the round meeting table. He'd written some notes on the list I'd given him and now had a yellow legal pad with even more scribbled notes, and he was scrolling through his phone. I handed him his coffee and the bag with his blueberry muffin, along with a chipper smile.

"I had them warm the muffin for you. Hope that's okay. There are some butter pats in the bag, if you want them."

His forehead wrinkled in confusion. "Yeah, that's great. Thanks."

I took the seat across from him and peeled back the plastic tab on my coffee before picking up my pen. "Why don't we start with my list? And when we're done, you can tell me how things went with the union yesterday and what I can do to help there."

"Okay..."

For the next hour, I ran Weston through the issues I'd discussed with Louis. After I finished, he slumped back in his chair.

"We have our work cut out for us."

"Yes, but I think we'll make a good team, and we'll be able to whip this place into shape in no time."

"You do?"

"Absolutely. If anyone knows hotels, it's us. We both grew up in them, years before we even started working for our families. It's in our blood. I've already reached out to two contractors we've used at Sterling properties before, and I set up a meeting with one of them at two o'clock this afternoon to discuss the construction that needs to be finished in the ballroom."

"Why your contractors? I was in one of your buildings for a meeting last month, and the place wasn't looking too hot."

My immediate gut reaction was to get defensive, but I tamped that down and managed to ignore the insult, focusing instead on working together.

"Well, I'll tell you what. We obviously need to get a few quotes, so why don't you call in one or two of your people. We can see what they all come up with, and how fast each one thinks they can get it done."

Again, Weston hesitated. "Yeah, okay."

We discussed a few other priority issues, including how to handle an employee Louis thought was dipping into the petty cash, and filling five key vacant positions, two of which were assistant manager jobs. I also had a team of CPAs and lawyers coming this afternoon to start due diligence on The Countess so my family could formulate its offer to purchase the minority share.

Without too much disagreement, Weston and I even decided which conference rooms we wanted to set up our teams in. We then threw around some counteroffer proposals to the union's offer we'd discussed earlier. All in all, it was a damn productive morning.

"Okay, well..." I shuffled the papers I'd spread out in front of me into a pile and neatened them into a stack. "This was a good meeting. I'm going to go talk to Louis about setting me up in an office somewhere, and I guess I'll see you upstairs when the first contractor arrives."

"You don't want this office?" he asked.

I stood. "You look like you've already settled in. I can find another one. No big deal."

We were about two minutes away from Weston feeling my forehead. Suspecting I'd made his head spin enough for the morning, my job here was done. "See you at two?"

"Yeah. I might be a little late. But I'll meet you up there."

Now it was my turn to be suspect. "Do you have something else planned?"

Weston got up and walked back to his desk, avoiding eye contact. "I have a meeting. But I'll be back after."

"A meeting? What kind of a meeting?"

"The kind that's none of your business. I'll be back as soon as I can."

Unable to hide how annoyed his response made me, I left the office. I'd just laid all my cards on the table, and that little shit probably had something up his sleeve that he was doing behind my back.

This being friendly thing wasn't going to be easy after all.

Sam Bolton had been doing construction in New York for my family since I was a kid—though I hadn't known Bolton Contracting was now Bolton and Son. Travis,

Sam's son, introduced himself and shook my hand. He was handsome, in more a clean-cut-boss type of way than a contractor-who-swings-a-hammer look, but definitely nice looking.

"It's nice to meet you," he said. "I didn't realize William had a daughter."

Travis meant no harm with his comment, but it hit home.

"That's because he's still hoping I'll come to my senses and tie on an apron and stay at home, preparing for my husband's arrival from work, like a woman should."

Travis smiled. "I hope you don't mind my saying so, but I've worked with Spencer, your brother, and I believe they make aprons to fit his size, too."

I liked Travis already. "*Half-brother,* and I'm pretty sure he'd burn anything he tried in the kitchen."

If I wasn't mistaken, I thought I caught *that look* in Travis's eyes. You know the one, a bit of a sparkle that shines when someone is interested in more than just your business. Though he was a perfect gentleman and did nothing inappropriate as I showed him around the construction space. Travis had been early, so a few minutes later, his father arrived. I'd also invited Len, the head of hotel maintenance, to join us, and he led the tour of what had been done and what still needed to be completed.

"What happened to the original contractor?" Travis asked.

"There were apparently multiple inspection issues that came up," Len said. "Ms. Copeland was unhappy about the frequent delays, so she fired the contractor with the intention of bringing on a new one. At one point, she told me she gave a new contractor a deposit, but nothing was ever started."

Great. Note to self. Add find out if a contractor was paid to start work and pulled a no-show to my to-do list.

"Everything pretty much came to a halt fourteen months ago when Ms. Copeland's health took a turn."

"And when do you need all of this done?" Sam Bolton asked.

"Three months," I said.

Travis's eyebrows jumped while his father blew out a deep breath and shook his head. "We'd have to have crews here around the clock. That means paying night differential, two foremen working overtime in twelve-hour shifts, and all sorts of extra benefits the union would require."

"But it is possible to get it done?" I asked. "We have events lined up starting in three months and really don't want to have to cancel them."

Sam looked around, scratching his chin. "It's possible. Not going to lie, I don't like working like that. I won't cut corners to get things done. Many times I'm at the mercy of subcontractors, so there's always a chance something could go wrong, too." He nodded. "But yeah, with those extras I think we could shoot for three months. We'd need to get down to the building department right away and see what the issues were with the last inspections and also take the blueprints with us today. But we can give it a shot."

"How fast could you get me an estimate?"

"A couple of days."

I sighed. "Okay. Well, let's do that."

Weston showed up just as we were finishing—more than a *little* late. Nevertheless, I kept the peace and even managed to smile as I made the introductions. He and Sam got into a discussion about people they both knew and jobs they were both familiar with. I told Len from maintenance he could go, and that left Travis and me talking.

"Do I hear a bit of a British accent?" he asked.

I didn't think I had one. But he wasn't the first person to ask me that. I'd only lived in London for six years.

"You're very perceptive." I smiled. "I was born and raised in New York, but spent the last few years living in London. Apparently I picked up a few things while I was there."

"What brought you to London?"

"Work. We have hotels there, and my father and I get along best when we're on different continents."

He smiled. "What made you come back?"

"This hotel. Plus, the timing was right. I was ready for a change."

Travis nodded. "And not one that entails an apron around your waist, I take it?"

I laughed. "Definitely not."

From the corner of my eye, I caught Weston looking over at Travis and me. It was the second or third time in five minutes. He was definitely monitoring our discussion.

After the Boltons left, Weston shook his head. "Those two are definitely not right for this job."

"What? What are you talking about? They said they could get us an estimate in a few days and meet our crazy timeline. My family has worked with them many times over the years. They're absolutely reliable. What else could we hope for at this point?"

"I just didn't get the right vibe from them."

"The right vibe? What vibe did you get?"

"I don't know. Just an untrustworthy one, I guess."

"That's insane!"

"They can submit their bid on the job. But I wouldn't count on my vote to give them the work."

My hands flew to my hips. "And who, exactly, do you think is right for this job? Let me guess, one of *your* people."

Weston shrugged. "I can't help it if we use better contractors."

"Better? How the hell do you know anyone is better than anyone else at this point?"

"Maybe if you paid a little more attention to what was going on around you, instead of checking out the contractor's son, you'd be in the same mindset as I am."

My eyes widened. "You've got to be joking!"

He shrugged. "Lust is blind."

"Obviously! Why else would I have slept with you!"

Weston's eyes darkened, his pupils blocking out most of the soft blue color of his irises. I could feel my face heat with anger, and... *Oh my God,* my damn belly did a little flutter.

Is my body insane?

It had to be. A sheen of cold sweat broke out on my forehead, and my body started to light up like a Christmas tree.

What the hell?

Seriously?

No. Just no.

As my head reeled from my body's crazy response, Weston's eyes dropped to my chest. I was mortified to find my nipples protruding. The traitors were standing at full attention, saluting this asshole through my blouse. I folded my arms across my chest, but it was too late. My eyes lifted to find a giant, wicked smirk on Weston's face.

Taking a deep breath, I closed my eyes and counted to ten. When I opened them, Weston was still sporting a smug smirk, but his brows were pinched together, and his forehead was wrinkled.

"If you were hoping I'd disappear, I'm sorry to disappoint you," he said.

I know I'm not that lucky had been on the tip of my tongue. But instead, I plastered on a sparkling smile.

Well, I was going for sparkling, but the look on Weston's face told me it came out more maniacal Joker than anything. Yet I rolled with it.

Speaking through my teeth, I said, "Why would I want you to disappear? You're so helpful. I look forward to meeting with your contractor."

Since I wasn't sure how much more I could take without losing it, I turned on my heel and walked toward the door. Without looking back, I said, "Have a good afternoon, Weston."

He yelled after me, "I will. And don't forget dinner tonight, Fifi."

CHAPTER 8

Sophia

I arrived at Le Maison fifteen minutes late on purpose.

Weston stood as I approached the table. "I was starting to think you weren't going to show."

I took my seat and folded a napkin across my lap. "I said I would, so I'm here. Though, why couldn't we just have dinner in one of the restaurants at The Countess?"

"This one has dancing. I thought you might enjoy feeling my body pressed up against yours when we're in public. I mean, we know how much you like it in private."

"I'm not dancing with you."

Instead of my refusal annoying him, Weston flashed his million-dollar smile. He really had a fantastic smile... which was irritating beyond belief. But I was hellbent on maintaining my composure this evening.

A waiter came over and asked if we'd like to see the wine menu. I took it and gave it a quick once-over, but decided rather than having hundreds of calories of wine to relax, I'd nurse one low-cal drink instead. I handed my menu back to the waiter. "I'll have a vodka and cranberry with lime, please. If you have diet cranberry, that would be even better."

"I'm sorry, we don't have diet. Would you like regular?"

"Sure. Thank you."

The waiter nodded and turned to Weston. "And for you, sir?"

"I'll take a Diet Coke, please."

This was the third time we'd been together and I'd ordered an alcoholic drink, yet Weston hadn't. I considered questioning it, but thought that might just shine a light on my drinking on a weeknight, so I kept my mouth shut.

After the waiter disappeared, Weston looked me over. "Don't forget about number two of our deal."

It took me a few seconds to recall what the terms of our dumb deal even were. We'd agreed to me calling him Weston, dinner once a week, and me...wearing my hair up twice a week.

"Why do you care how I wear my hair, anyway?"

"Because I like to look at the skin on your neck. It's creamy."

I opened my mouth to respond, then shut it. His comment seemed sincere. I knew how to fight with this man. I knew how to discuss business with him, even civilly. But I had no idea how to take a compliment when he was being nice.

"Don't say things like that," I finally grumbled.

"Why not?"

"Just don't."

Since business was a safe topic of conversation, I folded my hands on top of the table. "I made an appointment for a second contractor to come tomorrow at nine AM."

"I have Brighton Contractors coming tomorrow at eight. I'm sure we can cancel your appointment after we meet with Jim Brighton."

"I think I'll refrain from making that decision until after we meet with both. Unlike you, I have an open mind and have no problem considering all competent contractors, regardless of who brings them in."

Weston dropped his napkin on the table and stood. He held out his hand. "Dance with me."

"I told you, I'm not dancing."

"Just one dance."

"No."

"Give me one good reason why not, and I'll sit back down."

"Because it's unprofessional. This is a business dinner, not a date."

"So is fingering you while my belt is tied around your wrists. And you didn't seem to object to that as unprofessional. Though, if you ask me, leaving me in the state you did the other night wasn't your most professional moment."

The waiter arrived to deliver our drinks. Weston continued to stand and wait for me to agree.

When we were alone again, I said, "I've clearly had a few moments of insanity. But those are in the past, and I intend to keep things between us professional from now on."

Weston studied me for a moment. I was surprised when he took his seat again without more of an argument. His thumb rubbed back and forth over his lower lip as he continued to consider me from across the table. After a minute, his face lit up. The only thing missing was a light bulb in a bubble above his head.

He grinned. "You think if we play nice, you won't wind up with my cock inside you anymore."

I shifted in my seat. "Must you be so vulgar?"

"What did I say?" He seemed genuinely confused.

I leaned forward and lowered my voice. "*Cock*. Do you have to say it like that?"

He grinned. "I'm sorry. Can you say that again? I didn't hear you."

I squinted. "You heard me. I know you did."

He leaned forward and lowered his voice. "Maybe. But I really liked hearing you say *cock*."

A busboy walked by our table just as Weston spoke. The guy looked our way and smirked, but kept going.

"Keep your voice down."

Needless to say, he didn't. "Is it just *my cock* you don't like talking about? Or is it *all cocks* in general?"

I rolled my eyes. "God, you're such a twelve-year-old boy."

He shrugged. "Maybe. But I know what game you're playing now. You think no fighting equals no fucking."

"I do not," I lied. "I'm merely trying to maintain a professional relationship that started out on the wrong foot."

Weston plucked a breadstick from the middle of the table. "I like the foot it started out on."

"Regardless, we're going to do things my way."

He bit off a piece of the breadstick and waved it at me. "We'll see."

Over dinner, I somehow managed to steer our conversation back to business. While we were waiting for the check, I said, "I had Len, the head of maintenance, join me to show the contractor around this afternoon. He was gone before you got there, but I was glad I'd invited him. He was able to walk Sam and Travis through where things were left off with the electric and sprinkler systems that I wouldn't have known. I asked him to join us tomorrow for the other contractor I have coming in. Perhaps you should invite him to the eight-AM meeting with your guys."

"Alright, I'll do that."

Talking about this afternoon reminded me just how late Weston had been to the meeting. Since we were getting along and doing so well at sharing information, I figured I'd press.

"By the way, why were you so late this afternoon? You never mentioned what your appointment was for."

Weston's eyes jumped back and forth between mine before he looked away. "You're right. I didn't."

I sighed. "Whatever. I just hope you're not playing games, like when you went to the union behind my back."

"It won't be a problem."

The Countess was five blocks from the restaurant, so we walked back together, side by side. On our way, we passed a bar called Caroline's. I noticed, and immediately looked over to see if Weston had noticed it, too. I found him staring at the illuminated name above the bar. His eyes slanted to mine as they lowered. It felt odd not to say anything.

"I was very sorry to hear about your sister," I said quietly.

He nodded. "Thank you."

Caroline Lockwood was two years older than Weston, but only a year ahead of us in school because of how frequently she was absent. She'd suffered from leukemia from the time we were kids. I knew there were different subcategories of the disease, and wasn't sure exactly which type she'd had, but she'd always looked tired and too thin when we were in school. When we were about eighteen, right after we graduated, I remembered hearing she'd had a kidney transplant. Her family and friends seemed very optimistic that things would get better from there. But about five years ago, while I was living in London, I'd heard she passed away.

Weston stopped when we arrived in front of The Countess. He looked up at the beautiful façade and smiled. "Caroline would have loved this place. She studied architecture at NYU and got a job at the New York City Historic Preservation Society. She thought it was her personal duty to protect the character of the City's oldest buildings."

"I didn't know that."

He nodded, still looking up. "She was also obsessed with Christmas—thought it was her job to sprinkle it on everything for two full months each year. If she were here, she'd have us both already in planning meetings about how we were going to decorate The Countess at the holidays."

"I know a little trivia about Christmastime at The Countess, actually. And it involves our families. When I was researching the hotel, I came across some old pictures where there was an enormous Christmas tree in the lobby. I also read a few hundred of the hotel's reviews on Tripadvisor so I could get a sense of what people thought about their recent stays, and I noticed there were quite a few reviews written during December where people noted that the hotel had no tree and very few holiday decorations. I asked Louis about it, and he said the first few years they were open, our grandfathers would go out in search of the biggest tree they could find, and the three of them would personally decorate the tree from top to bottom. It was one of Ms. Copeland's favorite things to do. After everything happened between the three of them in 1962 and they parted ways, there was never another tree lit in the lobby. Grace loved having a big tree, but couldn't bear to put one up because of the memories it brought. She always felt bad that she'd caused the destruction of our grandfathers' friendship, and she hoped one day they'd bury the hatchet and a tree would again be lit in the lobby."

"No shit?"

I nodded. "Yup. So there hasn't been a tree or any real Christmas spirit here since before we were born."

Weston was quiet for a while as he continued to look up. "I guess Grace and I have something in common, then."

"What do you mean?"

"I haven't put up a tree or decorated since Caroline died either. When we were kids, she would make me spend hours helping her decorate the house. As she got older, she made me come over on her birthday, November 2nd, and spend the entire day helping her decorate. She did it on her birthday because it made it harder for me to say no."

I smiled. "I love the relationship you two had. In high school, I remember seeing you guys walk home together all the time, or I'd see you laughing together in the hall at school. It used to make me wish I had a sibling."

Weston looked at me with a warm smile. "What? Good old Spencer doesn't count?"

I laughed. "Not a chance. Plus, even if we did get along, he grew up in Florida where my father stowed his second family. So I didn't get to know him too well. And maybe he never had a chance with me because of how he came into my life."

Weston seemed to consider something for a moment. "Would it help you to have some dirt on him?"

"Help? I'm not so sure. But would I enjoy it? Absolutely."

He smiled and leaned in a bit, even though the sidewalk around us was empty.

"Your half-brother with the sweet, Southern fiancée and the engagement announced by her pastor father in *The New York Times*—well, he's screwing a stripper in Vegas who's a well-known dominatrix."

My eyes widened. "I knew you had dirt on him the other day at lunch."

"They stay at a small hotel-casino on the outskirts of town. I guess so nobody will notice them. Don't think

Spence knows I'm a silent partner at The Ace. Saw them together with my own eyes. Then I asked around. It's been going on for a while."

I shook my head. "I guess the apple doesn't fall far from the tree."

Since Weston had shared, I thought I'd let him in on a secret of my own. "You want a little dirt most people don't know?"

Weston smiled. "Absolutely."

"Spencer and I are only six months apart. He's a year younger in school, so people don't realize that. My upstanding father had both his wife and his mistress pregnant at the same time."

He shook his head. "I never liked your father. Even when we were kids, he struck me as shady. Your grandfather, on the other hand, always seems like a decent guy."

I sighed. "Yeah. Grandpa Sterling is really special. I don't see him often enough now that he moved down to Florida. After my dad left my mom, he really stepped up for us. He never missed a school recital or a tennis match. A few afternoons a week, I used to follow him around one of his hotels after school. Even back then, I saw the difference between how my grandfather and my father treated staff and how staff treated them. Grandpa Sterling's employees revered him, much like Grace Copeland's staff seems to have loved her. Whereas the staff feared my father more than respected him."

"I guess every family has its black sheep."

I nodded. "They sure do." Realizing I'd shared a lot more about my screwed-up family than he had, I asked, "Who's your family's black sheep?"

Weston shoved his hands into his pockets and looked down. "Me."

I almost laughed. "You? You're the prince of the Lockwood family."

Weston rubbed the stubble on his cheek. "You want to know a Lockwood secret?"

I smiled. "Absolutely."

"I was never the prince of the Lockwood family. They only had me for spare parts."

My smile faded. "What do you mean?"

Weston shook his head. "Nothing. Forget it." He paused and then tilted his head toward the door. "I'm going to check on something in the office before I call it a night. I'll see you in the morning?"

"Umm... Yeah. Sure. Have a good night."

CHAPTER 9

Sophia

The next morning was busy. Weston and I brought the two contractors through the construction site together, and then I headed down to where our legal and accounting team were set up in a conference room. The smile on my face as I opened the door wilted almost immediately upon entry. My father sat at the head of the table. I hadn't even known he was back in town...or perhaps he'd never left.

"I thought you went back to Florida?"

My father gave me a stern look. "I'm obviously needed here."

"Oh?" I folded my arms over my chest. "Did someone tell you that?"

I realized there was a room full of men with their heads swinging back and forth, watching the exchange between my father and me. I tilted my head toward the door. "Could we...talk outside for a minute?"

Dear old Dad looked like he *really* wanted to say no, but instead he let out an exasperated sigh and marched to the door.

Outside, he spoke before I had the chance to. "Sophia, you're in over your head. You can't run a hotel *and* lead a team to perform due diligence so we can make the winning bid to that shareholder."

I shook my head. "I thought we discussed this at dinner. If I need assistance, I'll call you."

As usual, my father ignored me. "You should be focusing on getting information out of the Lockwoods."

"What information?"

He sighed, as if he couldn't believe he had to explain everything to me. "We agreed to a sealed-bid process. But it would be helpful to know what the Lockwoods will be bidding so we can best their offer without losing our shirts."

"And how would you like me to do that?"

"That young blood who came to your defense the other day thinks you're a damsel in distress. Use that against him."

"What are you talking about?"

I wanted to think I didn't understand him, because it was unbelievable to me that a father would suggest such a thing to his child. Or maybe I didn't want to believe that mine cared more about money than whoring out his only daughter.

"Use your feminine wiles, Sophia. Lord knows you inherited those from your mother."

I felt my face heat. "You're serious?"

"We all have to do things at times for the sake of the family."

I gritted my teeth and took a deep breath before answering. "Which family are you doing things for today, Father? Would that be the one you walked away from when I was three weeks old, or the one where your mistress was *nineteen* when she got pregnant?"

"Don't be a smartass, Sophia. It's very unbecoming of you."

As per usual, trying to have a professional conversation with my father proved fruitless. I had better things to do than stand here and argue with him, so I gave in...for now. He could win this battle, but I knew exactly what I needed to do to win the war. Plus, the valuation of this hotel was going to take weeks, and my father's wife would never tolerate him being gone that long. I'd outlast him for sure.

"You know what? Why don't you work with the valuation team? I have plenty of other stuff to keep me busy."

He gave a curt nod. "Good. I'm glad we understand each other."

I extended a plastic smile, though my father had never spent enough time with me to understand my sarcasm. "Oh, I understand you perfectly, Dad. I'll see you later."

"I saw Billy Boy is back."

I'd been working behind the counter at the lobby reception desk when Weston walked up behind me. He stood a little too close, so I moved to a computer three spots over and hit the space bar to wake up the operating system.

"You seem to have a lot of free time to wander around the hotel and check out what my family and I are up to," I said. "It's too bad you don't use that time to do something helpful. While Louis is working on filling the open positions, the staff is short-handed. I'm sure they could use you to clean some toilets, if you have nothing to do."

Weston followed me over to where I'd moved and leaned one elbow on the counter, facing me while I typed. "Doesn't look like you're too busy yourself, moving around from computer to computer."

I sighed and motioned with my hand. "Do you see anyone else here? I'm helping out so Louis can do interviews upstairs for the assistant manager positions. One of the two reception clerks is in the back working on assigning rooms for new check-ins, and the other is at lunch."

"Trying to win employee of the month already?" He chided. "Such a kiss ass."

Renée, the woman who worked the reception desk, came out from the back. She looked at the two of us and said, "I'm sorry. I can come back."

"No, no. It's fine," I assured her. "You're not interrupting anything. What can I do for you?"

She held out one of those little cardboard room key holders with a plastic swipe card inside. "I switched your room. Would you like me to have housekeeping go up and move your stuff?"

I shook my head and took the key, slipping it into my pocket. "No, that's fine. I'll pack it up and move later. Thank you, Renée."

Once she walked away, Weston squinted at me. "Why are you changing rooms?"

"I wanted a bigger one. When I checked in, no suites were available."

"They weren't when I checked in either. Where are you moving?"

I knew my answer wasn't going to go over well. "One of the presidential suites."

"I asked for a suite when I arrived, too. How many are available?"

"Just the one."

"So why do you get it?"

"Because I'm the more diligent employee and followed up first thing this morning. Where were you? I saw you disappear bright and early out the front door."

"I had a meeting."

I perked a brow. "Another meeting? Let me guess. This one is secret, too?"

Weston's lips pressed into a straight line.

I offered a knowing smile before walking down to the other end of the counter. "That's what I thought."

He followed yet again. "If two guests checked in and both requested an upgrade, how would you decide whom to give it to?"

"I'd give it to the one who requested it first."

"That's right. So that's what we should do here."

I'd had to wait for my checked luggage after our flight while I'd watched Weston breeze right out the door at JFK. I didn't see him again after that until the next morning, so it was safe to assume he'd checked in first. He was technically right on what *should* happen here. But I'd had a lot of trouble falling and staying asleep the last week, and I thought having separate rooms to work and sleep in might help my mind relax better. Every time I looked over at my growing pile of work or my laptop, it made me think of ten other things I needed to jump out of bed and write down on my to-do list.

I sighed. "Could we at least alternate? A week at a time, perhaps?"

"Or...we could share it. We both know how much you enjoy being alone with me in the bedroom."

I scoffed. "I don't think so."

He shrugged. "Suit yourself. Your loss."

I shook my head. "I'm sure I'll be kicking myself for turning down such a generous offer."

Weston moved to stand directly behind me as I looked down to type into the reception computer. "You look beautiful with your hair up, by the way. Thank you. I appreciate it."

He was so close that I felt the heat from his body on my back. "I didn't do it for you to appreciate. Just living up to my part of the agreement we made—regardless of how stupid I think it is."

Weston inched closer. His breath tickled my neck when he spoke again. "So you didn't think of me at all when you were looking in the mirror getting ready this morning? I think you did."

I *had* thought about him while I was putting my hair up. He'd told me he liked to look at my neck, and the thought that he might get off on it today had made me anticipate seeing him all morning. But I would never admit any of that.

"Contrary to your belief, the world doesn't revolve around you. Especially mine."

"Do you want to know why I love your neck so much?"

Yes. "I don't really care."

"I love your skin. When you wear your hair up, I can stare at your neck without you knowing I'm looking. Like this morning, while you were getting your coffee at six twenty."

Maybe it should've felt a little creepy hearing he'd watched me grab my morning coffee, but for some reason, it didn't. Oddly, I found it kind of erotic that he stole glances when he could. Though I tamped down that feeling. "I think you need a hobby, Weston."

"Oh, I have one I quite enjoy." He leaned closer and lowered his voice. "Next time, I think I'm going to fuck you while you look in the mirror you use to put your hair up. So whenever you stare at your reflection, you won't be able to see anything but me watching you come while I'm buried deep inside you."

I was certain that if I backed up a few inches, I'd bump right into a steely erection. And though I was currently wearing my hair up as part of a bargain to keep what had happened between us private, I had the strongest urge to take a step back and find out, even while standing in public for anyone to see.

Luckily, a couple walked through the revolving door and headed right for the front desk, shaking me out of my moment of almost-insanity. Weston took a few steps back as they approached and then disappeared altogether while I checked them in. I took a deep breath and tried to focus, though the short training Louis had given me this morning on the hotel's guest registration system seemed to have gotten lost in my lusty haze of a brain, and I had to get Renée from the back to help me finish.

Not too long after that, I got back in the swing of things. I spent a few more hours working the front desk, and then went to check in with my family's team working on the valuation in the conference room upstairs. To my happy surprise, my father was no longer there. I sat with Charles, the senior manager of the audit team, who was in charge of the project. Three men and one woman sat around the table, buried in paper as they combed through the hotel's assets. Charles told me he would be bringing in a few art evaluators to assess the market value of some of the paintings scattered throughout the hotel, as well as an antiques expert. My hour-long conversation added a dozen more things to my to-do list, and when I looked down at the time on my phone, I couldn't believe it was almost six o'clock.

"Did my father say if he was coming back tonight or tomorrow?"

Charles shook his head. "I don't think he was planning on coming back today. But he did say he'd see me in the morning."

I sighed. "Great."

Charles smiled sympathetically. "If it helps, you're doing fine on your own. He didn't ask a single question you hadn't hit us with yesterday."

That made me smile a little at the end of a long day. "Thanks, Charles."

Since it was getting late, and I knew the housekeeping staff went down to a skeleton crew soon, I figured I should move to my new room so the old one could be cleaned and put back into inventory in case we had any walk-in guests tonight. The hotel wasn't sold out, but there weren't that many vacant rooms.

On the eighth floor, I packed up my clothes, toiletries, and all the work I'd spread out across the desk. Grabbing the stuff on hangers from the closet, I laid the garments over my arm. I'd stop back here to replace these with some empty ones from my new room on my way down to let the front desk know I'd made the switch.

With my purse, laptop, one big and one small suitcase, files, and a dozen hangers, I probably should have made two trips rather than one. Accessing the upper floors of the hotel required inserting a key into the elevator panel, so once I was inside, I attempted to balance everything while I dug my new swipe card out of my pocket.

The thirty-second floor of the hotel was the top floor, and all suites. The two largest ones, the presidential suites, were located in the corners on opposite sides of the building. A full row of diamond-level suites stretched between them. Finding room thirty-two twelve, I dropped a file on the floor while trying to scan the card in the electronic door reader. Bending to pick it up, I lost two of my dresses from their hangers. I barely managed to make it inside as more stuff started to spill from my arms. Using my hip to hold the door open, I dragged each of my bags inside the room and let whatever fell to the floor stay there. Sighing, I left everything at the front door and walked down the hall into the suite.

Wow. Totally worth the pain in the ass to change rooms.

To my right was a full living room, with a fireplace, floor-to-ceiling views of Central Park, two couches and two chairs, and a tremendous flat-screen TV. A set of French doors led to a small office, and another door on the left led to the bedroom. I walked there first, and a king-size bed with plush linens greeted me. On one side was a pretty settee, a love seat, and another fireplace. The other side of the room had the same floor-to-ceiling windows as the living room and—*what is that in the corner on top of another chair*?

It looked almost like luggage.

I stepped closer, and my eyes widened, confirming that it indeed was luggage.

Oh my God.

They'd assigned me a suite that wasn't vacated yet!

I hadn't noticed a sound since I walked in the door, but suddenly I heard the shower running, loud and clear.

Oh my God! I'm in someone's suite.

While they're in the freaking shower!

I froze for a few heartbeats, and then darted for the door. In my panic, I fumbled half of my belongings as I tried to toss them all out into the hallway before the guest got out of the shower.

But unfortunately, I was too slow.

A deep voice stopped me dead in my tracks.

"Going somewhere?"

Though, it wasn't just any deep voice.

No. *Of course not.*

Only one man had that thick, hard-edged, confident tone that simultaneously irritated the shit out of me and made me want to slide my damp panties down my wobbly legs.

I didn't even have to turn and see the face to confirm who it was.

In fact, I probably should have just finished tossing my stuff into the hall and bolted.

But I didn't.

Instead, I took a deep breath and ever so slowly turned around.

Only to find Weston standing in nothing but a towel wrapped around his waist.

The sight made my brain stutter.

"I knew you'd eventually come around." He smirked. "You should have just joined me in the shower. Though I do love undressing you myself."

I hadn't gotten a good look at Weston fully undressed before. The first time we were together, he was behind me most of the time. And the second, he'd had on an unbuttoned dress shirt and pants. I'd obviously felt his chest pressed against me, so I knew his body was firm, but seeing all of his sculpted flesh up close and personal was an entirely different experience. Beads of water traced their way down carved pecs onto washboard abs, and I had the strongest urge to catch each drop with my tongue. It was nearly impossible to lift my eyes and deprive them of such a magnificent view. But I forced myself to snap out of it.

"What the hell are you doing in my room? I thought Renée had accidentally assigned me a suite that hadn't been vacated yet."

"*Your* room? We decided to alternate weeks."

"Yes, but the first week was mine!"

"Who said? You agreed that the first guest to request an upgrade is the one who gets the room."

"But I had the key already. You knew that! You watched Renée hand it to me earlier."

Instead of answering me, Weston's eyes dropped to my breasts. I had no idea how the man managed it, but somehow it felt like his fingers were grazing over my skin as his gaze traveled over my body.

Did it suddenly get warm in here?

My heart thundered in my chest while emotions ran through my head. Disgust—a little at him and a lot at me—anger, conflict, confusion, and a heaping dose of *Jesus Christ, if that isn't the sexiest thing I've ever seen.*

Weston took a few slow steps toward me. Acting on self-preservation, I raised a hand and showed him my palm. "Stop. Don't come any farther."

He froze mid-step and raised his eyes to meet mine. The beautiful sea of blue irises disappeared as black, stormy pupils pushed their way in. We stood there for a long moment in an intense stare-off. Weston seemed conflicted about his next move—until his eyes caught on something to my right. They lingered there for a few heartbeats, and when his eyes slid back to meet mine, the air shifted. He could barely contain the grin he attempted to hide, and his eyes glinted with renewed mirth. I turned to see what had caused such a change and found myself staring at my own reflection. A giant mirror hung in the hallway, above a half-moon-shaped table.

Shit. I closed my eyes.

The sound of something soft falling to the floor caused a sharp intake of my breath. I didn't need to look to know what it was.

Weston's towel.

"Turn around. Hands on the table. Ass out, sweetheart."

I didn't budge. A war raged inside me. Was I really this hard up that a firm body could have me listening to commands barked by a man I couldn't stand? *Again?* What the hell was I doing? The door was only three feet away. Surely I was capable of putting one foot in front of the other and leaving this jerk with nothing but his misplaced confidence and a painful erection to take care of himself. Yet... I couldn't deny that my body wanted him. *Outrageously* so. It felt like my skin was on fire, waiting for his touch.

He moved closer, and the heat from his body radiated behind me. Unable to make a decision to flee, but also not ready to give in, I kept my eyes closed tight.

Weston gripped my hip and his fingers dug into my skin. "You're going to have to give me something. A nod, a yes, bending over and showing me what you want, a moan—I'll take a few blinks, if that's all you can do. I'm into role-playing you not wanting me to touch, if that would work for you. But only after I'm sure you're giving me permission, Soph."

Weston's other hand raised to my neck. He trailed a finger over my throat and traced my collarbone. I lost the little resolve I'd been holding on to.

Opening my eyes, I looked into his tempestuous ones. "Fine. But this is it. I'm not kidding, Weston. This needs to stop."

"Whatever you say."

"I'm serious."

"So am I. Now turn around. Grip the table. Eyes in the mirror at all times."

It was kind of hard to feign righteous indignation when you were about to bend over and let a man have his wicked way with you. But I was a trooper. I kept my face stoic.

"Hey, Soph?"

My eyes met Weston's in the mirror.

He grinned. "*To come or not to come, that is the question.*"

I did my best not to smile. "Let's just get it over with."

Twice.

I sighed, smoothing down my hair. For a man who had wanted me to wear my hair up so badly, he sure had no problem ripping it down. Weston was definitely a hair puller. And to my utter disgust, I loved every last tug. Though, this was the part I hated. Within two minutes of him straightening my skirt and disappearing into the bathroom, the cold air of rationality replaced the warmth of absurdity. In the heat of the moment, I couldn't get enough. It was as if my lungs couldn't take in enough air when Weston came near me with that darkness in his eyes. But as soon as it was over, a flood of oxygen had my brain firing again.

I rushed to gather my belongings before he came out of the bathroom, though I didn't quite make it. Standing in the hallway, I was reaching for my suitcase when Weston covered my hand with his on the handle.

"Give me two minutes, and I'll be out of here."

I turned. "You're going to give me the suite?"

He nodded. "I just need to pack up my stuff."

I studied his face. "You sure?"

Weston grinned. "I'm game for sharing, if you prefer."

I rolled my eyes, feeling more like the Weston and Sophia I was comfortable with. "Go pack your shit."

He smiled and disappeared into the bedroom as I rolled back inside. A few minutes later, he walked out with his zipped suitcase in one hand and his dress shirt in the other. Setting down the case, he raised his arms to slip into his shirt, and I noticed for the first time a large scar running down the side of his body. It was faint, only a shade lighter than his tanned skin. Earlier, all I'd been able to see was a mass of perfect muscle, so I guess those outshined any minor flaws.

"Is that from a surgery of some sort?" I asked.

Weston frowned. He looked down and began to button his shirt. "Yup."

Clearly, he didn't want to talk about it. But I was curious. "What kind of surgery was it?"

"Kidney. A long time ago."

"Oh." I nodded.

He picked up his suitcase, not bothering to finish buttoning or tuck his shirt in. "I left you something in the bedroom."

"What?"

"You'll see."

Weston seemed unsure how to say goodbye. Eventually, he said, "You know I'm only rushing out because I can take a hint, and I know you don't want me here after, right?"

"I appreciate that."

"While I'm at it, I love your ass, but I wouldn't mind looking at you while I'm inside you at some point in the future. Maybe even tasting those lips that like to yell at me." He winked. "Bite 'em a few times."

I sighed and looked away. "There can't be a next time, Weston. This really needs to stop."

I didn't need to look up to know he was smiling. His voice said it all. "'Night, Feef."

CHAPTER 10

Weston

"How are you, old man?"

Mr. Thorne grumbled. "I got a hemorrhoid the size of a golf ball sticking out of my ass, haven't been laid since the Clinton administration, and the only person who comes to visit me is you. How do you think I'm feeling?"

I smiled and pulled a chair up to his bedside. "Two out of three of those I could do without knowing. But that last one—you're a very lucky man."

He waved his hand at me. "Did you bring me the goods?"

I shook my head, pulled ten scratch-offs from my inside suit jacket pocket, and dug a quarter from my pants. Grabbing a book off his nightstand, I set it up on his lap so he could work on his lottery tickets.

Mr. Thorne started to scratch off the gray latex and pointed to the nightstand without looking up. "Make sure you take the ten from my money over there."

"Okay."

Same conversation we had every time I came by since I'd been back in New York, and I wasn't even sure he knew I'd never taken a dollar from him. The ten bucks was the least I could bring him for listening to my ass over the last few years.

While he was fiending on his lotto tickets, I swiped the remote from next to him on the bed and flicked to CNN.

"Hey. I was watching that."

I arched a brow. "You were? Let me save you the trouble. It's not the big guy with the shaved head's kids. It's the scrawny dude with the mullet and crooked teeth's spawn."

Mr. Thorne spent most of his day watching Jerry Springer and other similar programs. I had no idea if this particular episode was about paternity or not, but all those stupid shows seemed to end the same way.

"Smartass," he grumbled.

"You know what they need to do on one of those shows?" I said. "Have a minimum income of a million dollars a year for guests. Change up the scenery a bit. Maybe I could sign up a few members of my family. Airing the dirty laundry of rich assholes is just as entertaining as the dirty laundry of people who don't have a pot to piss in."

Mr. Thorne scoffed. "Like anyone could relate to your problems, spoiled rich kid."

Someone looking in from the outside might think I had reason to be insulted by the way the old man talked to me. But it was just his way—his way of reminding me my problems could be a hell of a lot worse.

He finished scratching off his tickets and tossed one at me. "Won five dollars. Only cost me ten. Give me back my ten and take this and a five. You can cash it in next time you stop to get my tickets. Bring me one of those ten-dollar scratch-offs next time instead of ten one-dollar ones."

I tucked the winning ticket into my suit jacket. We sat quietly for the next ten or fifteen minutes, watching a story on CNN about some pharmaceutical company being investigated for selling a knock-off Viagra that supposedly caused some people to stay hard for up to four days. I wasn't impressed; Sophia had done that shit even longer using nothing but her attitude.

Mr. Thorne clicked the TV off. "So, talk to me, kid. How are the urges these days?"

My gut reaction was to respond the same way I would if my father or grandfather had asked that question, which would be to lie and say I was doing great. But there was an old saying about the four people you always tell the truth: your wife, your priest, your doctor, and your lawyer.

But that was the sober man's creed. The rest of us had five: your sponsor.

"I've had my moments. I paid the cleaning woman at the hotel where I'm staying a hundred bucks to take all the little liquor bottles out of my room the other day."

He nodded. "Have you been going to meetings?"

I shook my head. "Not in the last two weeks, but I've gone to the shrink my grandfather is making me see a few times."

Mr. Thorne wagged a crooked finger at me. "Get your ass to a meeting. You know the drill. You don't have to talk, but you need to at least listen. That reminder is key in your recovery."

I tried to make light of things. "I'm here listening to you. Why can't that count as my daily listening torture?"

But Mr. Thorne took his sobriety very seriously. "Because I'm fourteen years clean, and the only way I can get myself a drink is by flinging my shriveled-up body off this bed and dragging these useless legs to a store. Which we both know, I don't have the strength for anymore. But you, you have temptation all around you. Temptation right at your fingertips. Hell, you don't even have to get up off your ass to get yourself a drink. Just lie in your fancy bed, in your fancy hotel room, and pick up the phone and call room service."

I ran a hand through my hair and nodded. "Yeah. Okay. I'll find a meeting."

Walter Thorne and I went way back. Nine years ago I'd wandered into his hospital room drunk one night when I'd meant to visit my sister. I'd tripped over my own two feet and woke him up, laughing hysterically from the floor beside his bed. Turned out, I hadn't even been on the right floor of the hospital. But the ornery bastard nevertheless sat up and asked me what my problem was.

I spent the next three hours unloading shit to him that I'd never said aloud to another soul. When I was done, I was pretty much sober, and Mr. Thorne proceeded to tell me he was in the hospital for his sixth surgery in five years since becoming a paraplegic when he crashed his car into a tree while drunk.

I didn't visit my sister that day. But I came back sober the next day and sat with Mr. Thorne for a few hours after I visited Caroline. In fact, I visited with Mr. Thorne for ten days after my sister was discharged. He spent half our time together telling me dirty jokes and the other half lecturing me about sobering up. It would be a much better story if I could say that had been a turning point for me. But it wasn't.

A few weeks later, I was back to partying, and I'd tossed the number Mr. Thorne gave me in the back of a drawer somewhere. Then five years ago, I dug it out and called him the night Caroline died. We started talking, and eventually I let him help me get sober.

"How are things between you and that jackass grandfather of yours?"

I forced a smile. "Everything's pretty good. As long as he continues to get outstanding reports from the shrink, and I live up to the twenty other things I had to agree to in order to get my job back."

"He's just looking out for you."

It was way more complicated than that; it always was with my family.

"How are things going with that lady friend you mentioned a while back?"

I had no idea who he was referencing, but I didn't need to in order to answer. I shrugged. "It was just a date. Nothing more."

"Boy, by the time I was your age, I was married with two kids."

"That's probably why you were divorced by the time you were thirty-five."

"Nah. My Eliza divorced me because I was a drunk who couldn't hold a job more than three months. Can't blame the woman. A good woman deserves a good man, and eventually she sees right through an imposter."

His comment made me think of Sophia. As much as I didn't want to think so—because it made my situation easier—she was a good woman. Mr. Thorne was the only person I could admit all my ugly shit to, and he wouldn't look down on me or judge me. Maybe it was because he had his own ugliness, or maybe it was because he was confined to this bed, and the only people who visited him were the nurse who got paid to take care of him and me. But whatever the reason, I trusted him with anything. In a lot of ways, he'd taken Caroline's place. She was the only person I ever felt like myself around.

Blowing out a deep breath, I said, "I've actually started seeing a new woman. Well, she's not really new, considering we've known each other since we were kids. And I guess technically we aren't seeing each other, but whatever. There's a woman."

Mr. Thorne nodded. "Go on."

"There's not much to tell. Her name is Sophia, and she's basically my enemy."

"So, you're telling me you're sleeping with the enemy, like the movie?"

I laughed. "A different kind of enemy. Basically, my family and her family hate each other."

"But you two get along?"

I shook my head. "Not exactly. Most of the time, she's about five seconds away from kicking me in the balls."

Mr. Thorne's bushy brows dipped down. "I'm confused. So, you're not sleeping with this girl?"

"No, I am."

"But she wants to kick you in the balls?"

I smiled. "She does."

"And that makes you smile? I don't understand this generation at all."

"She doesn't like me. But her body does. We're like a tornado and a volcano. It's rare the two meet. But when they do, it's explosive."

"Explosive, huh? That sounds more like destructive to me."

He had a point. But it was okay. Sophia wouldn't get hurt, since she was the tornado, and they tended to move on quickly. It was the volcano that sat around dormant for years on end.

"Be careful. That sounds like the type of thing that can jeopardize your recovery."

"Don't worry about me. I got it all under control."

Our eyes met for a moment, and we both knew this wasn't the first time I'd uttered those words and been wrong. Though I appreciated him not reminding me of that.

I stood. "How about we get your lazy ass into the wheelchair, and I take you outside for a walk? It's beautiful out."

Mr. Thorne nodded and smiled. "I'd like that."

Later that afternoon, I hit up an AA meeting on my way back to The Countess. After, I sat in my office thinking about what Mr. Thorne had said. I'd assured him I had things under control, and that was accurate in regard to my drinking, but the truth of the matter was that Sophia Sterling was getting under my skin. If I wasn't watching her from afar, I was thinking of excuses to go talk to her, which inevitably led to an argument I'd get off on. My days had become centered around watching her or interacting with her, and our nights together fulfilled my fantasies. If I couldn't goad her into a fight that heated things up between us, I sat in my room alone, jerking off to the memory. I'd even arranged it so when I moved out of the presidential suite, I moved into the room she'd just vacated and declined housekeeping. So now my sheets smelled like her, and every time I went into the shower, I imagined her standing in the exact same spot bringing herself to orgasm. Between that and how I liked to secretly watch her in line at the coffee shop and working behind the reception desk, I was turning into a real creeper.

So when Sophia knocked on my open door, I felt like a kid caught with his hand in the cookie jar.

I cleared my throat. "Yes, Fifi?"

She rolled her eyes and walked in. "Why did you start calling me that in high school, anyway?"

I leaned back in my chair and tossed my pen onto the desk. "I don't know. I said it once and saw that it got a rise out of you, so it stuck."

She sighed. "Some things never change, huh?"

"Well, technically they do. These days you're the one getting the rise out of me, aren't you?" I winked.

Sophia smirked, but ignored my comment. She took a seat in a chair on the other side of my desk and crossed her legs.

Was it me, or did her skirt ride up a little higher today? This morning, when I watched her from afar at the coffee shop, she'd had her hair down, but it was pulled to the side so I had a clear view of the beautiful skin on the back of her neck. While she stood in line, her perfectly manicured nails gently grazed up and down from her hairline into her silk blouse. I'd assumed it was my vivid imagination, and she wasn't intentionally trying to drive me crazy, but this afternoon's skirt *was* a bit on the short side.

When my eyes rose to meet hers, I could've sworn they held a hint of a gleam. Yet she was all business when she spoke.

"So, I received the two quotes from my contractors. The estimates aren't that different, but only one feels they could get the job done in the timeframe we need. Any chance your quote came in?"

"Actually, it did. I've only glanced at the bottom line, so why don't we take a look at all three and see where things stand."

We moved over to the round conference table to spread out, and Sophia and I exchanged estimates. It only took a quick look to realize both of her estimates were significantly lower than mine. While my contractor felt comfortable committing to get the work done in three months, he'd included a number of rush charges throughout. The only extra fees Sophia's contractors charged were for things like required night differential and overtime.

While we were reviewing the estimates, Sophia's cell phone rang. She quickly sent the call to voice mail, but not before we both read the name on the caller ID.

I felt a stab of jealousy in my chest. "I thought things were over between you and the boring Brit?"

She sighed. "Can we both pretend you didn't see that just now?"

My jaw flexed. "If that's what you want."

Sophia nodded and went back to reading the estimates. A few minutes later, she pushed the papers aside. "Well, I think it's obvious who we should use."

Maybe on paper it was. But I hadn't forgotten the way Travis Bolton looked at her. "It's not always about the lowest bidder."

Her tone was defensive. "I know that, but the Boltons are also the most confident that they can get the job done, and they have a great reputation and have never let my family down."

"I'll need to make some calls to ask around about them."

Sophia's lips pursed. "Whatever you need to do. But obviously the sooner we decide the better."

Fuck. I wanted to suck on those puckered lips. We had an obvious history of our attraction heating up when we were pissed off, but at the moment I was confused as to what the hell I was even pissed about. Was it because my estimate was clearly the shittiest one? Or because her asshole ex had just called her? Or did the thought of Travis Bolton hanging around her while doing the construction here drive me a little bit nuts?

Sophia's cell phone interrupted my thoughts again. We simultaneously read the name *Liam*, and I put my hand out, palm up. "How about I answer?"

Her eyes widened, and she sucked in her bottom lip. "What would you say?"

"Is it over?"

She nodded. "I want to bury the body deeper than eight feet."

I flashed a wicked smile. I could easily have picked up the phone from the table, and I doubted she would have stopped me. But I wanted her to hand it to me.

"Give me the phone." My hand was still extended, waiting.

I felt a surge of pride when she dropped it into my palm. The cell rang for a third time, so I swiped to answer and brought it to my ear.

"Hello."

"Who is this?"

"This is the man fucking your ex-girlfriend. And we're busy at the moment. So what can I do you for, *Liam*?"

Sophia's eyes looked like they might bulge out of her head. She covered her mouth with both hands.

The asshole on the other end of the phone had the balls to sound indignant. "*Put Sophia on the phone.*"

I leaned back. "No can do. She's a little tied up at the moment, if you get my drift."

"Is this a joke?"

"A joke? No, the joke's on you. I bet you didn't even know our girl likes to be tied up, did you? Such a shame. Maybe if you had taken your time exploring what the beautiful woman needs, she wouldn't be moaning my name at night. But that's not your thing, is it? You're only into fulfilling your own needs. You know, like with her cousin."

I kept quiet for a few heartbeats and waited to see what good ol' Liam had to say about that. Though, apparently I'd stumped the idiot. I could only hear him breathing loudly. So I figured I'd end on a fun note.

"Okay, then. It's been great chatting with you. And Liam, lose Sophia's number."

I swiped to end the call and offered the phone back to a very stunned Sophia. She continued to stare at me, bug-eyed, even as she took her cell. From the look on her face, I thought a tirade was likely on the way once she managed to get her bearings again.

"Too much?" I asked, lifting a brow.

Sophia's mouth hung open. But then her lips slid into a giant grin. "Oh my God! That was awesome!"

"Glad you think so. I was beginning to think you were going to lay into me. Although, that would turn into a big fight, and we both know where that seems to take us. So it wouldn't be such a bad thing."

We had a good laugh, and then Sophia swept all the papers on the table into a neat pile. I thought we were going back to business.

"Can I ask you something?" she said.

I nodded, and again, she chewed on that bottom lip.

"How did you know Liam had never tied me up?"

"The way you reacted when I asked your permission to use my belt. You wanted me to, but you weren't comfortable admitting that. If it hadn't been your first time, you would have reacted differently."

She nodded, but went quiet again. Eventually, she said, "But how did you know I wanted you to?"

Man, that Liam really was a dipshit. Didn't the fucker ever read what she wanted and try to satisfy her? I couldn't believe she had to ask me that question. Though I didn't want to make her feel foolish, so I did my best to answer without any hint of judgment in my voice.

"It's just something I sensed from you."

She shook her head. "How? Do I appear weak or something?"

"Just the opposite. You seem very much in control, which is why I thought it might work for you to let go a little. What you like in the bedroom in no way reflects who you are as a businessperson."

Sophia was quiet again. "Is this your thing? You're a dominant or something?"

I shook my head. "No. It's not *my thing*."

"Oh. Okay."

I leaned close and wound a lock of her hair around my finger until she looked up at me. Then I smiled and gave it a good, firm yank. "But it appears to be *our thing*."

CHAPTER 11

Sophia

I wasn't sure what bugged me more—the fact that in three short, intimate encounters, Weston had figured out something Liam had no clue about after more than eighteen months together, or that he'd figured out something even I wasn't aware of. But either way, he was right. While I wanted to argue about business with Weston, and challenge him on everything, what I seemed to like in the bedroom was how he took charge. Sex with Weston was light years better than what things had been like between Liam and me. I'd chalked it up to the spark that came with our arguing, but there was more to it than that, and the revelation pretty much freaked me out.

So for the next twenty-four hours, I did my best to avoid Weston. And I was successful, too. Until I came out of the office supply store a few blocks away from the hotel at close to eight o'clock at night, and I happened to see Weston up ahead on the opposite side of the street.

Since he was walking the direction I had to go, I kept him in my line of sight for the next two blocks. I figured he was on his way back to the hotel, like I was, but when he turned right instead of left at the next corner, I realized that wasn't the case.

Standing at an intersection, I looked left and could see The Countess one block over. To my right, I watched Weston continue to walk. Conflicted, my head swung back and forth a few times before I finally sighed and decided a little extra walk tonight would do me some good.

I let more distance gap between us as I followed him from the opposite side of the street. Whereas before we'd both been heading toward the hotel, and if I got caught behind him, I had a legitimate excuse, now I was just a plain old stalker. I tailed him for a solid ten minutes, turning left and right with no idea where the hell we were going. Eventually, he turned in to an office building. I caught up and watched from across the street as he walked through the glass doors and headed straight for the elevator. With the show over, I probably should've turned around and weaved my way back to The Countess. But curiosity got the best of me.

Looking both ways, I jay-walked across the busy street toward the building. My heart sped up as I made my way to the glass doors. Weston had disappeared into the elevator, and I had no idea what the hell I was looking for. Yet for some stupid reason, I was willing to get caught to see if I could figure out where he was going.

In the lobby, I studied the building directory. It read like a typical Manhattan skyscraper, with dozens of doctors, lawyers, and corporate offices. Weston hadn't stopped to check the directory, so he'd clearly been here before, or at least knew where he was going. Disappointed–though I had no idea why I'd followed him to begin with–I turned to leave. The last thing I wanted was to get caught when my snooping hadn't even produced any good information. As I returned to the front door of the building, my cell buzzed. So I dug it out of my purse while I kept walking.

But my feet froze as I read the text that had come in.

If you wanted to know where I was going, all you had to do was ask.

Oh God. I felt nauseous.

But it couldn't be from Weston. He didn't have my cell phone number, as far as I knew. I racked my brain trying to figure out who else could have sent me such a text. Everyone I knew was in my contacts, and this message had come from an unknown number. It *had to be* Weston. Nothing else made sense. Though, I was so freaked out that I hung on to hope.

My hands were shaky as I hit reply.

Who is this?

I held my breath as the little circles jumped around, waiting for the reply to come through. When it did, my mouth went dry.

You know who it is. Meet me in my room in one hour.

I practically ran back to the hotel. All I wanted to do was hide. In my suite, I looked down at my phone and realized fifteen minutes had passed since the text came in, yet I didn't remember any of the walk back.

Sitting down on my bed, I read Weston's text over and over again.

Meet me in my room in one hour.

Was he crazy? I was *not* going to his room. What was the point? To make it easy for him to torture me about being caught? And how did he even know I was following him? Even if he'd seen me somehow, I could've had an appointment in the same building. The entire thing could be a complete coincidence. For all he knew, I'd been walking to an appointment and never even noticed him up ahead on the other side of the street. His damn ego was so big that he just *assumed* I was following him?

Yeah, that's what happened. At least that was my story, and I was sticking to it.

In fact, the more I thought about it, the more it annoyed me that the arrogant bastard thought I'd been following him. He had absolutely no proof of that. Feeling a strong mix of pent-up anger and anxiety, I decided to take a bath to relax. Weston Lockwood was a damn egomaniac, and there was no reason to get myself all worked up over him. He had a lot of nerve barking at me to come to his room.

Turning on the bathwater, I pulled my hair into a ponytail and slipped out of my clothes while the tub filled. A good, long soak would make me forget all about the stupidity of this evening.

Except when I settled into the warm water, I couldn't relax one bit. I just kept grumbling different rants, over and over, about Weston. Not only was he a cocky jerk for thinking I'd followed him, but now that I'd thought about things, I decided he'd also had a lot of nerve saying those things to me in his office yesterday. The man made a lot of assumptions that weren't true.

Meet me in my room in one hour.

What did he think was going to happen? That I'd show up and spread my legs because I was so infatuated with him that I'd had to follow him?

I bet that's exactly what he thought.

And that made me even angrier.

So much so, that I decided to show up at his door—to deliver a piece of my mind, not a piece of my ass. Abruptly getting out of the tub, I splashed water all over the floor. I dried off and threw on a pair of jeans and a T-shirt. Grabbing my phone and room card from the counter, I didn't bother to check the time. I wasn't the least bit concerned whether I was early or late to his designated meeting time.

In the elevator, I jabbed the buttons on the panel and headed down to the eighth floor. Adrenaline surged through my veins as I raised my hand and rapped my knuckles on his door. I was so pumped up and ready to go that I started to rant before the door even swung all the way open.

"You have a lot of nerve. How dare—"

Oh shit.

This man was definitely not Weston.

He had on a bathrobe and slippers, looked to be in his seventies, and his white eyebrows drew down.

"Can I help you?"

"Umm... I think I might have the wrong room. I was looking for Weston?"

The man shook his head. "Think you got the wrong fella."

"I'm so sorry to disturb you."

He shrugged. "No problem. But take it easy on your Weston when you find him." He smiled. "Most times us men mean well. Sometimes it's just hard to see with our heads stuck so far up our asses."

I smiled. "Thanks. And sorry again."

After the man closed the door, I double-checked the number. This was definitely the one Weston had been in when our rooms were on the same floor. I was sure of it, because it was only two doors down from mine. But perhaps another suite had become available, and he'd moved, too.

As I waited for the elevator again, I decided it was probably for the best anyway. I didn't need to waste my time and energy on Weston. I might as well go back to my room. When the doors slid open, I was greeted by Louis.

"Hey. You're here late tonight," I said.

Louis smiled. "I'm just on my way out now."

I stepped into the elevator car. "Oh good."

"Did you get off on the wrong floor? Forget you changed rooms?"

I shook my head. "No, actually I was supposed to meet Weston. But he must've moved rooms, too. I think maybe a suite became available. I know he was also waiting for a bigger room."

Louis nodded. "He moved rooms. I was downstairs when he came down to change out his key the other day. But he didn't take an upgrade. He's just two doors over on this floor, in your old room."

"My old room?" My forehead wrinkled. "Had his room been reassigned after he checked out or something?"

Louis shook his head. "Not that I'm aware of. He just asked to move to the room you'd vacated. I told him housekeeping hadn't made it up there yet, but he said not to worry, he'd take care of it. I assumed you were aware."

The elevator doors had started to slide closed, but I stuck my hand in at the last second, stopping them.

"Ohhhh, that's right. I totally forgot about that. Sorry, Louis, it's been a long day. I'm going to get off here to go see him after all. You have a good night."

I walked down the hall to my old room, feeling completely confused. Why the hell had he changed rooms? The anger that had started to dissipate came rushing back with a vengeance.

This time I banged on the door like I meant it. *Bam. Bam. Bam.*

Weston opened the door wearing a smirk and immediately stepped aside. "Somebody's anxious," he purred.

"Why the hell are you in my old room?" I stomped past him.

"I think the better question is why are you following me?"

"I was not following you, you egotistical ass!"

Weston's smile widened. "Right."

"I wasn't!" My voice came out so high, it screeched a little at the end.

"Have a seat, Sophia."

I ignored him. "Why are you in my old room?"

Weston leaned against the desk and crossed his feet at the ankles. "I'll tell you when you tell me why you were following me."

"I was *not* following you. And you're totally delusional about why I do things. I happened to be at the same building as you because I had an appointment. While I'm at it, I also did not have sex with you because I like when you boss me around."

The smug bastard looked amused. He folded his arms across his chest. "No?"

I folded my own arms. "No."

We stared at each other. Weston had a gleam in his eyes, and I could see the wheels turning in his head as we waged an unspoken battle of who would blink first.

"Have a seat, Sophia."

"No."

He smiled. "See? Just because you like me to be in control when we have sex doesn't mean you want me to boss you around when we're not. One doesn't equate to the other. I promise you, it doesn't make you weak in my eyes that you like being dominated sexually."

"I do not."

Weston pushed off the desk and walked toward me. The air in the room began to crackle. As pissed off as I was, or as pissed off as I wanted to be, I couldn't deny that I was incredibly attracted to this man, in a way

I'd never experienced before. Something about having him near made me feel like I might combust if he didn't touch me.

He gripped my hip with one hand and looked up at me. Though he held me firm, I still knew without a shadow of a doubt that if I told him to take his hand off of me, he absolutely would. Our interactions were so bizarrely confusing.

"If I told you to remove your hand right now, what would you do?"

He looked me straight in the eyes. "I'd remove my hand."

"So how can you say I want to be dominated by you?"

"You're confusing domination with control. You can want to be dominated, and still keep control. In fact, you've been the one in control of what's going on between us every time we've been together."

I struggled to accept that, and Weston saw it in my face. "Just stop thinking about it and go with it, if you enjoy it."

I looked away, but turned back and caught his eyes. I didn't know why it was so important, but I had to ask. "Where were you going tonight? What was in that building?"

Weston was quiet for a moment. "I see a shrink. She has an office in that building."

Oh wow. That was the *last thing* I'd expected him to say.

He watched while I processed his answer. After giving me a minute, he tilted his head. "Any other questions?"

"No."

"Good, then it's my turn. Were you following me?"

How could I not be honest when he'd just admitted something so personal to me?

My smile was sheepish. "Yes, I was."

"Why?"

I thought about it. My answer came out on a laugh. "I have no goddamn idea. I saw you on the street when I came out of the store and just did it."

Weston smiled, and my insides melted a little.

"Where were you all day?" he asked. "I looked for you, but you weren't in your office. I couldn't even properly stalk you this morning while you were getting your coffee."

I grinned. "I hid in my room most of the day so I didn't have to see you."

The biggest, most honest smile spread across Weston's face. You would've thought I'd just told him how great he was rather than I'd spent the day avoiding him.

We again had a little stare-off, but this time Weston broke it. He reached down to unbuckle his belt. The sound of the metal clanking shot straight between my legs.

"Down on your knees, Sophia."

Oh God.

He put his hands on my shoulders and gave me a little nudge, encouraging me to kneel. To my utter disgust, I did. I dropped down and reached for his zipper.

"Hey, Soph?" Weston said.

I looked up.

He grinned. "I've been waiting a while to use this one. *Parting is such sweet* swallow."

CHAPTER 12

Weston

"I'm glad you agreed to come back today so we could pick up where we left off when we ran out of time yesterday. How was your evening?" Dr. Halpern asked.

"I didn't drink anything or do anything stupid, if that's what you're asking. I'm guessing you have to include that in your weekly report to my grandfather?"

Actually, I suppose stupidity was in the eye of the beholder. Some people might think sleeping with the enemy was stupid, but I happened to think what was going on between Sophia and me was pretty damn phenomenal.

"The reports I send your grandfather each week focus on your progress and the stability of your mental health. I know you signed a waiver of confidentiality, but that waiver is very limiting. You should know that I cannot legally, and I do not, provide any details of what we talk about. I simply report whether you're continuing to make progress, and whether I believe your emotional state puts you at risk for relapse."

I actually *hadn't* known that. I'd signed whatever legal mumbo jumbo my grandfather had put in front of me without reading it the day he'd agreed to give me another chance. For all I knew, he was entitled to keep my firstborn. I'd spent more time deliberating over whether I was willing to take weekly piss tests than whether I was willing to see a shrink. When I'd agreed to my grandfather's conditions to get my job back, I'd thought this would be the easy part. Go tell some quack a load of bullshit each week, meet regularly with my sponsor, and hit up some AA meetings. I'd be back in grandfather's good graces in no time. I didn't count on having the urge to actually talk to this woman.

"How has it been seeing Sophia every day at work? Last time we talked about her, I thought she might be a reminder of some difficult times in your life."

If Sophia had reminded me of Caroline initially, that definitely wasn't what I thought about when I saw her these days. In fact, it was nearly impossible to think of anything other than the sight of Sophia down on her knees in front of me last night. This morning, I'd nearly thrown myself into a diabetic coma with the amount of sugar I'd dumped into my coffee. Normally I put two sugar packets in, but this morning while I stalked her getting her coffee, I couldn't stop remembering the sound she'd made with my cock down her throat. It was a cross between a hum and a moan, and every time I thought about it, my balls tightened. Even now, I had to discreetly adjust my slacks.

"Working with Sophia has proven to be... interesting."

"Oh? How so?"

I looked over at the doc. "You really can't repeat anything we discuss in these sessions to my grandfather?"

Dr. Halpern shook her head. "Nothing. I only relay your overall mental stability."

I took a deep breath. "Okay. Well, Sophia and I... we've found a productive way to put the energy we create disliking each other to good use."

Dr. Halpern jotted something in her notebook. I wondered if it might be *fucking the enemy.* When she was done, she folded her hands on her lap. "So you and Sophia have entered into a personal relationship?"

"Something like that."

"Have you made her aware of your history?"

"You're going to have to be a little more specific there, Doc. What history are we talking about? Me sleeping with half the showgirls in Vegas? The abuse of alcohol? That my family is pretty much done with me unless I clean up my act? Or do you mean that I have babysitters who report back to my grandfather each week?"

I liked that Dr. Halpern rarely reacted—not even to my sarcastic questions. Instead, she just responded with no judgment.

"I was referring to your struggle with alcohol."

I shook my head. "No, that hasn't come up."

"Are you concerned it might be an issue for her, and that's why you haven't mentioned it?"

"It's just not the type of relationship we have."

"Well, many relationships start out as one thing and grow into something else. Sometimes when people wait too long to share something, there are hard feelings when it finally comes out. The person who was in the dark can feel an element of distrust."

"Trust me, our relationship isn't growing into anything more than it is."

"Why is that?"

"She's a nice girl—the kind who dates struggling playwrights, not recovering alcoholics who let down their family and can't remember the names of half the women who've been in their bed."

"When you say you let your family down, do you mean in a business sense, because your drinking interfered with your job? Or are you referring to Caroline?"

"All of it."

Dr. Halpern picked up her trusty pad and jotted a few notes again.

"What if I wanted to see those?"

"My notes?"

I nodded. "You're always writing, and it makes me curious."

Dr. Halpern smiled. Again, she folded her hands on her lap. "You're welcome to see my notes if it's causing you stress to not know what I'm writing. But I'm not sure reading them will make it clear why I thought whatever I've written down was important. How about, if you're curious, just ask me, and I'll tell you what I wrote and explain why I wrote it."

"Okay... What did you write down when I said I felt I'd let my family down?"

She looked down at her pad and then back up at me. "I wrote *misplaced guilt over Caroline's death.* And the reason I wrote that is because what seems to be at the center of your mental health issues is your sister."

I shook my head. "You're wrong."

"Meaning you don't think some of your struggles deal with the death of your sister, Caroline?"

"Oh no. I didn't mean that. Most definitely I struggle with my sister's death. What I meant was you were wrong in writing down *misplaced* guilt. My guilt is exactly where it belongs."

The hall lights in the executive office corridor were on a timer. After seven, sensors at various points would activate them only when motion was detected. Since I'd had a mostly unproductive afternoon, I decided to call it a night and go get something to eat at seven thirty. Closing up my office, I noticed the hall didn't illuminate right away, and it was easy to see that all the office doors were either closed or the lights were off. So as I walked down toward the elevator, I assumed Sophia wasn't in her office. But as I passed, I caught something in my peripheral vision that caused me to back up to her doorway.

"You're still here?"

The lights in Sophia's office flickered on. She must've been sitting so still that the motion sensors couldn't detect her.

"Were you sleeping or something?"

Sophia's eyes seemed to focus. "No, I guess I was lost in thought and didn't even realize the lights had turned off."

Yeah, I know the feeling.

I nodded. "I made some calls today and asked around about your contractor. Let's just go with the Boltons."

"Oh, great. I was going to ask you about that. Travis called me today to follow up."

Hearing that the asshole had called her made me want to change my mind. "What time did he call?"

"I don't know, maybe about eleven. Why?"

"Then why didn't you ask me?"

Sophia's lips puckered, while mine twitched to a grin. "Avoiding me again?"

"Just busy, Weston. Just once, can you not make something about you?"

"Sure, when I don't think it actually is."

Sophia rolled her eyes. "Is it difficult to carry around an ego that size? It must get heavy."

I laughed. Tilting my head toward the elevator panel, I said, "I was going to go downstairs to get something to eat. Did you have dinner yet?"

Sophia shook her head.

"Want to join me?"

She nibbled on that pouty bottom lip. "I still have a lot of work to do."

"I'm not asking for your hand in marriage, Fifi. Two people who work together can share a meal. If it makes you feel any better, we can discuss business while we eat. I spoke to the union again today and can fill you in."

She hesitated, but eventually sighed. "Okay."

I shook my head. "Such a sacrifice. You'll probably get into heaven with how good you are to me."

Sophia tried to hide her smirk, but failed. "I need to run to the ladies' room first. I'll meet you down there."

"Alright. If you want to avoid being alone with me in the elevator, I can understand that." I winked. "I'll get us a table downstairs at Prime."

"So do you miss London?" I asked, picking up my water. The waiter had dropped off the wine menu, and Sophia was busy perusing it.

She looked up and sighed. "I do, in a lot of ways. But in ways I didn't expect, I also *don't* miss it. How about you? Do you miss Vegas?"

I shook my head. "Not at all. Me and Vegas didn't mix well."

Sophia laughed. "Not even the nonstop parties? I know New York is the city that never sleeps, but it's different than Las Vegas. Maybe it's because I've only ever spent time in the touristy areas, but everyone in Vegas seems to be on vacation and having a great time. Whereas here, people walk around in suits to go to work."

I ran my finger along the condensation of my glass. "Especially the parties."

Sophia looked down at the wine list again and offered it to me. "Do you want to share a bottle?"

I hesitated, but our eyes caught, and somehow the truth tumbled out of my mouth. "I'm an alcoholic, and I'm in recovery."

Sophia's eyebrows jumped. "Oh! Wow. I'm so sorry for asking. I had no idea."

"It's fine. No need to apologize. And order your wine. Don't *not* indulge because of me. I'm good with sitting with someone who's having a drink and not having one."

She looked uncertain. "Are you sure? I don't need to have one."

Just then, the waiter walked over. "Can I get you something to drink or a glass of wine to start?"

I looked to Sophia, and she seemed torn. So I took the menu from her hands and handed it back to the waiter. "She'll have a glass of the 2015 Merryvale merlot, and I'll have a seltzer with lemon, please."

He nodded. "Very well. I'll give you a few more minutes to look at the dinner menu."

After he walked away, Sophia was still looking at me.

"It's fine, really. Stop thinking you're going to cause me to relapse or something."

She smiled. "You're giving me too much credit. I wasn't worried about your sobriety at all. I was actually wondering how you knew which wine I liked?"

"You left a half-full bottle in your room when you moved up to the suite."

She nodded. "That reminds me, you never did say why you moved into my room when I asked the other day."

I smirked. "You're right, I didn't."

She chuckled. "Seriously, was something wrong with your room?"

"No. My room was just fine."

"Was it too noisy?"

"Nope. It was pretty peaceful."

"So why would you move, then?"

"It's going to drive you nuts if I don't tell you, isn't it? Sort of like why you followed me the other day. You're a little on the nosy side, aren't you, Fifi?"

She squinted. "And you're a little on the annoying side. So spill it. Why did you move?"

My eyes dropped to her lips for a few heartbeats before returning to meet her gaze. "I figured it would smell like you."

Sophia sucked in a sharp breath. "That's why you told them not to make up the room?"

I leaned toward her. "The sheets still smell like you. I like to imagine that you laid in them completely naked with your fingers inside yourself."

Sophia's face flushed. Her lips parted, and her breathing was a little faster and a lot shallower. The look was so fucking sexy. It made my mind race, and I wondered if she would stop me if I slipped my hand beneath the table and fingered her.

Lucky for both of us, the waiter returned. Oblivious to the tension, he set down Sophia's wine and my drink. "So have you decided? Anything jump out at you that whets your appetite, or would you like to hear the specials?"

My eyes slanted to meet Sophia's. "Oh my appetite is whet, alright."

There was a sparkle in her eye, but she cleared her throat and folded her hands. "Actually, I'd like to hear the specials."

The waiter droned on for a few minutes...some fish...some Japanese beef...some fancy names to justify the lofty price tag. But basically whatever he said went in one ear and out my other. My brain was too busy to catch words as I imagined Sophia trying to keep a straight face while my fingers moved inside her and the waiter stood there talking. At some point, the masculine voice stopped and a higher-pitched one started, and then there was silence. It took a few seconds to realize both Sophia and the waiter were looking at me.

"Umm... I'll take the same thing she's having."

The waiter nodded. "Very good, sir."

After he disappeared, Sophia lifted her wine glass to her lips, hiding a smirk. "You have no idea what you just ordered, do you?"

I shook my head. "Not a damn clue."

A few more interruptions followed. The busboy brought bread, balsamic vinegar, and olive oil, and the restaurant manager walked over to introduce himself. Everyone at the hotel recognized us now. Unfortunately—or maybe fortunately for Sophia—the moment had fizzled by the time we were alone again. And even if it hadn't, the direction Sophia took the conversation certainly would have killed it.

"Can I ask how long you've been in recovery?"

"Fourteen months."

She nodded. "Good for you. I honestly had no idea. And here I thought our families did such a good job tracking all the gossip on each other."

"That's only true of the stuff they want people to know. But we all bury the things that might blemish the family name too much." I took the lemon off the side of my glass and squeezed it into my seltzer. "As far as the world knows, your mother divorced your father in an amicable split. If we hadn't spent that night together after the prom, I wouldn't have even known he'd left you guys."

Sophia tilted her head and studied me for a moment. "You never mentioned what I told you that night to anyone in your family, did you? I don't think I realized until this moment that you could have leaked the truth as gossip. I'm sure your father or grandfather would have shared it if you'd mentioned it to them."

I sipped my seltzer. "You told me that while we were lying in your bed. Give me a little more credit than that."

Sophia looked away but nodded. "So...the psychiatrist you go to, is that part of your recovery?"

I nodded. "It's part of my grandfather's recovery plan for me, anyway."

"What do you mean?"

"If I want to keep my job, I have to do what he says. Fourteen months ago, I wound up in the emergency room after nearly drinking myself to death. I did thirty days in rehab to dry out. During that time, my father and grandfather personally stepped in to take over the properties I ran. Las Vegas hotels have to be watched like a hawk. You tend to get a lot of gamblers with money problems as employees, and the theft and embezzlement can run rampant if no one's minding the store."

I shook my head. "They had to clean house while I was gone. I'd been too wasted most of the time to notice people stealing right under my nose. A woman I'd been sleeping with tried to blackmail my family with videos of me doing stupid shit, like taking a piss in the hotel's fountain. It wasn't pretty. The day I got out of rehab, my grandfather gave me an ultimatum: '*Do exactly what I say or you're on your own.*' Psychiatrist, AA meetings, random piss testing—you name it. I'm a puppet, and he holds the strings."

"Wow. Well, if it makes you feel any better, I'm pretty sure if I spiraled out of control and wound up in the emergency room, my father would hang up on the call and never even come."

I forced a smile. But really, her father pissed me off more than my own family did. At least mine had reason to treat me like dirt. I was a fuckup.

The waiter showed up with our food, and I was glad to move on from this conversation. I cut into my steak and steered things in an entirely different direction. "So, have you heard from the playwright since he and I had a nice chat?"

"He sent me a text, basically saying I had a lot of nerve letting another man answer my phone. I blocked him from calling or texting after that."

I smiled. "Good for you."

"What about you? Any disastrous relationships since we parted ways prom night?"

"I think those are the only kind I've had over the last twelve years."

"No serious girlfriend at all?"

"There was one. Brooke. We were together for a little over a year."

Sophia wiped her mouth with a napkin. "What happened there?"

"I fucked it up. We got together a few months before Caroline died five years ago. I spun out of control after that. Eventually, she didn't want to put up with my crap anymore." I shrugged. "I don't blame her."

I saw sympathy in Sophia's eyes and hated it. I guess I hadn't steered us in the right direction after all. "Not to change from the happy topics we've been discussing, but I'm down to two issues with the union—number of sick days and the quota for how many rooms the cleaning crew are required to clean per shift."

"Oh, that's great. Anything I can do to help?"

"I have a sit-down scheduled for the end of this week." I debated how to handle that. "If you'd like to join me, you're welcome."

Sophia smiled. "I'd like that. Oh, also, I have a friend coming in from London. Scarlett is staying here. She arrives this Friday, so your mention of the union meeting reminded me. If you see a woman with bright red lipstick that matches the bottoms of her shoes and looks like she stepped out of a *Vogue* magazine, that would be her."

"Sounds interesting."

"Oh, she is." Sophia lifted her glass and tilted it toward me. "You know, now that I think about it, in a way, she's sort of the female equivalent of you."

"How so?"

"She's arrogant and confident. The sea kind of parts when she walks into a room."

I perked a brow. "You better watch it there, that almost sounded like a compliment."

Sophia shook her head. "Let's not go crazy. But since it seems like you're in a pretty good mood, would it be okay if I kept the suite a few days longer than my week? At least until Scarlett leaves? Then we can switch, and you can keep it for as long as I did. Scarlett and I like to sit around and talk late at night, so it would be nice to have the living room while she's in town."

"No problem. I wasn't planning on making you alternate with me anyway."

"You weren't?"

I shook my head. "I never even requested an upgrade when I checked in. I just said that to screw with you."

Sophia's eyes widened. "Oh my God. You're such a jerk."

I chuckled. "You say that like you're surprised. But you can't honestly tell me that's news to you."

"No, definitely not. But thanks for coming clean and letting me keep the suite while Scarlett is here anyway."

After dinner, we walked to the elevator bank together. I kept my distance on the other side of the car and shoved my hands into my pants pockets. We'd had a nice evening. It was the first time I felt like Sophia had let her guard down. So as much as I wanted to back her up against the elevator wall and push the emergency stop button, she seemed vulnerable in a way that made it feel wrong to go there.

At the eighth floor, I hesitated as I got out—especially when I looked over at Sophia and could have sworn she looked a little disappointed about how our evening was ending. I had to force one foot in front of the other to make myself get off the damn elevator.

Looking back, I caught her eyes one last time. "Sweet dreams, Fifi."

She shook her head. "Goodnight, Weston."

CHAPTER 13

Sophia

I rolled over in bed, unable to fall asleep after half an hour.

It bugged me that Weston hadn't even attempted to persuade me to go back to his hotel room or worm his way into mine. I knew it was stupid to lose sleep over it, but I couldn't stop wondering why. He could have just been tired or not in the mood, but neither one of those seemed likely for Weston. So the only logical conclusion I could come up with was that he'd grown bored.

It shouldn't have been a shock to figure out he was one of those types of guys—the ones who enjoy the chase more than the prize itself. In fact, now that I thought about it, that actually made a whole lot of sense. We'd had a nice dinner, good conversation—dare I say the evening was friendly? I'd mistaken Weston's attraction to the chase for an attraction to me.

But that was fine. Really, it was—even if accepting it caused a weird ache in my chest. Absolutely no good could come from the craziness between us anyway. In my head, I knew we were better off keeping our distance.

Yet I still couldn't fall asleep.

So rather than further analyze our dangerous attraction, I thought back to the things Weston had shared tonight. He was an alcoholic. And if I read between the lines correctly, things had gone bad after his sister died. Those two had been thick as thieves. I considered myself an only child, since I didn't count my half-brother, Spencer, so I didn't have any experience with a relationship like those two had. I would imagine growing up in either of our big, yet lonely families caused siblings to grow even closer—us against them. Then add Caroline's illness, and I could see how Weston would've taken the protective, big-brother role, even though he was younger. Losing it after she died didn't seem like a negative thing. There was something beautiful about him caring for someone so deeply that after she was gone, he became self-destructive. In a weird way, I was kind of envious of that kind of love and dedication to another person. I'd been close to my mother, but she'd died before I was even really an adult.

Thinking about that side of Weston gave me a warm feeling. And also made me feel a little unsettled. So maybe it was for the best that he'd seemed to lose interest. Because the last thing I needed was to grow feelings for a member of the Lockwood family.

The next day, I'd just hung up my phone when Weston popped his head into my office.

"Meeting with the union is Friday at two o'clock."

"Oh, okay. That's great. Thank you. I was actually going to come by your office to see you."

He grinned. "Miss me already, huh?"

"How could I miss you when I saw you a few hours ago standing behind the column in the lobby watching me get my coffee?"

Rather than deny anything, Weston's grin widened to a smile. "Some guy was standing in my normal spot."

"I find it interesting that you don't even try to hide your stalking. Is this a hobby for you? Stalking, I mean."

"You're my first." He winked. "You lucky girl, you."

I shook my head. "Anyway, I spoke to the Boltons a little while ago, and they were able to get all the outstanding permit issues cleared up so they can get started. There are a few things they wanted to discuss over lunch today, if you're available."

Weston rubbed his bottom lip with his thumb. "They called you, huh?"

"Yes."

He tilted his head. "Which one called? Sam or Travis?"

I knew what he was getting at, but I wasn't going to make it easy for him. "Travis."

"So he called you, but specifically asked you to invite me along as well?"

I rolled my eyes. "Get over yourself, Weston. Your big ego shouldn't bruise that easily if someone prefers to call me over you. It makes sense since my family has worked with him before."

"Sure...right..."

I sighed. "Are you going to join us or not? I'm going to call downstairs and reserve a table for one o'clock. Should I make it for two or three?"

"Definitely three. There's nothing I enjoy more than being a third wheel." He rapped his knuckles against my door. "See you later, Fifi."

A few hours later, I'd lost track of the time and arrived at the restaurant at ten after one. Travis and Weston were already seated. They stood as I approached the table.

"I'm sorry I'm late. I'm not sure where the morning went."

Both men went to pull out the chair between them at the same time. It was awkward, but Travis backed off.

"Thank you," I said, taking my seat. "I hope I didn't miss too much."

"Not at all." Travis smiled. "It gave Weston and me a chance to get to know each other a little."

My eyes slanted to Weston's. He picked up a glass of water and brought it to his lips. "It made my day."

I scowled. Luckily Travis either didn't notice Weston's sarcasm or was professional enough for both of them and ignored it.

"I was just starting to tell Weston we can start as soon as tomorrow, if that's alright with you both. All of the open issues with the building department have been cleared, and the missing paperwork filed. I had to renew the permits because they'd expired already, but I took the liberty of putting down tomorrow as the start date. So we're ready to go, if you give us the all clear."

Weston and I agreed the sooner the better, and we went on to discuss how many shifts we wanted working and the dates Travis thought we might want to leave the rooms directly below the construction open because of higher noise levels. We ordered, and by the time our food came, Weston's attitude seemed to have relaxed a bit.

Travis picked up the ketchup and twisted the top. Removing the bun from his hamburger, he said, "You know, my fiancée and I looked at the Imperial Salon after we got engaged." He smiled. "Once we got the cost estimate, we realized we'd have to cut our guest list in half to hold our wedding here. But I think if the rooftop had been open at the time we were looking, my fiancée would've talked me into taking out a loan to snag this place. I really think it's going to be beautiful, once it's done."

Weston perked up. "Where did you wind up having your wedding?"

Travis shook his head. "We didn't. Things...didn't work out exactly as planned."

Weston sent a gloating smile my way. "You like the single life, then? Some people just aren't the marrying type."

"Oh, no. I'm definitely the marrying type. I hate the bar scene and prefer a quiet night at home after a long day's work. My fiancée, Alana, passed away." He shook his head. "Breast cancer."

I put my hand on Travis's arm. "I'm so sorry. I didn't know that."

I didn't miss the way Weston's eyes zoomed in on my hand.

He grumbled between gritted teeth, "Sorry for your loss."

A little while later, we'd gotten on the subject of college, and Travis mentioned that he'd dropped out. Again, Weston seemed to perk up and commented that not everyone could hack finishing their education. Travis then replied that he'd dropped out to help his dad, who needed back surgery.

There were a few more odd exchanges like that, and I could've sworn Weston enjoyed hearing a potential negative about Travis, and it pissed him off every time when it turned out to be something noble.

When our lunch plates were cleared, the waiter came over and handed us dessert menus. "We also have a wonderful array of spiked coffees—Irish coffee with Bailey's, French cappuccino made with Grand Marnier, and Italian Classico made with amaretto."

Full from lunch, I passed on dessert but ordered a cappuccino. Weston ordered a regular coffee, and the waiter turned to Travis.

"How about you? The spiked coffees are delicious. Can I tempt you?"

Travis held up a hand. "No, no temptation for me. Thank you. I'll have a regular coffee."

"I guess it's not such a good idea to add liquor to lunch when you work around heavy machinery," Weston said.

Travis nodded. "Actually, I don't drink at all. Seen too many guys go down a rabbit hole from alcohol. It's just a personal choice."

Weston's jaw flexed. He tossed his napkin on the table. "You know what? I just remembered I have another appointment to get to. I'll see you tomorrow,

Travis." He nodded to me. "I'll take care of the check on my way out. You two enjoy yourselves."

CHAPTER 14

Sophia

"Oh my God, it's worse than I expected. What is that dreadful thing you have on your arms?"

"Scarlett! You're early!" I rushed out from behind the reception desk and wrapped my arms around my friend. After we hugged, Scarlett pulled back and held my shoulders.

"Is that *brown*?"

I glanced down at the blazer I wore. "It's part of the hotel's uniform. I wear it when I'm behind the front desk. What's wrong with it?"

Scarlett seemed confused at my question. "It's *brown*."

I laughed. As expected, Scarlett looked like she'd just stepped out of a fashion magazine instead of off a seven-hour flight. Her shoulder-length blond hair was styled in roaring-twenties finger waves. She had on wide-legged cream slacks with a simple navy silk blouse, but the six or seven layers of pearls wrapped around her neck, oversized men's Rolex on her wrist, and bright red pointy shoes on her feet made the outfit scream *fashionista.* Scarlett was a good five inches shorter than me, standing at only five foot two, but I doubted anyone knew that since her heels were always sky high. Her skin was as pale as mine, yet she could pull off bright red lipstick like no other. I think when your mother names you Scarlett, you might not really have a choice.

"We all can't look picture perfect like you. How was your flight? And I thought you were bringing another person?"

"I did. He had to go straight to a meeting. I told him I had a pressing engagement and he'd have to handle it alone."

I pouted. "I hope you aren't gone too long. I was looking forward to having drinks. I haven't found a new Friday night happy hour buddy yet."

Scarlett draped her arm around my neck. "You *are* my pressing engagement. Why else would I take such a dreadful early-morning flight?"

I smiled. "Oh, great! That's exactly what I need."

It was the first time in a few days that I hadn't felt a bit blue. I hated to admit it, but the lack of attention from Weston had left me feeling almost melancholy. It was stupid, I knew that, but logic didn't pep me up any. Sadly, our fighting—and what came *after* our fighting—had been the highlight of my last few weeks. Ever since our lunch with Travis two days ago, Weston had been scarce. He'd even been keeping the door to his office shut now, which he'd never done before.

Granted, we were both really busy. Between the construction, the meeting we'd had with the union, our legal teams holed up in conference rooms and constantly requiring us to chase things to continue their due diligence, and just the general time constraints of trying to run a hotel you're barely familiar with, it was a wonder either of us had time to notice the other one's absence. I really hated that it bugged me at all.

Scarlett's visit couldn't have come at a better time. There was no better cure for feeling down and out than a heaping dose of Scarlett's sarcasm.

I grabbed one of her two oversized wheelie bags. "How long are you staying? You only had me book four nights. This looks like enough luggage to last two months."

"Darling, I'd need a separate plane for my bags if I were staying two months."

I laughed. "Come on, let me show you to your room. I already checked you in. I'll let you settle, and then we can enjoy happy hour at the main bar upstairs. It has a beautiful view of the City."

"Come meet my new friends." Scarlett swiveled on her bar stool as I walked back into the lounge. I'd been called down to the basement to deal with a broken pipe. When I returned, two very handsome men were seated to her left, and both stood.

"You must be Sophia." The taller of the two smiled, extending his hand. "I'm Ethan, and this is my business partner, Bryce."

I looked to Scarlett to fill in the blanks. I'd only been gone for about twenty minutes. Perhaps they were people she knew here for the fashion show. "Nice to meet you."

"Ethan and Bryce are in the travel industry, too," Scarlett said. "They own private planes that are rented by people who aren't satisfied flying first class commercially. I told them they could buy our next round." She picked up her drink and swirled the straw. "What more does a girl need than a best friend who owns beautiful hotels and two new friends who own private planes? Sounds like a match made in heaven, if you ask me."

There were no seats left at the bar, so Bryce motioned to the one he'd been sitting in. "Please, take a seat."

Scarlett caught my eye and wiggled her eyebrows discreetly. The men were handsome and obviously successful, but I'd been looking forward to some alone time with my friend. Though Scarlett seemed excited about our new companions, so I smiled and took a seat.

"What can I get you to drink?" Bryce asked.

Just then the bartender, Sean, walked over. He set a napkin down on the counter in front of me. "You want a vodka and diet cranberry, Ms. Sterling?"

"Ohhh. That sounds good. You have diet cranberry today?"

He nodded. "Sure do. Mr. Lockwood made sure we ordered a case of it the other day."

"He did? Are we adding a special drink to the menu that uses it?"

"Not that I'm aware of." He shrugged. "He just told us to make sure it's in stock from now on because that's what you like."

It had felt odd to take a seat and agree to have drinks with these two men. But I quickly chalked that up to being out of practice. Liam and I were together for a long time, and I hadn't jumped back into the dating world yet. Well, not really. Obviously Weston and I had had our dalliances. But the bartender's mention of Weston doing something so small, yet sweet, made me realize the reason I felt uncomfortable sharing a drink with a man had nothing to do with being out of practice.

Forcing that thought from my head, I said, "Vodka and diet cranberry sounds perfect, Sean. Thank you."

Bryce smiled. "I guess it's hard to buy a woman a drink in a hotel she owns, huh?"

I smiled, and the four of us fell into easy conversation. Eventually, the seat to my left opened up, so Bryce sat down next to me. It allowed the conversation for four to turn into two more intimate conversations of two.

"So, I take it you live here in the City?" he asked.

"Right now, I live here in this hotel. My family just recently became partial owners of The Countess. I'd been living in London the last few years and moved back to help transition things here."

"Does that mean you'll go back to London after things are settled?"

I shook my head. "No, I don't think so."

Bryce smiled. "I'm happy to hear that. New York is my home base, too."

His flirting was innocent, yet it made me feel guilty to participate. Obviously, Weston and I hadn't talked about seeing other people. Not that he and I were actually seeing each other. I wasn't naïve enough to think there was anything other than a physical relationship going on, and even that seemed to have fizzled as of late. So, I forced myself to stay open-minded, even though all I really wanted to do was go back to my suite with Scarlett and tell her all about me and Weston.

I sipped my drink. "So your office is here in the City, then?"

"Only a few blocks away. I've never been inside this hotel though." He looked around the bar and out the tall wall of windows nearby. "The view is amazing. I have to admit, Ethan wanted to come here for drinks to celebrate a new contract we just signed, and I didn't feel like it. Now I'm glad I did."

Bryce and I sat together for a half hour, our conversation flowing pretty easily. I learned that six months ago he came out of a two-year relationship, and I shared that my long-term relationship had also recently ended.

"We got a dog together," Bryce said. "Or rather, she picked out a dog, and I got to feed it and walk it."

"What kind of a dog was it?"

"*Is*, not was. I got the dog in the breakup. Sprinkles is a shih tzu. She was the one who wanted the dog, yet she showed up at my apartment with some clothes I'd had at her place and the dog. Said if I didn't take it, she was going to the vet to get him put down. What kind of a person does that? Anyway, now I have a girly-looking dog named Sprinkles."

I laughed. "Did you not want the dog to begin with?"

"I wanted a dog, but I'd been thinking more along the lines of a black lab named Fred." He shrugged. "The little guy is a damn yapper, but he's grown on me. He sleeps on my pillow right next to my head and likes to lick my ear at five o'clock in the morning. If I'm being honest, it's pretty much the only action I've seen in a while." Bryce laughed.

I had a smile on my face until I saw the man walking toward me. Weston did *not* look happy. His long strides ate up the distance between us.

"The front desk said you would be here. I didn't realize you were on a *date.*" He didn't *say* the word date so much as *spit* it at me.

"I'm not—I mean, I wasn't... We aren't..." I shook my head. Motioning to Scarlett, who'd turned around, I said, "Scarlett and I came for happy hour."

Weston glanced over at Scarlett, gave her a curt nod, and returned his angry glare to me. "You were dealing with a busted pipe in the laundry room?"

"Yes, why? Once the plumber arrived, I came back to finish my drinks with Scarlett. Is everything okay?"

Weston's eyes slanted to Bryce and back to me. "The plumber wants you to sign off on the repair estimate since you hired him. I told him I could take care of it, but apparently you're the only one capable of making such a decision in his eyes."

I stood. "Oh. Okay. I'm coming."

Weston did another sweep of our group, and his jaw flexed. "Scarlett." He nodded, turned around, and marched back out of the bar.

"Umm..." I stood. "I'll be back as soon as I can."

Bryce stood also. "Was that your manager? He was a little gruff the way he spoke to you. Do you want me to walk with you to meet the plumber?"

I held up my hands. "No, I'm good. It shouldn't take too long."

Weston was nowhere in sight as I made my way down to the basement laundry room. At first, when he'd walked in and found me sitting at the bar talking to another man, I'd felt guilty. But as I rode the elevator, my mindset started to shift.

What an asshole.

How dare he storm into the bar and give me such an attitude?

He hadn't even spoken to me the last few days.

He'd been completely unprofessional.

By the time the elevator doors slid open in the basement, whatever misplaced guilt I'd been feeling had morphed into anger. My heels echoed loudly on the floor as I marched to the laundry room and swung open the door.

Finding Weston inside, I tossed him a dirty look and walked over to the plumber, wearing the fake smile I usually reserved for when my father was around. "Hi. Mr. Lockwood said you wanted my approval on the estimate?"

The plumber had been kneeling on the floor packing away his tools. He snapped the top of the metal box shut and stood, extending a piece of paper to me. "I capped off the water that goes to the two machines on the end for now. But you got some pretty bad rusted pipes overhead." He pointed to the ceiling where a few tiles had been removed, exposing the plumbing. "Looks like you have original pipes in here. They should have been replaced twenty years ago. You've been lucky. I gave you an estimate for re-piping all the machines to the main and an estimate for just getting these two machines up and running again."

Great. Rotted pipes.

Looking down, I eyeballed the bottom line on the estimates. My family kept a database of approximate prices of most repairs. Managers could approve up to five percent more than the average, based on the job. When the pipe had burst earlier, I'd checked the average cost of replacing a broken pipe in the laundry room, and the repair estimate in my hand was in line with that. But I hadn't checked what re-piping an entire laundry facility should cost.

I looked over at Weston. "Do you have any thoughts on this?"

He didn't even glance at me as he responded. "I hopped on a washer and took a look at the pipes in the ceiling myself. No point in doing just a repair when everything up there is rotted. It's a fair price."

I nodded and spoke to the plumber. "When can you start a full re-piping?"

"Tuesday. Can you handle being down two washers until then, or do you need me to get those up and running tomorrow when the plumbing supply store opens?"

I shook my head. The Countess had at least twenty washers and as many dryers. "We should be fine until Tuesday."

He nodded. "Okay, then. I'll see you next week."

Weston opened the laundry room door for the plumber and extended his hand for the man to walk out first, though he didn't follow. Instead, he pointed down the hall. "The elevator is just down the hall to your right. Have a good night." He barely waited until the guy started to walk away before shutting the door.

With the two of us alone in the laundry room, the big space suddenly felt very small. Weston stood with his back to me, facing the door, for a long time. Neither of us said a word. The basement was so quiet that I could hear the clock on the wall ticking. It felt like I was listening to the countdown for a bomb about to explode.

Tick. Tick. Tick.

More silence.

Tick. Tick. Tick.

I didn't realize I'd been holding my breath until Weston reached out and put his hand on the doorknob. Then I exhaled a sigh of relief.

But I'd breathed too soon...

Instead of turning the handle, Weston twisted the lock.

The loud clank of the bolt fastening into place echoed through the room, and my pulse took off like a rocket.

Weston turned around. Without a word, he slipped off his suit jacket, tossed it on top of one of the dryers, and began to roll up his shirtsleeves. My eyes were glued to his corded forearms as my heart ricocheted against my rib cage.

He finished one sleeve and began to work on the other. "Are you planning on fucking the nice man you're having drinks with, Fifi?"

I glared at him. "What business is it of yours if I am?"

"I'm spoiled. You've said so yourself, right? Well, us spoiled people do not like to share their things."

"Are you insinuating that I'm a *thing*? You're such an asshole."

Weston calmly finished rolling up his second sleeve and finally looked up at me. The smile that spread across his ridiculously handsome face could only be described as sinister. "You are so much more than a thing. In fact, you're *every*thing. That's why I have no intention of sharing you."

I folded my arms across my chest. "That's not exactly your choice."

He took a few steps toward me, and my body began to vibrate. "No, you're right. It's not my choice who you give your body to." He twirled a lock of my hair around his finger and gave it a strong tug. His eyes locked with mine. "But you don't really want anybody but me."

I was about to argue with him, but we both knew where that would take us. So instead, I straightened my spine and decided to make this conversation useful.

"Why have you been avoiding me the last couple of days?"

Weston looked away. He seemed to consider my question. "Because you're a nice woman, and you deserve better than a playboy alcoholic."

"You're not an alcoholic. You stopped drinking fourteen months ago."

He shook his head. "That's not exactly the way it works. Once an alcoholic, always an alcoholic."

"That's a technicality, a definition for a word. You're not drinking anymore. That's what's important, isn't it?"

He looked up into my eyes. Sexual tension radiated between us, but he seemed to be listening. And I had more I wanted to say.

"And as for being a playboy, are you currently sleeping with any other women?"

Weston shook his head.

"Okay, then. So you're not currently a playboy or a drunk. Now that we've established that, are there any other reasons you've been avoiding me?"

Weston stared into my eyes. "You deserve better."

"Maybe I don't want better. You know, I'm pretty much an only child. So if anyone is selfish, it's me. You might not want other people touching your *things*. But I want what I want."

Weston's eyes dropped to my lips. He reached a finger to my neck and traced my pulse from jawline to my collarbone. "Fine. But no fucking other men while your spoiled ass is getting what she wants."

I squinted at him. "Fine."

"Slip off your panties, Fifi."

I blinked a few times.

He repeated himself, this time more gruff and each word spoken in a staccato burst. "Slip. Off. Your. Panties."

Goose bumps broke out all over my body. I needed my head examined. A nice, handsome man who wasn't a Lockwood sat upstairs in the bar waiting to get to know me, and here I was in the dingy basement with a man who'd just referred to me as a *thing*. Yet my arms shook as I bent and reached under my skirt. Hooking one finger over each side of the lacy fabric, I shimmied my underwear down my legs. Letting them drop to the floor, I stepped out, one dramatic foot lift at a time.

Weston's eyes glittered. He side-stepped around me to one of the washers and twisted the dial. The machine turned on and began to hum. Turning back to me, he ran his tongue across his bottom lip as his eyes swept over my body from neck to toes.

"Hike up your skirt."

My eyes jumped to his. "What?"

"Up around your ass. Hike it up."

I hesitated, but honestly, I was so turned on that there wasn't much he could ask that I wouldn't do. Grabbing the hem of my skirt, I bunched it up until the material was gathered around my waist. Standing with everything from my waist to my toes completely on display left me exposed in so many ways.

Weston stepped forward, gripped my waist with two hands, and lifted me off my feet. He carried me over to the washing machine he'd turned on and gently set me on top.

"Spread your legs."

I opened them a little.

Weston shook his head slowly. "Wider. One leg on each side of the machine. Straddle it for me."

At that moment, the empty washing machine began to vibrate. It started slow, but quickly ramped up to jumping around like a Mexican bean.

Weston saw the concern on my face and smiled. "It's fine. An empty washer on spin cycle isn't going to buck you off, so spread those legs for me."

It might've been the strangest thing I'd ever considered. Nevertheless, I did as he instructed and spread my legs wide enough to straddle the machine, one leg hanging over each side.

Weston smiled. "Now, lean forward a little bit."

I gripped the front edge of the washing machine and shifted my weight from my ass to my hips. The sensitive skin between my legs met the cold metal, but I quickly realized why he wanted me to tilt forward.

Oh my God.

Oh wow.

My eyes wanted to roll back into my head.

The empty washing machine vibrated and bumped around. When I tilted forward, all of the sensation hit my most sensitive spot. It felt like I was holding a vibrator between my legs, only better. For the first time in my life, I might've felt all eight-thousand nerve endings firing at once. My jaw went slack, and a sheen of sweat broke out over my skin.

Weston's eyes were glued to my face. The heat emanating from him blazed off the charts. I thought for sure this was just a quick bit of foreplay, but then he walked over to one of the out-of-service washing machines on the far side of the room and climbed on top.

"Wha... What are you doing?" I asked. With the vibration between my legs, I could barely string together a few cohesive words.

Weston reached above his head to the ceiling and started screwing with the tiles the plumber had left displaced.

"Fixing the ceiling."

"Now?" I screeched.

He chuckled. "Trust me, we both need a few minutes. Seeing you with that douchebag got the best of me. That machine is giving you foreplay you wouldn't be getting from me. You have no idea how much I need to pound the thought of that guy from the bar out of your head. Plus, I was on edge already and wouldn't have lasted for very long."

Since I was in no condition to argue and it felt so damn good, I closed my eyes and figured I'd enjoy the ride. A few minutes later, I felt Weston's hot breath on my neck.

"We still playing by your rules?"

The question confused me because it seemed like Weston was the one making up the rules for whatever game we were playing.

He must've seen the question on my face.

Pushing a lock of hair behind my ear, he said, "No kissing. Only from behind."

In the moment, I really wanted him to kiss me. Yet something inside me felt like that wouldn't be a good idea. So I swallowed and nodded.

Weston's lips flattened to a line, and the muscle in his jaw flexed. Yet he gave a curt nod, lifted me off the washing machine, and set me on my feet. "Turn around. Bend over the washer."

My skirt had fallen into place, so he hiked it back up to my waist. The sound of his belt unbuckling, zipper teeth separating, and the foil of a condom wrapper tearing coiled tension in my lower belly. Weston leaned over me, covering my back with his front, and I felt him nudge at my opening. He settled his mouth at my ear and bit before grumbling, "Dumb fucking rules. You better hold on tight."

Remember the first time you walked into your house after you'd been out drinking with your friends at age fifteen and you found your parents in the living room, still awake? You weren't sure whether you should do a quick wave and attempt to escape to your room or if that in itself might raise suspicion. But if you went and sat down on the couch, there was a distinct chance your parents would either smell the alcohol on you or you'd slur your speech.

Well, I might've been twenty-nine now, and Scarlett might've been my best friend instead of my parents, but that was exactly how I felt walking back into the restaurant from the laundry room.

I'd been gone for over an hour, so I wasn't even sure if Scarlett would still be at the bar. She was, though I was relieved to find her alone now.

Her back was to me as I approached, so I smoothed down my hair and did my best to act normal.

"I'm so sorry. That took way longer than I expected."

Scarlett waved me off. "No problem. Our friends just left five minutes ago anyway. So I had good company."

I settled into the empty seat next to her and relaxed a little. *Okay, maybe Mom and Dad won't suspect a thing*. "You must be starving by now," I said.

"I had a..." Scarlett trailed off and her eyes roamed my face. They suddenly widened. "*Oh my God*. You just shagged that tall glass of testosterone!"

I debated denying it, but felt my skin starting to flush, even as I went over my options.

Scarlett clapped her hands. "I almost went looking for you. That gorgeous man's face was murderous. Now I'm relieved I didn't, or I would've walked in on him putting that anger to good use."

I covered my face with both hands and shook my head. "I think I've lost my mind."

"Well, I wouldn't mind losing mine, too. Any chance your man has a pissed-off friend for me?" She smiled.

The bartender came over. "Can I get you another vodka and diet cranberry, Ms. Sterling?"

I was about to say yes. Alcohol sounded exactly like what I needed at the moment. But Scarlett responded before I could.

She leaned in and lowered her voice. "Sean, my love, any chance we could persuade you to slip us a bottle of the wine I'm drinking, a bottle of vodka, and one of those diet cranberries? I haven't seen my best friend in a while, and I think we could both use a change into our pjs and some room service."

Sean smiled and nodded. "I'll do you one better. Why don't you ladies head upstairs, and I'll send the bottles along?"

Scarlett leaned across the bar and planted a kiss on Sean's cheek, leaving behind a smear of her trademark red lipstick. "I love America. Thank you, darling."

I thanked him and dug a fifty out of my purse. "Please put everything on my room."

"Not necessary." He shrugged. "The gentlemen left their tab open for you ladies. They said to make sure all of your drinks and any food you ordered were put on their bill."

Well, now I just felt like shit. Nevertheless, Scarlett and I headed up to our rooms. She went to change in hers, and fifteen minutes later knocked at my door wearing *Duck Dynasty* footie pajamas.

I chuckled as she walked into my suite. "I'll never understand how the woman who abhors television and walks around like she just stepped off the runway could be so obsessed with those pajamas."

"You're just jealous I can rock it." Scarlett settled into the couch.

Room service had delivered a tray with a bottle of wine, two silver cocktail shakers filled with chilled drinks, an unopened bottle of Tito's vodka, a full bottle of diet cranberry, and an assortment of nuts, pretzels, cheese, and crackers.

She grabbed a handful of cashews and tossed a few in her mouth before pouring a drink for each of us into glasses. "Tell me again why you weren't living in one of your hotels in London? Because I can surely get used to this service. Especially if there's a resident stud who takes care of the hotel's and my pipes."

I took my drink from the coffee table and sat down on the chair across from her. Tucking my legs beneath me, I sipped. "Trust me, that life sounds more glamorous than it is. Living in a hotel turns into a very lonely existence pretty quickly."

"Oh? You weren't looking very lonely when you walked into that restaurant. Seriously, Soph, Liam used to stay over at our house. I don't recall you ever looking as properly fucked by that bore."

I sighed. "I guess that's because sex with Liam was never half as good as sex with Weston."

Scarlett smiled. "I am over the moon for you. This is exactly what you needed."

I arched an eyebrow. "To canoodle with a sworn enemy of my family while trying to come up with the winning bid that will allow me to force him out of any management of the hotel?"

"First off...*canoodle*? Now I know you're American, but as far as I know, you are not over the age of seventy. So let's give what's going on the proper amount of respect, shall we? Shagging, fucking—I'll even permit *getting it on* from that car-accident-waiting-to-happen of a show you Yankees loved, *Jersey Shore*. And secondly, it's your grandfather's ax to grind, not yours, correct? Did the angry Adonis ever do anything to you personally? Other than give you what I assume are spectacular orgasms?"

"Well, no... But...we aren't even nice to each other."

Scarlett sipped her wine, looking at me over the brim. "Being nice isn't a requirement for good sex."

"I know. But..."

Ever since the moment Scarlett figured out what was going on, the smile hadn't left her face. Until now.

She set her drink on the coffee table and shook her head. "You're growing feelings for him, aren't you?"

I shook my head. "No... Definitely not... I mean, I don't know."

Scarlett sighed. "It would be easier if you could keep feelings out of it."

I nodded. "Trust me, I've tried. And it started out that way. I didn't like him the slightest bit when this first started—well, that's not true. I might've liked *some* parts of him. But it was purely physical. Every time we argued, we'd wind up having pissed-off sex. He's the absolute last person I'd ever pick to go out with. Aside from the fact that we're competitors and our families have been at war for a half century, he's a playboy, arrogant, not exactly stable, and has more emotional baggage than I do."

"Well, you've spent the last ten years picking men you thought would be good for you. How did that turn out?"

I made a disapproving face. "Thanks."

"As much as you thought Liam checked all of your required boxes, I always thought he was a selfish slug. Whenever we all went out together, it was on his timeline and to a place he liked. He never seemed to ask what you wanted. We've never discussed your sex life, but I would venture to guess he wasn't generous in that arena either."

She wasn't wrong. Toward the end, it had been a special occasion if Liam put in more than three minutes of foreplay. And him giving me oral sex was essentially a birthday or Valentine's Day gift, even though he knew my orgasms from that were incomparable to any other. I worked weekdays. He worked weekends. Yet the only time we ever went out late was on the days he didn't have to get up, even though I did.

"I've definitely noticed that Weston is more attentive sexually. He pays attention and figures out what works for me. Liam had his little routine, and it worked for him—sometimes it worked for me, too. But I can chalk that up to experience. I haven't asked for a headcount, but I'm certain Weston has been with more women than Liam."

Scarlett pointed to my drink. "How is that with the diet cranberry?"

"It's great. You don't even taste the difference." I held the glass to her. "You want to try it?"

Scarlett tilted her head. "Did *Liam* ever stock his fridge with what you liked?"

I knew what she was getting at. "That *was* very thoughtful of Weston. But..."

"Listen, Soph. I don't know this man from Adam, so I could be totally off base. But I get the feeling that if you really think about it, you'll see there's more to it than just Weston ordering diet cranberry juice and making sure you finish first. And the same goes for Liam. If you think back, I have no doubt you'll see you were second on his priority list. Liam was always number one."

CHAPTER 15

Sophia

Oh no. Nothing good could come from this pairing.

The next morning I walked over to the seating area off the lobby, where Weston and Scarlett were having coffee and laughing.

"Good morning, sleepyhead." Scarlett sipped from her mug through her grin.

"This is late for you," Weston chimed in. His eyes gleamed. "Must've been worn out last night."

"What are you two doing?"

Scarlett feigned an innocent face. "Having coffee. What does it look like we're doing?"

I rolled my eyes. "I need coffee to handle you two at the same time. Be right back."

"I'll take another caffè macchiato with one pump of vanilla, please." Scarlett held up her mug.

Weston shrugged. "I'll take a tall, black coffee."

I squinted. "Not that I asked..."

I heard them chuckle as I walked away.

After a long wait in line, I put all three drinks on a plastic serving tray and walked back to where Weston and Scarlett were still looking cozy.

"What are you two talking about?" I handed Scarlett her coffee and then Weston. "You look like you're enjoying yourselves a little too much."

"I asked Weston if he knew of any good clubs nearby. We need to go out dancing. He told me about a place a few blocks away that's become a celebrity hangout."

"Oh really? I didn't realize Weston was a club hopper."

He sipped his coffee. "I'm not. Not anymore, anyway. Church is owned by one of my buddies from grad school. He built it in a closed-down cathedral. It's all he posts about on social media."

"Wes is going to get us in, so we don't have to wait in line."

"*Wes*?"

Weston grinned. "It's what my friends call me. Maybe someday you'll get around to calling me that, huh, Fifi?"

I sighed. This new bond made me a little nuts, which they clearly enjoyed. "When is this happening? Going clubbing, I mean."

"Tonight." Weston stood. "I'll make sure both your names are added to the VIP list and let them know you'll be there about ten. How does that sound?"

"That sounds fabulous," Scarlett said.

"All right, then. I need to get upstairs to the conference room." Weston buttoned his suit jacket and gave a slight bow in Scarlett's direction. "Thank you for your company, Scarlett. It was enlightening."

Weston grinned at me. "Have a great day, Sophia."

I plopped down into Weston's chair and scowled at my friend. "Enlightening? What were you two talking about?"

Scarlett waved her hand in the air. "A little of this and a little of that. He's lovely."

"Please don't try to matchmake. What Weston and I have—occasional, meaningless sex—is perfect the way it is."

"I agree." Her tone was totally patronizing.

"Scarlett..." I sighed. "Even if you're right and he's a great guy under all the layers of cocky arrogance, I just came out of a relationship. I'm not looking for another one. Especially not one where the new guy has baggage and our families hate each other. It's too complicated. Sometimes things are better kept simple."

She smiled wider. "Okay."

I squinted at her and stuck out my tongue.

"Very mature," she gloated.

"I actually need to get upstairs to the conference room where my team is working, too," I told her. "What time is your fashion show?"

"Eleven. I'm going to head over to Bergdorf's first, as soon as I finish this second cup of coffee. But I should be back tonight by about seven."

I stood and leaned down to kiss my friend's cheek. "You drive me nuts, but I'm so glad you're here."

That night, I realized it had been a long time since I went to a club. I put on a pair of jeans, a cute navy blouse, and a pair of wedges I knew I'd be able to dance in. Scarlett knocked on my hotel room door at nine forty-five.

"I thought we were meeting downstairs in the lobby at ten?"

She looked me up and down and walked in with her arms full. "We were. But then I realized you'd be dressed like *that* without my help."

I looked down at my outfit. "What's wrong with what I'm wearing?"

Scarlett sighed. "You screwed a man in the laundry room yesterday. You're not boring, yet you insist on dressing like you are."

"This is an expensive shirt. And I'm wearing tight jeans and heels."

She ignored me and held up a sparkly, *flimsy* silver blouse that draped into a V-neck in one hand and a pair of sparkly, strappy silver heels in the other.

"I like this one best," she said. "But this one..." She tossed the silver garments on the bed and held up a bright green halter-top in one hand and a pair of sky-high black shoes I'd never be able to walk in in the other. "This one would look fabulous with your hair."

I knew better than to argue with Scarlett when she didn't approve of my outfit. Plus, I couldn't deny that both of her choices were more exciting than what I had on.

"Fine." I picked up the silver items from the bed, acting like it was a sacrifice.

But when I looked in the mirror after I'd changed, I realized my friend was totally right. The other outfit was *nice*, but this one was *fun night out clubbing*. And if I were being honest, it was kind of exciting to be dressed a little sexier.

I turned for Scarlett's approval.

She shrugged. "I'd fuck you, if you had a dick."

I laughed and looped my arm through hers as we headed toward the door of my suite. "You know, I thought I missed you. But actually, I think I missed your closet."

Weston had done more than get us skip-the-line entry. We had a roped-off table in the upstairs VIP area with a bucket of champagne waiting when we arrived. The waitress told us she was our personal attendant for the evening, and a VIP host handed us keys to a special VIP ladies' room that was always empty.

Scarlett and I took full advantage. We sipped champagne while scoping out the bodies swaying to a live DJ on the dance floor below and getting the feel for the place. Then we hit the dance floor like it was nobody's business. One song led to the next, bodies pressed close all around us, and my heart seemed to beat in rhythm to the thump of the bass. After an hour, the back of my neck was slick with sweat, and my hair had pasted itself against it.

Throughout the night, various men tried to dance with us, but we were enjoying our time together and not interested in meeting anyone. Most took the hint. Though, at one point, a very good-looking guy walked over to Scarlett during a song transition and said something I couldn't hear. Whatever it was made her laugh, and he started to dance with us. Unlike some men, who think a woman smiling on the dance floor means they have a license to dry hump you, the guy kept a gentlemanly distance, and we formed a small circle together, even though he clearly had eyes for Scarlett.

A friend of his joined us a few minutes later, and that led to us getting coupled into dance parties for two. The guy with me wasn't trying to grope me or anything, so I kept dancing. I closed my eyes and swayed to the music, but a hand snaking around my waist from behind spoiled the moment. My eyes flashed open. I assumed it was the guy I'd been dancing with getting too friendly, but he was still right in front of me. I whipped around, preparing to tell some asshole to get his hands off me, but halfway through my first word, I realized it wasn't just any asshole. It was *my* asshole.

Weston.

He tightened his grip and leaned over my shoulder to speak to the man in front of me.

"She's here with someone."

It was a total alpha move, but somehow he pulled it off without seeming obnoxious. The guy I'd been dancing with looked at me for confirmation, and I sighed but nodded. He politely disappeared without a scene.

I turned around to face Weston. "What are you doing here?"

He shrugged. "Dancing. What does it look like?"

"Here? You just happened to feel like dancing tonight?"

He grinned. "Nope. I was invited by Scarlett."

I searched through the crowd to find my friend. When our eyes caught, I glared at her. She grinned and wiggled her fingers.

Cute. Very cute.

Weston took the opportunity to slip his hands around my waist again. His hard chest pressed against my back as he started to sway. Leaning over my shoulder, he lowered his mouth to my ear and whispered, "Relax and dance with me. You already know we have good rhythm together."

I didn't really have an opportunity to say yes or no. Weston just started to lead from behind, taking over the same way he did when we had sex—the same way I loved so much. It felt good, and our bodies really did move well together. So for once, I didn't bother to fight it. I shut my eyes. One of Weston's hands trailed possessively down my side as we moved, tracing its way from my ribs down over my hips to caress the top of my thigh. I lifted one arm and hooked it behind his neck, where his other hand held it in place.

We stayed that way for a few songs, and I could feel him swelling against the top of my back as time went on. Heat built inside of me, and I wondered to myself if the VIP bathroom was soundproof.

Weston leaned down and spoke into my ear again, "Want to take a break and get something to drink?"

I nodded. The music on the main floor made it

virtually impossible to communicate unless there was a mouth right next to your ear. So we went back to the VIP table upstairs where we could hold a conversation.

The waitress came over the moment we sat down. She used tongs to pluck a chilled face cloth out of a basket and handed one to each of us. I used mine to wipe off the back of my neck, while Weston cooled off his face. We dropped them back into the basket and the waitress asked, "What can I get you to drink? Would you like more champagne?"

I smiled. "I'd love some. Thank you."

"Just a water for me, thanks."

I'd completely forgotten until that moment that Weston didn't drink.

"I'm sorry. I wasn't thinking."

Weston shook his head. "It's fine. I'm the only one who needs to remember."

"Isn't it hard for you to be in this environment?"

He shook his head. "I avoided clubs and bars for the first six months. But now I'm okay with it. At least when it's early. I loved the three-AM crowd when I was drinking. The later it got, the crazier the shit that happened. To me, that was the witching hour. I sometimes wouldn't go out until one in the morning, so I could get shitfaced by three and be ready for the action. It's funny, the first time I was in a bar at that time sober, I realized the people I'd thought were so much fun were really just a bunch of obnoxious assholes."

"You had beer goggles on."

"More like rum goggles, but yeah."

I was so warm from dancing. I gathered the back of my hair into a ponytail and fanned myself to cool my skin.

"Hot still?"

"Roasting." I looked down at the time on my phone. "I think Scarlett and I were on the dance floor for close to two hours."

Weston nodded. "You were."

My brows drew together. "How do you know?"

"I watched you from up here for at least an hour. Do you have one of those hair ties in your purse?"

I shook my head. "I wish."

The waitress returned with my champagne and set down Weston's water. "Can I get you anything else?"

Weston nodded. "Do you think you could find us one of those hair ties like you have in, to make a ponytail?"

She smiled. "Sure. No problem."

"And can we maybe get another one of those cold towels, please?"

"Coming right up."

After she walked away, Weston draped one arm casually along the top of the booth behind me.

"Thank you. I wouldn't have thought to ask her for that."

"I'm here to serve." He winked. "Any other needs I can fill?"

I laughed. "Not at the moment, but I'll let you know."

When the waitress came back with a hair tie and fresh cool towels, Weston ordered me a glass of water.

We sat looking down at the dance floor, but my mind wasn't on the club or the people swaying to the music below. I was thinking about what Scarlett had said about Weston last night—how she'd noticed that he put me first, and Liam never had. Tonight alone, Weston had made arrangements for us to get into the club, made sure we got set up with VIP treatment, scored me a ponytail holder to put my hair up because I was hot, and asked the waitress for more cool towels and water. Even watching us dance from a distance and cutting in when two guys got a bit more friendly than most—Weston had a protective nature to him. Some of that was good old alpha-male, territorial behavior, but it wasn't overly obnoxious. I found his jealousy kind of sexy.

Weston leaned forward. "You cooled off now?"

I nodded. "The ponytail holder really helped."

He inched closer to me, and the hand that had been stretched along the top of the bench seat slid over to my shoulder. He gently nudged me to lean back against him, and I did. We'd seen each other naked plenty of times, but this simple cuddle was more intimate than we'd been in a lot of ways. Weston traced his fingers back and forth over my bare shoulder, and I felt my body relax into his touch. It felt good, really good even, and my head lolled back to rest against his chest.

I'd been staring down at the dance floor, not paying attention to anything in particular, when I saw Scarlett extend a hand to the guy she'd been dancing with. He took it and leaned down to say something. A few seconds later, his smile had wilted, and he walked away with his shoulders slumped. Scarlett raised her arms in the air, shut her eyes, and went back to dancing happily by herself.

"Did you catch that?" Weston asked.

"I did. Guess she was done with him." I laughed.

"I like her a lot. She says what's on her mind."

"That's Scarlett. People either appreciate that about her and love her, or don't."

"I'm guessing the ones who don't she doesn't consider a loss."

"Definitely not. She jokes that I'm her only friend, and she's been auditioning replacements ever since I left. But people would line up to be closer to her. She doesn't let many into her circle, though."

"You two seem to have a lot in common."

I nodded. "I thought I would miss a lot about London, but she's the only thing I truly miss."

"Not Liam?"

I didn't have to think about that. Shifting my eyes from the dance floor to meet Weston's, I said, "Liam who?"

Weston smiled, and his eyes dropped to my lips for a moment. The music pumped loudly around us, and there had to be a few hundred people in the club, yet it felt like just the two of us. Weston had a way of making me feel special and desirable that didn't require any words. My eyes fell to his mouth, and for a change, I didn't overthink my actions. Leaning in, I pressed my lips to his. He wrapped a hand around my neck and kissed me back, but didn't try to make out with me. Instead, we shared a very tender first kiss. After, he pulled back.

"You broke your own rule?"

"*Eh.* Fuck the rules."

A smile spread across his face, and his eyes grew darker. "Yeah?"

I nodded. "Yeah."

He squeezed my neck and tugged my face back to his. The second kiss wasn't tender; Weston kissed the living shit out of me until I was breathless.

After, he dipped his mouth to my ear. "How about we keep one of your rules? You *come* first."

It was after two by the time the three of us walked back into the hotel lobby. Scarlett had kept us entertained the entire way with the worst pickup lines she'd heard tonight, plus some memorable ones from over the years.

Weston pushed the up button to call the elevator, and stepped aside for us to enter first when the car arrived.

"What's your go-to line, Wes?" Scarlett asked.

He shrugged. "I usually go with...hey."

Scarlett snorted. "I guess that's all you need when you look like you do, pretty boy."

Weston winked and tilted his head in my direction. "Worked on this one."

I'd been standing in front of the button panel on the right side of the elevator, but forgot to push our floors. After a minute, Weston noticed we weren't moving.

"Helps if you tell the elevator where you want to go, Soph."

"Oh shit. Yeah." I hit all three of our floors, and the car started to move.

Scarlett's room was on the third floor, so her stop came first.

"Thank you for a lovely evening, Weston. I had a blast."

"Anytime. But I have a feeling you have a blast wherever you go."

Scarlett and I hugged, and then the elevator headed up to its next stop. Weston's room was on the eighth floor. The doors slid open, but he made no move to exit.

"Are you...getting off?" I said. "This is your floor."

Weston shook his head. "Nope. I'm going to your room to get *you* off."

CHAPTER 16

Weston

Sophia walked into the suite ahead of me and flicked the light on in the hall. In the living room, she turned on a lamp. I followed close behind her and turned it off.

Normally I didn't give a shit about mood lighting. In fact, I don't know that I'd ever considered it before. But the light in the hallway illuminated the room enough for me to see her, and anything more felt like a distraction.

"Do you want some water or something?" Sophia asked.

I shook my head and crooked my finger. "Or something. Come here."

Sophia bit her bottom lip, but moved closer to me.

I traced her pulse down her neck with one finger. "You have no idea what your skin does to me. It's so soft and perfect. Every day while I watch you get your coffee, I daydream about sinking my teeth into it. I want to suck on every part of your body and leave marks."

She laughed nervously. “But then it won’t be perfect anymore, will it?”

“Actually, the only thing that could make it *more* perfect would be marking it as mine.”

I cupped her cheeks and pulled her close. Now that I could finally kiss her, I never wanted to stop. The woman knew how to kiss. She sucked on my tongue, bit my lip, and tugged until I felt it straight down in my cock. But it was the soft mewl she let out that got to me. It traveled through our joined mouths, wrapped around my heart, and squeezed.

I grabbed her ass and lifted her off her feet. Her long legs wrapped around my waist as I carried her into the bedroom. I’d never wanted a woman missionary style like I wanted this woman. Actually, I’d never wanted *any* woman the way I wanted Sophia at this moment. I couldn’t wait to spread her out on that king-size bed and watch her beautiful face as she came undone.

Sophia’s fingers threaded through my hair, and she tugged. We were both still fully dressed, but the way I felt, I knew if I didn’t slow things down, I was going to break the one rule I’d told her we’d keep. So I forced my mouth from hers and broke the kiss.

She shook her head as I tried to pull away. “No. More.”

I smiled. “I want to take my time tonight.”

She groaned, and I chuckled as I set her on her feet. Taking a few steps back, I said, “Take off your shirt.”

Our eyes locked, and she pouted. “Can’t we both get undressed at the same time?”

The desperation in her voice made me feel like the king of the jungle. But she was giving me all of her tonight, and I wanted it to be good. We'd fucked plenty, though that was just our bodies. Tonight we'd upped the ante.

So I reined in my desire and repeated myself. "Take off your shirt, Sophia."

I managed to keep my eyes on her face while she slipped the silver top from her shoulders and let it fall to her feet. But *fuck*—she had no bra on. Her gorgeous, smooth skin was on complete display, and her full, real breasts had the sexiest natural curve to them. Deep pink nipples stood at full attention, coming to pert, hard points. My mouth salivated. I couldn't wait to bite them.

Raising my chin, I said, "The pants now."

The sound of the zipper of her jeans coming undone echoed through the room. This little striptease was supposed to give me time to get myself under control, but it was having the opposite effect. I was so hard it was growing painful.

Sophia slipped the denim down her sexy, toned legs and stepped out. Standing before me, she wore only a small triangle of black lace covering her pussy. God, I loved every one of her curves...the narrow of her waist, the slope of her hips, those smooth, mile-long legs.

My voice came out gruff. "You're so beautiful."

Though she was standing before me practically naked, my words seemed to make her blush.

"Thank you."

I started to undress myself, taking my time as the tension between us built. Like her, I let my shirt fall to the floor, and then removed my pants. Sophia's eyes dropped to the noticeable bulge in my boxers, and I practically growled when she licked her lips.

"Fuck, Soph. Don't look at me like that."

She sucked her bottom lip in. "Like what?"

"Like you want me to put you on your knees with your hair wrapped around my fist while I feed you my cock."

Her eyes twinkled, and her lips curved to a devilish smirk. "Take off your boxers."

Fuck.

I shook my head. "Get over here."

The minute she pushed her warm tits up against my chest, I lost my last sliver of self-control. With my hands in her hair, I not-so-gently tugged her face up to meet mine.

All hell broke loose after that. Sophia pushed down my boxers, her fingernails scraping my skin in the frenzy to get them off, and I took her taut nipple between my teeth and tugged until I heard her breath catch. She wrapped one leg around my waist and hoisted herself up, climbing me like a fucking tree. If I'd had any doubt whether she was ready, that went out the window. Her pussy was soaked as she rocked up and down, coating me with her juices.

"I want you," she groaned.

I sat on the edge of the bed with her in my lap. Sophia's arms shook as she wrapped her hands around my neck and lifted herself enough to take me into her body. I felt the heat of her warm pussy slip over the head of my cock, and then she stopped. We had no condom on. I was just about to say something, but Sophia beat me to it.

"I...I'm on the pill. And I got tested before I left London. There hasn't been anyone since."

And here I was thinking her letting me kiss her, letting me look at her beautiful face while I was inside her, was the biggest gift she could give me. But this—this was so much more. *Trust.*

I looked into her eyes. "I'm clean. It's been years since I've been with a woman without, and I get tested regularly."

Sophia nodded and leaned in to kiss me as she started to lower herself. But I wasn't having that. I'd let her take control, ride me as slow or as fast as she wanted, but I needed to see her tonight. So I held her face a few inches from mine. I saw the confusion in her eyes.

"I'm game for however you want it—fast, slow, on top, or underneath me, but I want to watch you."

Her eyes searched mine before she nodded. Then she lifted again and slowly pushed onto me. It took everything in my power to not buck my hips and surge up to fill her all at once. But she'd given me so much tonight, and I wanted to give her something I usually held tightly—control.

"Beautiful." I looked down between us and watched my cock inching into her pussy. "Just fucking beautiful."

She smiled so sweetly before closing her eyes. Then in one swift motion, she sank all the way down, sucking me into her body until her ass was flush with my lap.

"*Jesus Christ*," I muttered.

Sophia's eyes fluttered open. I probably sounded like the biggest pussy ever, but I swear the moment felt holy. Her eyes were glazed with lust, her skin so creamy and radiant, and a single ray of light shone across her body. She looked angelic, and even though she was on top, there was something in her face that let me know she'd just surrendered.

"I...I...." she said.

I smiled. "I know, baby."

We began to move together. Sophia rocked back and forth, and I thrust up and down. She was wrapped around me so tight, it felt like a fist gripping my cock.

"Weston..." she moaned. "More..."

Fuck yes.

I lifted her until the tip of my cock was barely inside her. Then in one swift motion, I pulled her down on top of me *hard*.

She moaned again.

So I did it a second time.

Another moan.

I lifted again, and this time, when I yanked her back down onto my cock, I thrust up at the same time.

She moaned louder.

Over and over, we grinded and gasped, pushed and pulled, slammed in and slid out, until I could no longer tell the end of Sophia's moan and the beginning of her next. It all became one beautiful song.

Her eyes rolled back in her head and the wall of her muscles clenched down around me. "Wes..."

"Right here, baby. Right here."

"*Please*," she moaned. "*Please*."

"Tell me what you want."

She stuttered. "Come...come inside me. Come now."

I didn't need to be told twice. With one last thrust, I planted myself to the root. My body shook, consumed with everything Sophia—her smell, her taste, the way she moaned my name over and over as she came all over my cock, the feeling of her nails digging into my back, her tits pressed against my chest, her ass cheeks resting on my balls. I was utterly and completely lost in this moment...in this woman.

"Soph..." I couldn't hold back any longer. "Soph... *fuck*."

A few tears might've leaked out as I unloaded inside of her. It was absolutely, positively, the most fan-fucking-tastic orgasm of my life.

After, Sophia was completely spent. Her body slumped into mine, and her head nuzzled against my chest as we attempted to catch our breath.

My dick apparently thought it was a volcano that had just erupted. It trembled with aftershocks, jerking and sputtering its last bits of hot lava.

Sophia looked up at me with a smile that could only be described as delirious. "Are you doing that? Making it move like that?"

I chuckled. "No. It's got a mind of its own."

She wrapped her arms around my neck, kissed my lips, and sighed. "That was really nice."

I arched a brow. "Nice?"

"Yeah. What else should I call it? Nice is...nice."

I clutched my hand to my chest like I was in pain. "That hurts."

She giggled. "Outstanding? Is that better."

"A little."

"How about orgasmic. Does that work?"

"You're getting warmer. Keep going."

"Epic. It was epic."

"What else you got?"

"Phenomenal? Earth shattering? Extraordinary?"

I shifted and gently lifted her off me. Cradling her in my arms, I stood, causing her to yelp in surprise. But the smile on her face told me she loved every minute of it.

"What are you doing?" She giggled.

I carried her to the top of the bed and laid her in the middle of it before climbing on top and nudging her legs open with my knee. "I'm going to fuck the nice out of you."

She answered through a laugh. "That might take a while. I'm pretty nice, you know."

I smiled. "That's okay. I'm good at what I do. You know, some are born great, some achieve greatness, and some get to have greatness thrust *inside* them."

Sophia giggled. "Pretty sure Shakespeare said some get to have greatness thrust *upon* them."

Weston winked. "Maybe later we can do that, too."

CHAPTER 17

Sophia

The next morning started the same way last night had ended—with Weston inside of me. Though something had changed between us. Instead of a frenzied race to cross the finish line, we took our time, exploring each other's bodies. There was an intimacy now that hadn't been there before.

I rested my head on his chest and traced the length of the faint scar on his abdomen.

"You said this was from a kidney surgery, right?"

Weston stroked my hair gently. "Yeah, the testing for this surgery was actually the day after our prom."

"It was? I don't remember you mentioning anything about an upcoming surgery."

"We didn't do so much talking on prom night, if I remember correctly."

Thinking back, I smiled. "Yeah, I guess you're right. What was wrong that you needed surgery?"

Weston was quiet for a moment. "Nothing. I donated a kidney to Caroline."

I turned my head to look at him, propping my chin on my hands. "Oh, wow. I had no idea. That's amazing."

Weston shrugged it off. "Not really. Three years after the transplant, she started showing signs of rejection. At first, we thought she had the flu. But it wasn't. The doctors tried to stop it by giving her immunosuppressants, but all that did was weaken her immune system. She struggled with being sick off and on for years. Eventually, she died from an infection because the antirejection drugs she was taking for my shitty kidney made her susceptible to so many things."

I felt an ache in my chest. "I'm so sorry."

"Nothing to be sorry about. It's not your fault."

Of course it wasn't. But something told me he did place blame on someone. "You know it's not *your* fault either, right?"

Weston looked away. "Sure."

"No." I touched his chin and tilted his face back in my direction. "You know it's not your fault, *right*?"

"I had one job in life, to make my sister healthy. And I couldn't even do that."

I searched his face. He was dead serious. Shaking my head, I said, "It wasn't your job to make Caroline healthy. I think it's incredible that you donated a kidney. But I'm sure you did it because you loved her, not because you felt obligated to."

Weston scoffed. "No, Soph. It *was* my job. I'm a savior baby."

My brows drew together. "A savior baby?"

He nodded. "Caroline was diagnosed at a year old. My parents conceived me through in vitro fertilization.

Only zygotes that were genetically compatible to my sister and free of all genetic diseases were implanted into my mother. I was a walking inventory of spare parts."

My mouth hung open. "Are you serious?"

"Three bone marrow transplant donations and a kidney."

I had no idea what to say. "That's...that's..."

Weston smiled sadly. "Fucked up. I know. But it is what it is. I honestly didn't think anything of it growing up. When my sister was sick, I had to stay in, too. I thought my mother was just nervous that I'd bring germs into the house and make Caroline sicker." He shook his head. "But she wanted to make sure I didn't get sick so if my sister needed another transplant, I'd be healthy."

"You and Caroline always seemed so close. I remember seeing you walk home from school together and studying in the library all the time. I was always kind of jealous of your relationship with her because all I had was my dumbass half-brother."

"We were close. I loved Caroline more than I loved myself. If there had been a way for me to be the sick one, instead of her, I would've changed places with her in a heartbeat. She was an amazing person."

I tasted salt in my throat. "That's beautiful. It really is. But that shows you didn't help Caroline because it was your job; you did it out of love."

Weston looked at me. He seemed to search my eyes before speaking again. "When I was born, my grandfather put five-million dollars into an account for me. I thought he did that for all of his grandchildren. The night of Caroline's funeral, I found out I was the only one with that kind of a trust fund. He'd set it up to compensate me for being Caroline's donor."

I blew out a ragged breath. "That's screwed up."

"My mother calls me twice a year—on Caroline's birthday and the anniversary of her death. She hasn't called me on my birthday in ten years."

"God, Weston."

He smiled and brushed a hand over my hair. "You thought your family was fucked up? They don't hold a candle, sweetheart."

I thought about how he'd gone on a downward spiral after his sister's death. What he'd just shared made the reasons so much clearer.

I dropped a tender kiss above his heart. "I'm sorry," I said. "Not for your loss—although obviously I'm sorry for that, too. But I'm sorry I judged you for so many years without ever getting to know you. Underneath the asshole exterior you wear so proudly is a really beautiful man."

Weston stared off at nothing in particular. "You're a good person, and good people look for the good in everyone."

"So? What's wrong with that? Is that such a bad thing? Wanting to find good?"

He turned back to look at me and smiled sadly. "It shouldn't be. But it skews what you see. Sometimes what people are showing you is really who they are."

I thought he was wrong. But I knew there was no point in arguing. I looked down and traced his scar again. "Can I ask you something personal?"

"Because everything you've asked me in the last ten minutes—or the last few weeks, for that matter—hasn't been?"

I laughed and smacked his abs. "Shut up, Lockwood."

He smiled. "What's your question, nosy?"

"Do you talk about these things with the therapist you go to? About losing your sister and how you felt responsible for her well-being?"

Weston frowned. "I go to the shrink because it's a condition of keeping my job. I'm not there to be fixed."

Silence stretched between us until eventually Weston cleared his throat. "I'm going to get going. I have to visit a friend this morning."

"Oh... Okay."

I shifted to my side so he could get up and watched as he got dressed. I wasn't sure if Weston really had somewhere to go or if our conversation had made him uncomfortable enough that he had the urge to flee. Either way, the air in the room had shifted. I pulled the sheet up to my shoulders to ward off the chill.

Weston leaned down and kissed my forehead. "I'll see you later?"

I forced a smile. "Sure."

A minute later, the door clicked closed. I laid in bed by myself, going over the last twenty-four hours. Sex with Weston was beyond a doubt the most amazing physical experience I'd ever had with a man. We had undeniable chemistry. I'd thought the intense spark came from the push and pull of our antagonistic feuding, but last night, there was no feud, and our connection and chemistry were more intense than ever. So maybe there was more to it than taking out our pent-up frustrations on each other.

For some reason, that thought made me nervous. Was I gun-shy after what happened between Liam and me? Or was my inner self-protective mechanism giving me a warning that had everything to do with Weston Lockwood?

It was a lot to think about. Luckily, my cell phone buzzed on the nightstand, interrupting what I was about to overanalyze. Scarlett's name flashed on the screen, making me smile.

"Good morning," she said. With just those two simple words, I could tell she was smiling on the other end of the phone. "Am I interrupting something?"

"No. I'm just lying here in bed, all by my lonesome, being lazy."

"All by your lonesome?"

I laughed. I knew what she was getting at. Scarlett didn't do subtle. "Yes, Weston just left a few minutes ago."

"Perfect. Then open the door."

My forehead wrinkled. "What door?"

A knock rang out in surround sound. It came through the phone and also from the other room of my suite. "This one. And hurry. Our breakfast is getting cold."

"So...anything interesting happen after I got off the elevator?" Scarlett's eyes twinkled.

I picked a piece of pineapple from the plate of fresh fruit and shoved the entire thing into my mouth. Pointing, I mumbled as if I couldn't respond because my mouth was full.

Scarlett laughed. "That's what I thought. Weston couldn't keep his eyes off of you all night at the club."

I sighed. "We definitely have good chemistry."

"That's it? Just good chemistry?"

I shook my head. "I honestly have no idea anymore. It started out as purely physical—we were basically hate-fucking, Scarlett. But things have changed. He's still a pain in my ass, but there's more to him than he wants people to see. Like, he goes out of his way to make me laugh. He knows my ex was a playwright, so he recites these Shakespearean quotes, only he turns them dirty. Like, *It's better to have been fucked once than never have been fucked at all*, or *To come or not to come, that is the question*. I just know he sits at his desk reading Shakespeare so I'll crack a little smile. It's oddly sweet."

Scarlett swiped a grape and popped it into her mouth. "So he's handsome, thoughtful, and funny. Sounds awful."

"He's also very protective of the people he cares about, though he doesn't seem to let many people in."

"Sounds like someone else I know..."

I nodded. "I always thought we were so different. But the more I get to know him, the more I realize we just choose to wear different masks."

"Wow... That sounds deep and boring as shit." Scarlett grinned. "And here I thought I was going to get to hear how he banged the shit out of you. But instead, I'm being subjected to feelings... Yuck."

I tossed a pillow at her and laughed. "Shut up."

"Seriously, I like this one."

"It's probably the dumbest thing I've ever done."

"Why?"

"Well, for starters, as I believe I've mentioned, his family and my family have been at war for half a century. But even if we put all of that aside, there's a million reasons it's a bad idea. I just came out of a long-term relationship. This thing between me and Weston has rebound written all over it. Come on—I hopped from a nice-looking, safe, stable playwright to the sexy-as-sin bad boy with a ton of baggage. Could it be any more cliché? Not to mention, we both have some pretty big trust issues." I shook my head. "Weston is like a bright star on a dark night. He can light up the sky, but eventually that fire burns out and all the pieces crumble. Then you're left in the dark."

"You do know the sun is a star, too, right? Sometimes we can rely on a star to come back every day."

I sighed.

"You'll figure it out," Scarlett said. "Just promise you won't let your family or Liam factor into your decision whether Weston might be right for you. Whatever you decide, it should be about you and Weston only."

I nodded. "Thanks."

After we finished breakfast, Scarlett talked me into going shopping. I went to check in on the construction, since we had crews running even on Sundays. Then I took a quick shower and tied my hair up while she sat in my suite having a third cup of coffee and reading bits and pieces of the news to me aloud. It felt exactly like a Sunday morning back in London. Which made me realize I wasn't going to lose our friendship because of the distance between us now. Where we were didn't matter; we'd always find a way. London just wasn't my home anymore.

"You ready to go shopping?" I asked when I was finally ready, grabbing my purse.

She looked down. "I'm wearing flats. What does that tell you?"

I smiled. While I often wore flats, and even sneakers sometimes, Scarlett almost always wore heels of some sort, unless she was exercising. Which meant we'd both be getting a full cardio workout today as we ran around the City.

Opening the door to my suite, I almost crashed into a bellman who had his knuckles raised to knock on my door. Startled, my hand flew to my chest as I stopped abruptly.

"Sorry. I didn't mean to scare you," he said.

"My fault. I wasn't paying attention to where I was going. It's Walter, right?"

"It is." He nodded and smiled, then held up a long white flower box. "I was just delivering this. Mr. Lockwood said I should put them in your suite if you weren't here."

"Mr. Lockwood asked you to deliver them?"

He nodded. "He was at the front desk when they were delivered a few minutes ago."

I was surprised, not just that Weston had sent me flowers, but that he'd had a member of the staff deliver them to me. For the most part, we'd been very discreet around the hotel.

"Oh. Okay, thank you."

Walter passed me the box and turned to go.

"Wait! Let me give you a tip." I dug in my purse, but the bellman held up his hand.

"Mr. Lockwood already took care of that. But thank you."

Scarlett was all smiles as I brought the box into the suite.

"Looks like your flash-in-the-pan star has a romantic side."

The box was tied with a big red bow, so I set it down on the living room coffee table and untied it. Inside were two dozen beautiful yellow roses. A small card lay on top. I didn't even realize I was smiling until I slipped it from the envelope and read. Then I felt my upturned lips droop to a frown.

The course of true love never did run smooth.

I miss you. Please call me back.

-Liam

Scarlett saw my face and walked over to peek at the card.

"It doesn't run smooth?" she said. "Yes, true love will hit some bumps in the road when you stick your dick in your girlfriend's cousin. God, that man truly is a tosser."

"The quote is from Shakespeare."

"Figures." She rolled her eyes. "Dull roses and recycled bullshit. The man never could be original. I bet if Weston sent you flowers, they'd be wildflowers or something as rare and unique as you are. And I'd prefer a card that said, 'Let's fuck' over some pretentious quote any day of the week."

Weston.

Shit.

I'd momentarily forgotten that the bellman said Mr. Lockwood had accepted the delivery and made sure they were sent right up to my room.

But something told me when I ran into him next, *he* wouldn't have forgotten.

CHAPTER 18

Weston

"Well, don't you look like shit."

Not even Mr. Thorne 's insults could make me smile this morning.

When I'd left Sophia's room, I'd felt conflicted. I didn't want her to think I was a good man, only to feel like she'd had the rug pulled out from under her when she got to know me better and realized I wasn't. That was exactly what her asshole of an ex had done. But by the time I'd showered and gotten dressed, I'd started to get over myself. The fantastic night we'd shared together pushed my concerns to the side, at least for the time being. I even ordered her damn flowers. I couldn't remember the last time I'd sent a woman flowers. But then I'd gone downstairs and happened to be at the front desk when a delivery arrived for her—and not from the florist I'd visited.

My morning was shot to hell after that.

I dragged a hand through my hair. "I didn't get much sleep last night."

The look on Mr. Thorne 's face told me what he was thinking. I shook my head. "I wasn't out partying. I did go to a club, but I didn't fall off the wagon."

He wagged a crooked finger at me. "You know better than that. Going to a place where everyone around you is indulging is asking for trouble."

I couldn't argue, because he was right—though I spent every day in one hotel or another that had a few bars. Some of our properties even had clubs in them. Unless I was changing my line of work, I wouldn't be avoiding places that served alcohol. Besides, I hadn't had the urge to drink last night. My mind had been too busy obsessing over Sophia.

"Yeah, I know. But it wasn't like that." I shrugged. "I wasn't even tempted."

Mr. Thorne shook his head anyway. "Did you at least bring my ticket?"

I grabbed the scratch-off from my back pocket and handed him the book from his nightstand he always leaned on. "One ten-dollar ticket, like you asked for."

He put on his reading glasses, grabbed a quarter, and went to work. "So...you stayed at this club all night? And that's why you look like a raccoon?"

I shook my head. "I spent the night with the woman I've been seeing, if you must know."

"Sophia?"

"Yeah, Sophia."

He finished scratching off the gray latex and brushed the scraps from the lotto ticket. "You two going steady now?"

"Considering it's not 1953 anymore, no, we're not going steady."

"You just hooking up then?"

His use of the term made me chuckle. But most of his vocabulary came from Jerry Springer, so I wasn't surprised he knew what it meant. "Yeah, I guess that's what we're doing."

"Don't you ever want to settle down? Meet a nice woman? Come home to her after a long day of work and share a nice meal she cooked for you? Maybe pop out a couple of rugrats?"

I could not picture Sophia wearing an apron and making me dinner, but I got what he was trying to say. I'd never given much thought to coming home to a woman or starting a family. But the truth was, I *could* envision that with Sophia. Albeit, my version of things wasn't exactly Mr. Thorne's. Instead of her cooking me a nice dinner, we'd have reservations for seven o'clock since we both worked a lot. I'd lose track of time and show up at the restaurant a half hour late, and she'd be pissed. I'd slide into the booth next to her, instead of across from her, and apologize. She'd tell me to stick my apology up my ass. We'd argue, and I'd notice how sexy she looked with fire in her eyes and slip my hand under the table. When the waiter came to take our order, I'd be knuckles deep inside her beautiful pussy, and she'd be angry when he walked away that I hadn't withdrawn. But then she'd come so hard she'd lose some of her fight. I'd whisper another apology when she softened, and she'd tell me not to let it happen again.

Though, that fantasy would never become a reality. Because sooner or later, Sophia was going to hate me.

I shrugged. "We don't really stand a chance."

Mr. Thorne's brows pulled together. "Why not?"

"It's complicated. Let's just say there are a lot of obstacles in our way."

Mr. Thorne steepled his fingers. "You know what obstacles are?"

"What?"

"They're tests to see if you deserve to win. How do you show someone they're worth fighting for unless you've knocked down whatever's in your way? If you're just gonna sit on your ass and not even try..." He shook his head. "Well, I guess you don't deserve the prize anyway. I thought you had more balls than that, kid."

I gritted my teeth and bit my tongue. "You want me to take you for a walk or what?"

"How about you take me over to that new fancy hotel of yours? I'd like to see it. You know, that's where I proposed to my Eliza."

"I didn't know that."

"They do that place up nice for the holidays. I took her over and proposed in front of the big tree on Christmas Eve."

"I guess you got engaged before 1962?"

Mr. Thorne's forehead wrinkled. "It was 1961. How'd you know that?"

"Because they stopped putting up a Christmas tree in 1962."

"No shit?"

I nodded. "Apparently, the tree was another victim of the Sterling-Lockwood feud. Grace Copeland, the woman who kept the hotel and died recently, leaving it to my and Sophia's grandfathers, never put up a tree after her split with them—for sentimental reasons."

"I guess that makes my proposal in front of the tree even more special then. That place was magical at the holidays."

I had never stepped foot into The Countess until my family had become part owner. But I could imagine the lobby looked pretty nice all lit up with a big tree. The weather was pleasant outside today. I could probably wheel Mr. Thorne there in a half hour or so—get him some air and let him reminisce a little. So I grabbed his wheelchair, locked the wheels in place, and got ready to lift him out of bed.

"Alright, old man. I'll bring you to see the hotel. But no telling dirty jokes to the staff, like you did when I took you to the live taping of that dumb talk show last month. You'll get my ass sued."

After I walked Mr. Thorne over to The Countess, I spent an hour showing him the hotel. I was glad we hadn't run into Sophia. My ass was dragging, so I took him to get some caffeine at the lobby coffee shop, and we sat in the same corner I often sat in early in the morning while I waited for Sophia to come down and get her coffee.

Mr. Thorne sipped an iced tea while looking around the grand lobby with a smile on his face. "This place is something special."

I nodded. "Yeah, it's nice."

He shook his head. "It's more than just nice, kid. It's magical. Can't you feel it?" He pointed to the two grand staircases that led up to the second floor from different directions. "That's where the tree goes. I got down on one knee right over there. Happiest day of my life."

I knew the last few years hadn't been easy for him. But it was pretty crazy that he could say proposing to a woman who was now his ex-wife was the happiest day of his life. "I don't get it. You're divorced. You've said yourself that things didn't end well. How could the start of something that ended badly be the happiest day of your life?"

"One good day with my Eliza was worth a hundred bad ones on my own. We only get one life, son. Chances are, I'm going to die alone sitting in this chair one day. But you know what? When I sit here, I do a lot of thinking back to the good times. So while I might be alone now, I still have memories to keep me company. Bittersweet memories are better than regrets."

Just then, out of the corner of my eye, I saw Sophia walk through the revolving lobby door with Scarlett. She had a shopping bag in her hand, but her friend had at least half a dozen. They were laughing, and it made me smile that she'd enjoyed her day.

The ladies were almost halfway across the lobby when Sophia looked around. It seemed like she sensed someone watching. Her eyes glided over to where I was sitting with Mr. Thorne, then flashed back in a doubletake. She leaned over to Scarlett to say something, and then they headed in our direction.

Clueless, Mr. Thorne elbowed me. "Don't look now, but two beautiful birds are coming our way. I call dibs on the one on the left."

I shook my head. "Don't think so, old man. That one's taken."

Sophia's smile was a mix of curious and amused as she approached.

"Hi."

I lifted my chin to Scarlett's bags. "Looks like you might need another suitcase for your trip home."

"The store is delivering the rest. I couldn't carry it all."

I smiled and shook my head.

"She's totally not kidding," Sophia said. "They really are delivering. I didn't even know they would do that type of thing."

Mr. Thorne cleared his throat next to me.

"Sorry. Sophia, Scarlett, this is Walter Thorne."

The women took turns extending their hands. "It's nice to meet you, Mr. Thorne," Scarlett said.

"Please, call me Walter," he replied.

"What the hell?" I said. "I have to call you Mr. Thorne and these two you just met can call you Walter?"

"If you were as pretty as they are, I'd let you call me whatever you wanted."

I rolled my eyes. "You're unbelievable. Maybe they should pick up your scratch-offs from now on, then."

Mr. Thorne waved me off. "An old man should be addressed formally, at least until using his first name is earned."

I hadn't really been annoyed until he said that. "And I haven't earned it yet?"

He tilted his head. "Not quite."

Sophia laughed. "I take it you two have known each other for a while?"

"Too long," I grumbled.

He leaned toward the women and lowered his voice. "Do you know what skinny jeans and a cheap hotel have in common?"

"What?" Sophia said.

"No ballroom."

The ladies both laughed, which only egged Mr. Thorne on.

"A man brought a lady back to his hotel room after their first date," he said. "Things were going well, and clothes started to come off. The man took his shoes and socks off, and the woman noticed his toes were all gnarly and twisted. She said, 'What's wrong with your toes?' to which the man replied, 'I had tolio.' She said, 'Tolio? Do you mean polio?' He shook his head. 'Nope, I had tolio.'

"A few minutes later, the man took off his pants, and the woman noticed his knees were all beat up. She said, 'What's wrong with your knees?' The man replied, 'I had the kneasles.' The woman replied, 'Kneasles? Don't you mean the measles?' Again, he shook his head. 'Nope. Had the kneasles.'

"Things were getting hot and heavy, so the man finally took off his boxers. The woman looked down and said, 'What a shame. You had small pox, too!'"

The ladies cracked up again, and I rubbed my hand over my face. "Alright. I think that's my cue that it's time to get out of here. Things will only get worse after that start."

We said goodbye, and Mr. Thorne opened his arms to Sophia. She smiled and leaned down for the hug he offered. I heard him give her more than that, though he tried his best to lower his voice.

"Don't give up on him too fast, okay, sweetheart?" he whispered. "Every once in a while he pulls his head out of his ass, and it makes all those rough edges smooth out nicely."

CHAPTER 19

Sophia

The next morning, Louis, the hotel manager, stopped by my suite to deliver a bunch of reports our legal team needed. He set them down on the desk and noticed the empty box of flowers there, as well as two dozen roses, blooms down, sticking out of the wastepaper basket next to it.

"Did I miss your birthday?" he asked.

"No. My birthday is in October."

When I offered no additional explanation, he took the hint and nodded.

"Why don't I take those with me? I'm on my way down to the loading dock next. The dumpster is out there. It'll get them out of your way and save housekeeping from carrying them down."

"Ummm...sure, that would be great. Thank you."

He picked up the box and stuffed the roses from the trash can back inside. "Did you throw out the others? I can grab those, too, if you want."

"Others?"

Louis nodded. "The ones from Park Florist, the place around the corner. They came about a half hour after these did."

"Are you sure they were for me?"

"I'm pretty sure. I could've sworn Matt, the usual delivery guy, said, 'Flowers for Sophia Sterling.'" Louis shook his head. "But maybe I misheard. I can double-check with Mr. Lockwood."

"Weston? Why would he know?"

"He walked over and said he'd take care of the delivery."

Hmm... Something in my gut told me Louis hadn't heard wrong. But who else would have sent me flowers, and why would Weston make sure these were delivered and not the others?

"Don't worry about it. I'll check with Weston. Thank you for letting me know."

After Louis left, I needed to get the reports down to my legal team, so I put off asking Weston. Then the morning got so busy that I forgot about it until I was on my way to grab a chopped salad for a late lunch and noticed the sign above the building a few doors down. *Park Florist.*

On a whim, I decided to go in.

"Hi. I had some flowers delivered yesterday. I think they were from this florist, but the card was missing, so I'm not sure who they're from."

The woman behind the counter frowned. "Oh no. I'm so sorry about that. Let me see what we have on file."

I smiled. "That would be great."

"Could I just see some ID, please?"

"Sure." I dug my license out of my purse and handed it to the woman.

She smiled. "Sophia Sterling. I remember the gentleman who came in and ordered these. He was quite the looker, if you don't mind me saying so, and was very particular in what he picked out. I should have the card in our system. We make our customers type their note into our iPad so we can print it out nicely and don't make any mistakes."

"Thank you. That would be great."

The woman typed into her computer and then walked to a printer and picked up a small, typed-up floral card. Handing it to me, she smiled. "Here you go. Sorry about that again."

I looked down and read it.

The lips on your face taste almost as good as the ones between your legs. Apologies for the abrupt departure. Let me make it up to you.

Dinner in my room at 7.

I wasn't sure if the florist had read it or not, but I felt my cheeks flush anyway.

"Uh, thank you. Have a good day." I rushed toward the door, but on my way out, the refrigerator full of colorful flowers caught my eye. I turned back. "What kind of flowers were those that you sent me? I'd never seen them before."

The florist smiled. "They're blackberry ripple dahlias. Beautiful, aren't they?"

I pretended I knew what they looked like. "Yes, they are."

"You know, being a florist is sort of like being a priest. We get people coming in seeking forgiveness for their sins, and others sending flowers to women who aren't their wives. You'd be amazed how many people tell us intimate stories while they're picking out an arrangement. We make a habit of keeping our customers' confidence. But I don't think there's any harm in telling you that when the gentleman who sent you those flowers walked in, he went right for those dahlias. I asked him if they were your favorite, and he said he wasn't sure, but they were beautiful and unique, a lot like the woman he was sending them to."

My heart did a little flutter. Only Weston Lockwood could make my emotions bounce around like a ping-pong ball. The other night had been amazing—beautiful and heartwarming and so physically satisfying. But the morning after, he'd seemed to shut down. Though, we'd talked a lot about Caroline, which wasn't easy for him. So after he left, I'd tried to chalk up what felt like a retreat to just a somber mood.

Then the flower delivery from Liam came, and the flower delivery from Weston *hadn't* come. And then there was Mr. Thorne. Who was he? In just the few minutes I'd spent with them, I could see there was an interesting dynamic there.

I smiled at the florist, feeling more confused than when I'd walked in. "Thank you for sharing that with me."

Outside on the street, I started to compose a text to Weston about the flowers, but decided I wanted to see his face when I asked him about the two deliveries. So instead, I sent a short, vague text:

Sophia: Need to discuss a delivery issue. Are you free?

By the time I'd picked up my salad and walked back to the hotel, my phone pinged with the response.

Weston: I'm in Florida. Is it something we can do over the phone?

What?

Sophia: When did you go to Florida?

Weston: This morning.

I don't know why, but I felt a little hurt that he hadn't mentioned the trip to me. But maybe it was an emergency and something was wrong. I knew his grandfather lived down there, on the opposite coast of my grandfather.

Sophia: Is everything okay?

Weston: Yes, fine.

I mulled over asking why he hadn't mentioned leaving. At a minimum, we were running a hotel together. So even if there wasn't anything personal going on between us, a heads-up would've been nice. But I didn't want to get into it over text. Instead, I opted to wait and have the discussion in person, along with the talk about the flowers.

Sophia: It can wait. Give me a call when you're back.

Two days later, I hadn't heard another word from Weston. His office door was still closed, and he hadn't called to let me know he was back like I'd asked him to. Scarlett had flown back to London this morning, and I'd spent the majority of the afternoon in with the legal and accounting team, trying to finalize the list of assets that still needed valuation. Our bid to buy out the minority share from the charity was due in less than three weeks.

Around seven o'clock, I went downstairs to the front desk to check in with the reception manager since Louis was off today. While I was there, a messenger delivered a package, and I overheard the bellman say to one of the employees, "I'm going to run this up to Mr. Lockwood. I'll be back in five minutes, in case anyone's looking for me."

The clerk nodded. "No problem. I'll keep an eye on your station."

I walked over and interjected, "Mr. Lockwood is out of town. But he has a mail bin in the manager's office in the back."

The clerk looked confused. "Did he leave again? I saw him a few hours ago."

"You saw Weston today?"

She nodded. "He came in about eleven this morning with his luggage."

What the hell? He's back? Where the heck had he been all day, and why hadn't he called me like he was supposed to?

I forced a smile and extended my hand to the bellman. "I'll take it up to him. I didn't realize he was back, and I have some reports to drop off also."

I stewed the entire ride up to the eighth floor. What the hell was his problem? If he wanted to back away from whatever was going on between us personally, that was one thing. But I'd told him I had business to discuss, and he hadn't even had the courtesy to let me know he was back in town?

At his door, I took a deep breath and knocked. The entire floor was quiet, including his room. After a minute or two and no sign of Weston, I wondered if maybe the clerk had made a mistake. Sighing, I headed back to the elevator with his package. But when the silver doors slid open, guess who was inside?

"You're back?" I said.

Weston stepped off the elevator. "Do you need something?"

"Did you get in this morning?"

"Closer to lunchtime. Maybe a little before noon."

"Where were you?"

"In Florida. I told you that the other day."

"No, I mean all afternoon. I came by your office earlier, and the door was shut."

He looked away. "I had a lot of work to do, so I kept it closed."

I squinted at him. "I thought you were going to call me when you got in."

He continued to avoid my eyes. "I was?"

"Yes, remember? I texted you the other day and said I wanted to discuss a delivery issue."

The adjacent second elevator doors dinged and slid open. A woman from housekeeping wheeled a cart out, and we all exchanged pleasantries. She parked her cart outside a guest room two doors down from the elevator and propped the door open.

I looked at Weston, waiting for his answer.

He shrugged. "It must've slipped my mind. What's up?"

The maid went in and out of the nearby room, bringing in sheets and taking out garbage, and I didn't want to have this conversation in the hall.

"Do you think we can have this discussion in your room?"

Weston seemed to hesitate a moment, but he nodded. We walked to his room together in awkward silence. I wasn't sure what was up, but I was now certain *something* was.

Inside his room, the first thing I noticed was the enormous flower arrangement sitting on the desk. It was still wrapped in paper, but it had the logo of Park Florist stamped all over it.

"Flowers?" I said, arching an eyebrow. "Do you have a secret admirer?"

He walked over to the minibar and grabbed a water. "I...uh...tried to deliver them to a guest for the bellman the other day right before I left for my trip. But the guest had checked out early. I was running late, so I just left them in here. I need to toss them."

"Oh really? That would be such a shame. What kind of flowers are they?"

Well, I'd learned one thing about Weston today. He was a really shitty liar. He couldn't seem to meet my eyes every time he spewed another one.

He shrugged. "Not sure. I didn't look."

I stared at him until he returned my gaze.

"What?" he asked.

"Nothing. Just seems like a shame to throw out perfectly good flowers. Maybe I'll take them. I love flowers." I was really enjoying screwing with him, so I added, "Unless they're dahlias. I'm not a fan, and they make me sneeze."

Weston had looked away again, but now his eyes came back to mine. I watched as the wheels in his head turned, trying to decide how to proceed.

In the end, he went with cautiously. "Dahlias only?"

I flashed a smile somewhere between smug and friendly, which only added to his confusion. "Yup. Just dahlias. In fact, the blackberry ripple variety are the absolute worst. I just sneeze and sneeze and sneeze..."

His already-squinting eyes narrowed even more. So I widened my smile and upped the ante.

Walking over to the flowers on the other side of the room, I fingered the card still stapled to the paper wrapping. "You weren't even curious what the card said?"

Weston stayed rooted to his spot. He looked about seventy-five percent sure I was fucking with him, yet the remaining twenty-five percent wanted to hold out before folding.

He shook his head slowly. This time when he spoke, his eyes remained locked with mine. "Nope. No interest whatsoever."

I fiddled with the card but left it attached to the paper. "Hmmm... Well, I am. Hope you don't mind if I read it."

Weston's jaw ticked as I called his bluff.

"It's an invasion of the sender's privacy," he grumbled. "Don't you think?"

I plucked the card from the paper wrapping and smiled. "Then you don't have to read it." Taking my sweet-ass time, I ran my nail across the back of the envelope and sliced it open. For full dramatic effect, I flashed my pearly whites at Weston as I slowly pulled the card out.

Before I could scan the first word, Weston was in my personal space. He snatched the card from my hand and gripped both sides of the desk around me, boxing me in.

His eyes gleamed. "Don't screw with me."

I lifted my hand to my chest and feigned innocence. "Why, whatever do you mean?"

"Ask what you want to ask, Sophia."

I tapped my fingernail to my lips, looking up at the ceiling. "Hmm... I have so many questions. I'm not sure where to start."

"Start wherever you want. Because you playing games just pisses me off. And you know what happens when we get pissed at each other." He leaned in closer. Our noses were only two inches apart. "Don't you, Soph?"

My mind immediately conjured images of me pressed against the wall with my skirt around my waist, and Weston with a fistful of my hair standing behind me.

When I didn't answer right away, he smirked. "Yes, that. Exactly what you're thinking."

I squinted. "Oh, you know what I'm thinking now, do you?"

"You were thinking of the first time we were together." He nodded toward the door. "I fucked you right up against that wall."

My mouth dropped open.

Weston ran his thumb along my bottom lip. "Well, we were both thinking the same thing a minute ago. But now with this beautiful mouth looking so inviting, I'm remembering a different evening."

Luckily, at that moment the smell of the flowers behind me permeated my nose, reminding me of the purpose of my visit. I cleared my throat. "Why did you buy me flowers and then not give them to me?"

Weston's jaw flexed. "It seemed you had another delivery, and I didn't think you needed two arrangements."

I tilted my head. "Why not let *me* decide which arrangement I wanted to keep?"

Weston relinquished his position and stood with his arms folded across his chest. "It pissed me off that another man felt he had reason to send you flowers."

"How do you know another man sent them? Maybe they were from a woman friend?"

"Because I read the damn card, Sophia."

I folded my arms across my chest, matching his stance. "Really? Didn't you just tell me that would be an invasion of the sender's privacy?"

"And if the roles were reversed? Can you honestly tell me if flowers came for me, you wouldn't sneak a look at the card?"

I thought about it and shook my head. "I'm not sure."

Weston gave me a curt nod. "You're a better person than I am. It happened. Can we move on, please?"

I shook my head. "From the flowers, yes...*after* you apologize for invading my privacy and intercepting my delivery."

He held my eyes for a few seconds before nodding. "Fine. I apologize for reading the card. The delivery I intercepted was the one I sent, so I had every right to do that."

I rolled my eyes. "Fine. I accept your half-ass apology. But I have other questions, aside from the flowers."

Weston mumbled under his breath, "Of course you do."

"Why did you leave the other morning so abruptly?"

Weston shook his head and blew out a deep breath. "Our situation is complicated, Sophia. You know that."

"Yes, I do. But we'd just had a really nice evening together. I thought we'd grown closer."

"Bingo. That, in itself, is the complication."

Everything about the two of us was complicated. Our relationship had been destined to be difficult before we were even born. But something inside told me that wasn't what had spooked Weston the other morning.

"So...it bothered you that our families have been feuding fifty years, and we're basically competitors?"

Weston looked away. "Yes, that's part of it."

I chuckled. "Just like you seem to be able to tell what I'm thinking, I can tell when you're full of shit."

Weston's eyes slid back to meet mine.

"What was the other part of it?" I asked.

He dragged a hand through his hair and exhaled harshly. "What do you want me to say? That I'm an alcoholic who's fucked up pretty much everything important in his life and you're too good for me?"

"If that's how you feel, yes."

He shook his head. "Of course it is. I'm not an idiot."

"Okay, well, at least if I know how you're feeling, I won't feel used."

Weston's face softened. "You felt used?"

I nodded.

"I'm sorry. I didn't mean to make you feel that way."

"It's fine. Obviously, we both have a tendency to jump to conclusions."

Weston nodded, looking down.

"Was your trip to Florida planned? Did you know about it when you left my room the other day?"

He shook his head. "I needed to speak to my grandfather about a few things. My grandmother isn't well, so he doesn't travel unless it's necessary."

"I didn't know. I'm sorry to hear that."

"Thank you."

We were quiet a long moment. We'd cleared the air, but some of what he'd said bothered me. I was probably just as hesitant as he was about getting involved. But none of the things that gave me pause had to do with him not being good enough, and I wanted him to know that.

"Can I ask you something?" I said.

"What?"

"Do you have one person you look up to more than anyone?"

He nodded immediately. "Caroline. She never felt sorry for herself, complained, or stopped smiling." He shook his head. "Hell, she spent more time listening to my problems and trying to cheer me up than bitching."

I smiled. "I wish I'd gotten to know her better. She sounds very special."

"She was."

"The person I look up to more than anything is my mom. She was an alcoholic."

"Really? I had no idea."

I shrugged. "Most people don't. God forbid anything real get out about the Sterling family. My father walked out on us without looking back, but he always made sure to cover my mother's tracks. After all, her last name stayed Sterling even after they divorced."

"Did she start drinking after they split up?"

I shook my head. "I wish I could say she did. It would give me something else to despise my father for. I had no idea she was an alcoholic until I was a teenager. After she found out she had cancer, I went to a bunch of doctors with her. A few suggested she go to rehab before she had her first surgery. Believe it or not, that confused me, even though I saw her drink every single day. My mom drank martinis out of expensive crystal glasses, so somehow it never dawned on me that she had a problem. Alcoholics swigged from the bottle, wore dirty clothes, and got sloshed and fell down. They didn't wear pearls and bake pies."

Weston nodded. "When I went to rehab, I was pretty surprised that half the people in there were over fifty and looked pretty damn normal."

"My mother did a different kind of scared-straight program. She kept getting headaches and blurry vision and probably attributed both to hangovers. It's what delayed her diagnosis. She had a tumor the size of a golf ball in her brain by the time she told the doctor about her symptoms. She was just so used to hiding things related to her drinking."

Weston took my hand and squeezed.

"Anyway, my point is, my mother was loyal, loving, kind, smart, and generous to a fault. She was the first person in her family to go to college, and even after she married my father, she continued to work part-time as an adjunct professor. Most people probably thought it was a fluff position, since she married into more money than she would ever need. But she took her entire paycheck and sent it to her parents every single week because they needed a little help. And when my father left us, she started teaching more classes and refused to take one dime from him, except for the cost of my education."

"Wow."

I smiled. "She was all those wonderful things. *And* she was also an alcoholic. I'm not gonna pretend there weren't days that sucked. Because there were plenty of those. But alcoholism is a disease, not a character trait, and it doesn't define who she was."

Weston stared at me. I could tell he was lost in thought, but I couldn't tell if he understood why I'd shared this. The look on his face was intense, and his Adam's apple bobbed up and down.

"Did you approve a fifty-thousand-dollar increase to our budget for the Boltons' construction?"

My forehead wrinkled. I had no idea what I'd expected him to say in response to my heartfelt admission, but this was certainly not it. "Yes. They needed an answer to avoid a delay, and you weren't around."

"Is your phone not working?"

I got angry. "I *had* called you once. You were supposed to call me when you got in, which you never did. They needed to add steel headers to a weightbearing wall in order to accommodate the extra weight on the roof above. It's not like I approved an invoice for decorating. If you want to be involved in every decision, I'd advise you to be here."

"Don't do it again."

My hands flew to my hips. "Then make yourself more goddamn accessible."

Weston's eyes darkened. "You're not well-versed enough in construction to make large financial decisions, especially ones that involve Travis Bolton. He's laying the charm on thick, and you fall for it."

Two minutes ago, I'd wanted to hug him, and now I was seriously considering punching him in the face. "Screw you."

He smirked. "Been there, done that."

My eyes widened. "Go to hell!"

He glared at me. "Turn around."

"What?"

"Turn around. Bend over the desk."

Had he been drinking? He had to have fallen off the wagon and hit his damn head if he thought I was about to have sex with him. "I have no idea what I was thinking being nice to you and opening up." I brushed past him and marched toward the door.

He called after me. "You're forgetting your flowers."

I halted and decided to show him what he could do with his flowers. Walking back to the desk, I picked them up with the intention of tossing them in the garbage. But before I could turn around, Weston had pushed up against me.

"I don't know how to do nice, Soph," he whispered in my ear. "*This* I know how to do."

My pulse raced. I'd been practically shaking with anger. "Are you joking? You baited me into a fight because you don't know how to be nice to me?"

He pushed his erection into my ass. "That depends on how you define *nice*. I would say giving you multiple orgasms is pretty nice."

I wanted to be mad, but I felt my resolve slipping. "You're an asshole, you know that?"

There was a smile in his voice. "Yes, I do." He paused. "Now bend over, sweetheart."

Sweetheart. One little word, and I turned to mush.

I stood there debating, wanting in the worst way to walk out the door, but somehow I couldn't get my feet to align with my head.

Weston brushed the hair from my neck and kissed his way up to my ear. "I missed you, babe." He snaked a hand around my waist and cupped between my legs, bunching the fabric of my skirt into his hand. "Tell me you're wet for me."

I was getting there, but I wasn't about to admit that. "You want me to do your job? Isn't it enough that I've been covering for you for two days?"

He chuckled. "I'm about to make it up to you."

Weston pushed my skirt and panties aside and stroked up and down once before pushing two fingers inside me. It took me less than three minutes to come on his hand, and ten seconds later I was bent over the desk as he pushed inside me. The second time I came, we shook the desk so hard the flowers tumbled to the floor. Weston said my name over and over again as he emptied himself inside of me. It was fast and furious, but just as physically satisfying as if it had been long and tender.

He leaned over my back as he attempted to catch his breath. "Thank you," he said.

"I should be the one thanking you. You did most of the work."

Weston pulled out and turned me around to face him. He pushed the hair off my face. "I wasn't talking about the orgasm. I was talking about what you said earlier."

I grabbed two fistfuls of his shirt and nodded. "There's no reason to thank me for that. It was the truth. Your struggles with alcohol don't have to define you. We all get knocked down at one point or another in our life. But you stood taller when you got back up. You should be proud of that."

He looked down for a while before his eyes returned to mine. "Have dinner with me tomorrow night."

We'd had dinner together quite a few times over the last few weeks. "Okay..."

"I don't mean dinner at the restaurant downstairs while we discuss business, or you eating with me because I'm blackmailing you to share a meal. I want a date—a real date."

I smiled. "That sounds nice. I'd like that."

"Let's not get carried away and call it *nice*. It's still going to end with my cock inside of you."

I laughed. "I expect nothing less."

Unfortunately, I still had a million things to do tonight, things that needed to get done by the morning for the valuation team. So I pressed my lips to his and said, "I need to get going now. I have a lot of work to do tonight."

Weston didn't hide his pout. I straightened my clothing and gave him one last quick kiss. At the door, I looked back.

"Oh, by the way, I threw out the roses the day they came, and I'm not allergic to dahlias. You know my room number, so clean up that mess and go get me some new ones."

CHAPTER 20

Sophia

The next day, the deliveries just kept coming and coming. They started at 10AM, and by two in the afternoon, I had four enormous arrangements of dahlias. Each was a different vibrant color, and each from a different florist.

Weston had been in the conference room with his team all day, so I hadn't even had a chance to thank him for the *first* delivery when he popped his head into my office. I was on the phone and held up a finger, motioning him to come in as I finished my conversation with my father.

"Yes, I'm doing that," I said. "They know our deadline, and I'm on top of them."

Weston shut the door behind him and made sure he had my attention as he reached back and twisted the lock. Meanwhile, my father was busy interrogating me about every decision I'd made here at the hotel and the laundry list of things I still had left to do. But his words started to fade away as I watched the man with the devilish smirk walk toward me.

Weston Lockwood was positively sinful. He had a jawline that would make a sculptor weep and eyes that were perpetually undressing me. But it was his crooked, dirty smile that always did me in. He walked behind my desk, leaned his ass against it, and casually started to take off his tie.

"And what about those open lawsuits?" my father snapped. "Has Charles gotten back to you about the potential exposure we have there?"

Weston tugged the tie from his neck and wrapped the ends around his fists.

"Uhhh... Yeah. He sent me an opinion on the slip and fall, but I'm still waiting for his review of the other two suits."

"There are f*our* lawsuits pending, Sophia!" my father barked. "What are you doing at that hotel? Do I need to be there every day?"

Weston held his hands up—his tie stretched between them. His hooded eyes raked over my body as if contemplating what he might tie up first. Distracted, I'd heard what my father said, but my response capabilities were running in slow motion.

"I think I need to get back on a plane."

That snapped me out of my haze. I shook my head, turning away from Weston. "No, no. That's not necessary at all. There're four suits. I knew that. I just misspoke."

"I want an update tomorrow morning," he grumbled.

"Fine. I'll talk to you tomorrow then."

As usual, he didn't bother to say goodbye. The line just went dead. Normally a conversation like that would leave me sitting and stewing, but it was impossible to feel angry with the glint in Weston's eyes.

I tossed my cell phone on the desk and swiveled in my chair to face him.

"I think you went a little overboard with the flowers." I smiled.

His eyes focused on my lips. "Have you ever had sex blindfolded?"

Okay, then...guess we aren't talking about the flower deliveries. I crossed one leg over the other. "No, I haven't. Have you ever blindfolded anyone?"

He shook his head, which surprised me. "You'll be the first."

I arched a brow. "Sure of yourself, aren't you?"

"How about in public?"

"Does in a car count?"

"That depends. Where was the car parked?"

"In a parking lot at the beach after it was closed."

Weston grinned. "Then, no. That doesn't count."

"What about you? Ever had sex in public?"

"Not while sober."

As ridiculous as it was, I felt a pang of jealousy. "Well, then you have, and I'm not looking to be another notch on your belt."

Weston's grin turned into a full-blown, cocky smirk. "You're cute when you're jealous."

I folded my arms across my chest. "I'm not jealous."

"We have a meeting now; otherwise I'd love to argue with you over who's right and wrong. Or at least prop you up on your desk and eat you out while you try to yank the hair from my scalp."

Oh... That sounded good.

Weston read my mind and chuckled. "Hold that thought. There's another problem with the construction, and I told Sam we'd come up to discuss it."

I should have been disappointed that we had another issue to contend with, but let's face it, I really just wanted to go deal with whatever it was and come back to pick up where we were leaving off.

I stood. "Okay. Let's go."

Weston didn't move out of my way. Instead, he slipped one hand around my neck and pulled me to him, placing a tender kiss on my lips. "You're welcome," he said against my mouth.

"What am I thanking you for?"

"The flowers. And, no, I didn't go a little overboard. You said you liked them, so you should have them."

My insides felt all mushy. "That's sweet. But four deliveries weren't necessary. The gesture was enough. Though I am looking forward to thanking you for each one."

"That's good." He winked. "Because you have a lot more than four coming."

Upstairs, the Boltons didn't even have to point us to the latest issue with the construction. The wide-open wall filled with dry rot was self-explanatory.

Weston and I were already looking at it when Sam and Travis walked over.

"This whole wall needs to come out," Travis said. "There're some leaky pipes above that must've been trickling for years. The wood is soft and warped."

The wall ran the length of the entire ballroom. It had to be at least a hundred feet.

"What about the leak itself?" Weston asked. "How much of the pipe needs to be swapped out?"

"We can probably contain the leak and fix the current problem, but that's only a Band-Aid. The pipes all along the ceiling should be changed. They're pretty badly corroded. Now's the time to do it since the walls are wide open. But that also means a delay of a few days at least and another plumbing bill."

Weston and I looked at each other. I shook my head. "Let's just do it right. The last thing we need is to start holding events in here and have leaks spring up."

Weston nodded. "I agree." He looked at Sam. "How soon can you get us an estimate?"

"I can start working on it now and bring it up to you by the time I get out of here tonight at eight."

"I won't be around this evening," Weston said.

Travis looked at me and smiled. "I can drop it off with Sophia."

Weston's jaw flexed. "She won't be around tonight either. We'll both be busy, *all night*. Tomorrow morning is fine."

Travis gave us a questioning look, but he knew better than to ask. Instead, he gave a curt nod. "All right. Sounds good."

On our way out, I teased Weston. "That was the equivalent of peeing on a fire hydrant."

"What are you talking about?"

"We'll both be busy *all night*? You might not have used the words, but it was pretty obvious what you were saying."

We arrived at the elevator bank, and Weston pushed the button. "Would you like to fight about it? We could cross sex in public off my to-do list. I'm sure it would make Saul in security's year. He's been working a lot of double shifts since we haven't replaced the night guard yet. I've been meaning to pick him up a bottle to say thank you. But I think he'd like listening to the way you moan much better."

I scowled at him as the elevator doors slid open. Weston put his hand on my back, guiding me to enter first.

"Why am I even having dinner with you tonight?" I asked. "You're such an ass."

He stood behind me in the elevator and whispered in my ear, "Because you like my cock."

I squirmed. "It's often the only part of you I like."

When the doors slid open on our office floor, I stepped off. Weston stayed in the elevator.

"Aren't you coming?" I said.

He smirked. "I will later. Be downstairs at six thirty, Sophia."

CHAPTER 21

Weston

Whose bright idea was it to go out to dinner all the way across town, to a fancy restaurant with appetizers, dinner, dessert, and dancing?

"This restaurant is beautiful." Sophia looked around. "Have you been here before?"

I shook my head. "Did you wear your hair up for me?"

"You do that a lot, you know."

"What?"

"I ask you a question, and rather than answer it, you respond with a question on a totally unrelated topic."

"I guess sometimes I have a one-track mind when I'm around you."

She smiled. "Yes, I did."

I was confused for a second. She'd jumped back to my question about her hair. "Thank you. But since you did that, you can expect me to be distracted all night."

Sophia looked even more gorgeous than usual. She wore a red dress with a halter top and a fuck ton of cleavage on display. The way the top wrapped around her neck showcased that collarbone I loved so much. My eyes bounced back and forth like I was in a tennis match, volleying from round, full tits to her succulent neck.

I'd had the menu in my hand for a few minutes with my head tilted down, though I still hadn't read a single word. So when the waiter walked over to take our order, I wasn't even sure what my choices were.

"I'm going to have the pistachio-encrusted sea bass, please," Sophia said.

I handed the waiter my menu. "Same."

When he walked away, Sophia sipped her drink with a smirk. "You have no idea what was on the menu, do you?"

"Nope. Guess I'm lucky I usually like what you like."

"What's going on in that head of yours that has you so preoccupied, Lockwood?"

"You sure you want the answer to that question?"

She giggled, and I swear a rush of heat seeped through my chest. I'd gone out with gigglers before, and Sophia was definitely not one of those. During the day, she wore conservative business clothing and worked hard not to let anything super feminine overshadow her capabilities. She laughed during a business lunch, and wore high heels, both of which I found sexy as shit. But something happened when she went into date mode. She let her guard down, and all that pent-up feminine stuff came flowing out. So, yeah, I was attracted to

Sophia the businesswoman. But Sophia the woman out on a date who allowed herself to giggle freely? She was absolutely mesmerizing.

"I definitely want the answer," she said.

I reached for my water and slugged half of it back. "All right. You know how I love your neck?"

"I do."

"Well, tonight you also have the most incredible cleavage on display, so my eyes can't decide where to look. You look absolutely gorgeous, Soph."

She smiled. "Thank you. But I have to admit, that's a lot cleaner than I expected."

I leaned toward her, over the table. "I wasn't finished yet. While looking at your beautiful tits and the creamy skin on your chest and throat, I'm envisioning what my cum would look like all over it. I've been busy debating if one spill would be enough to blanket everything I want to cover, or if I would need to unload twice to properly drench you."

Sophia's mouth dropped open, and she laughed nervously. "Oh, my..."

The only thing I liked better than feminine Sophia on a date was turned-on Sophia with her mouth hanging open. I put two fingers under her chin and nudged her jaw back up. "I'm going to get arrested if you don't keep this beautiful thing shut."

Lucky for me, the waiter came back to deliver our appetizers. He spent a few minutes telling us about all of their desserts since some of them needed to be ordered an hour in advance. I was grateful that Sophia passed on the soufflé, because I intended to eat my dessert in private.

When he was gone, it was Sophia's turn to guzzle some of her ice water. When she set it back down on the table, she immediately picked up the cocktail she'd ordered and drained half of that, too.

I chuckled. "I'm a little envious that I can't have something to take the edge off."

"I bet. You must walk around really damn tense from all the crap that goes on in your brain."

We laughed, which seemed to ease the dangerous sexual tension from a few minutes ago.

"You wore red on prom night, too," I said.

Her brows pulled together. "Did I? I can't even remember what my dress looked like at the moment."

I leaned back in my chair and shut my eyes. "Strapless. A little lighter than the color you have on now. It had a silver, sparkly belt that looked like a ribbon." I motioned in a circle with my pointer finger. "You wore these silver strappy sandals that wrapped around your ankle. You tried to take them off when we got back to your house, but I made you keep them on."

Sophia's face lit up. "Oh my God. That's right! How the heck did you remember that?"

"You don't forget what the dress of a woman you've spent half your life sneaking peeks at looks like when you finally get to slip it off of her."

"You...you used to sneak peeks at me?"

"Every chance I got. I thought you knew that. Though your face just told me I had that wrong. Guess I was pretty stealthy after all."

"Guess so. I really thought you hated me."

I smirked. "Oh, I did. But I also wanted to fuck your brains out."

She laughed. "So not much has changed, then?"

"Nah. Now I just wish I hated you." I shook my head. "You're impossible not to l—" I caught myself. "Like. You're impossible not to like."

Sophia didn't seem to notice my slip. Or if she did, she didn't call me out on it.

"As long as we're admitting the truth, I used to check you out all the time back in high school." She smiled. "Maybe even middle school."

"I was itching for a reason to clock that jackass you went out with, even before the night of the prom."

"Well, somebody took care of that for you. I'm not sure if you knew, but apparently he got into a fight after I left the prom, and his nose was broken."

"I'm aware. Cost my family twenty grand to stop him from pressing charges."

Sophia's eyes widened. "It was you? Why didn't you ever say anything?"

I shrugged. "I didn't think it was a big deal. He got what was coming to him. Plus, it wasn't like you and I were friends."

"I guess not." Sophia got quiet for a minute. She traced the condensation on her water glass before looking back up at me. "Are we friends now?"

"You tell me, Soph."

She took a moment before nodding. "When I think of a friend, I think of someone I can rely on, someone I trust and respect and also enjoy spending time with. So yeah, I think we're friends. You know, it's funny, I spent almost two years with Liam, yet I never felt like I could rely on him." She shook her head. "I once had a small fender bender, but my airbag went off, and it left me sort of rattled. I called Liam, hoping he would come, but he told me he was in the middle of a dress rehearsal and suggested I call Scarlett."

I shook my head. "That guy really was a dick."

She smiled sadly. "He was. You're definitely very different men. Somehow I know that if I'd called you like that, you'd have been there no matter what you were doing. You have a very protective way about you."

I nodded. "I'd show up for you, Soph. I would've even back in high school. Don't get me wrong, I'd bust your chops the entire time, but I'd show."

She smiled. "So...I guess that makes us...what then? Friends with benefits? Pretty sure our families would disown us if they found out."

"Fuck 'em," I said.

"Oh... You don't care?" She arched a brow. "So your family knows we're sleeping together and have become friends?"

I shook my head. "No, but that's mostly because I don't discuss my personal life with them. Neither my father nor my grandfather has ever taken an interest before, and I don't expect them to start anytime soon."

"Does that bother you? That they don't have an interest in getting to know you?"

I shrugged. "It used to. But I've spent way too many years trying to get them to see me. For a long time, I thought I was made of poison. Lately I've started to realize that venom can come from a family of snakes."

Sophia looked so vulnerable. Holding her hand out across the table, she nodded like she understood. And

I'm sure she did...a little, at least. Though I doubted she fully comprehended what my family was capable of.

Putting my hand in hers, I looked down at our entwined fingers for a long time. "Do you have plans for Labor Day weekend?"

She started to shake her head and then stopped. "Oh—actually, I do. I usually go to the Children's Hospital's charity event that weekend. My entire family does. Yours does, too, right?"

I leaned in and lifted her hand to my lips, placing a kiss on the top. "They do. Will you go with me?"

She looked surprised. "Are you asking me to go as your date?"

I nodded. "I am."

"With all of our family in attendance?"

"Why not? It'll be fun to see their faces."

Sophia nibbled her bottom lip for a minute before her face lit up. "Okay!"

I smiled. "Good, then I guess I have a new friend and a date for the event Labor Day weekend." I slipped my hand from hers and picked up my fork. "Now eat your damn food before it gets cold, so I can get you back to the hotel and decorate that neck."

"So how are things going?" Dr. Halpern asked. She set her pad on her lap and folded her hands on top.

"Fine."

"Have you been sleeping okay?"

My brows pulled down. "Same as usual. Why do you ask?"

"You look a little tired today."

I couldn't even try to hide my grin. "I was up late. But don't worry, you don't have to run to my grandfather. I wasn't drinking or doing anything stupid."

Well, I guess that would be a matter of opinion. My family would definitely think spending an entire night inside Sophia Sterling was stupid.

"I see. So you're seeing someone, then?"

I was hesitant to talk about Sophia with Dr. Halpern, even though she'd assured me nothing we discussed, except my general emotional state, went into her report to my grandfather. Doctor-patient confidentiality meant nothing when your resources were limitless—though I did want to work some things out.

"Yeah. I'm seeing someone."

"Tell me about her."

I thought about how to describe Sophia. "She's smart, beautiful, strong, and loyal. Basically, she's way above my pay grade."

"You think she's too good for you?"

I shook my head. "Not think, know. She's absolutely too good for me."

"What makes you say that?"

I shrugged. "She just is."

"Let's back up for a moment. You said she's smart. Do you feel you have inferior intelligence?"

"No. We can go toe to toe."

"Okay. You said she was beautiful. Do you consider yourself unattractive?"

I knew I wasn't. That wasn't what this was about. "I'll save you some time, Doc. We're not equals on the loyalty front."

"Is it because you have a tendency to stray and she doesn't?"

There was no damn way stepping out would be an issue with Sophia in my bed. "No, sex is definitely not an issue."

"So this is about you being someone she can rely on for things that are not physical?"

I let out a long, low sigh. "I don't exactly have a track record for being someone people can rely on. Plus... Let's just say things between us didn't exactly start off with honesty."

Dr. Halpern picked up her notepad and scribbled something. "Who do you feel you've let down in your life?"

I scoffed. "Probably easier to ask who I didn't."

She was quiet for a moment and then nodded. "Okay. Let's say everything you've just said is true, even though I'm certain it's not. Why can't this woman be the first person who experiences the new Weston Lockwood?"

"People don't change."

Dr. Halpern pursed her lips. "That would render my job useless, wouldn't it?"

I said nothing.

Dr. Halpern laughed. "You have manners, so you didn't answer the question with words. I appreciate that. But your face said it all. There are very few things I'll argue with a patient about, but having the ability to change is one of them. We all have the ability to change, Weston. Maybe not our DNA, but certainly the way we treat people is something we're all capable of modifying.

It's not always easy, but the first step is awareness—recognizing what needs to be changed and wanting things to be different. Whether what you believe about yourself is true or not is almost immaterial. What's important is that *you* believe it to be true, and you have the desire for things to change."

"No offense, Doc, but that sounds like a lot of psychobabble. If changing is that simple, why doesn't everyone do it? Prisons are filled with repeat offenders. I'm sure most guys who rob convenience stores don't walk through the gates on release day thinking, *I can't wait to go rob someone again and come back here.*"

"I'd have to agree with you. In that case, things are hard when they walk out of prison. They likely have no money, and the life they knew before has moved on without them. I never said it was easy to change. But if you hit the pavement eight hours a day, every day, willing to accept any minimum-wage job, most people will find something to cover feeding themselves and putting a roof over their head. The problem is, it's a lot harder to work forty hours a week washing the floor and scrubbing dishes than it is to point a gun at someone and steal a thousand dollars out of a register. So you truly have to want a clean lifestyle at any cost."

Dr. Halpern shook her head. "I think we've gotten off track, but the principle is still the same. There will be situations in your life that tempt you away from being loyal, and sometimes not taking the temptation will cost you something. It's a matter of how badly you want what you want and what you're willing to sacrifice to get it."

She made it sound so simple. It wasn't like I'd made a conscious choice in the past to screw things up. All of a sudden, I'd find myself someplace, and I usually hadn't realized where I was heading until I got there.

"I don't always see my bad choices before I make them."

She nodded. "That's understandable. But there are a few things you can start to practice that will lead you in the right direction."

"Like what?"

"For starters, express your feelings. Whether it's a good thing or bad thing, try to be open. Don't lie or omit things that are on your mind. And that's a task that's easier said than done. For example, does this woman know how you feel about her?"

I shook my head. "I'm not sure I even know how I feel about her."

Dr. Halpern smiled. "Are you sure? Very often, we tell ourselves we feel conflicted about someone or something because the thought of how we really feel scares us."

Fuck. I dragged a hand through my hair. She was right. I was falling in love with Sophia, and not the kind of fall that happened slowly. I was barreling head over heels, hard and fast, and it scared the living shit out of me. It took a few minutes for that to sink in, even though it had been there all along. My head pounded, and my mouth felt like the Sahara Desert. I looked up at Dr. Halpern and discovered she'd been watching me mull everything around in my head.

Frowning, I said, "Fine. Maybe you're not such a quack after all."

She laughed. "I think we've had a good session today, so I won't push you to discuss the feelings you have about this new woman. But loyalty is a two-way street, and it begins with honesty. Now that you've admitted what your heart holds, perhaps the next step is sharing it with the person who holds your heart."

CHAPTER 22

Sophia

The last few days had been crazy busy. My father was back in town, and the legal team had been working twelve hours a day as we loomed closer to the bid-submission deadline. Some nights I didn't finish working until almost midnight. And even then, the light was still on in Weston's office when I left. Though that didn't stop him from making his way to my bed when he finally called it quits.

This morning it felt like we'd barely fallen asleep, and now we were up again. The first light of the day streaked in through a gap in the curtains and sliced a ray of sunshine across Weston's face.

He petted my hair as I looked up at him, chin propped up on my fist. "There's a room key on the desk over there."

Weston's hand froze. "You want me to have a key to your suite?"

"Well, last night you woke me up about ten minutes after I dozed off. So I thought maybe you could just let yourself in."

He grinned. "I'm pretty sure you just invited me to slip my cock inside of you while you're sleeping."

I play-slapped his chest. "I meant let yourself in my *room*, not my body."

Weston leaned his weight to one side and rolled us. I was quickly on my back with him hovering over me. He pushed the hair from my face. "I like my idea much better."

I smiled. "I bet you do." We were both still naked from last night, and I felt him hardening against my thigh. "My father is leaving on an afternoon flight, so I told him I'd meet him downstairs at seven. Unfortunately, I have to jump in the shower now."

He leaned in and kissed my neck. "Is there anything I can do to convince you to be a few minutes late?"

I chuckled. "There's no such thing as a few minutes with you."

"You say that like it's a bad thing."

I shook my head. "It's definitely not. But it's also the reason I'm about to go into the bathroom and lock the door."

Weston sulked. It was adorable. He rolled to his back and blew out a frustrated breath. "Fine. Go. But don't blame me if there's a wet spot on your side of the bed when you get out of the shower."

I wrinkled my nose and stole the sheet from the bed as I stood. "My side? Why don't you make that mess on your own side?"

He tugged at the sheet I tried to wrap around myself. "Because it's your fault there will be any mess to begin with. If you'd just give me five minutes, I could make that mess where it belongs—inside you."

God, I had it bad for this man. What he'd just said was crude, yet I felt that mushy feeling in my belly, just hearing him say his cum belonged inside me. *Romantic, right?* But it was what it was.

I leaned back down to the bed and kissed his lips. "My father should be gone by noon. How about you meet me back up here for lunch at one o'clock, and I'll let you make that mess anywhere you want?"

Weston's eyes darkened. "*Anywhere* I want?"

Oh boy. That was a dangerous statement. But what the hell? I smiled. "*Anywhere*. Good luck concentrating today while you debate exactly where that will be."

"You and the Lockwood boy seem to have made friends," my father said.

It was just the two of us left in the conference room now that he'd rudely told the legal and accounting team to *make themselves scarce*.

Where is this leading? Dad rarely made observational comments that didn't have a purpose. He treated people as pawns in a chess game. I shuffled a pile of papers to a neat pile. "We've found common ground. It's not like we have a choice when we're running a hotel together."

"He's not focused on running a hotel with you, Sophia. His focus is on your ass. I'm not dumb. I see the way he looks at you when he thinks no one is paying attention."

I froze. "How does he look at me?"

"Like he's a pit bull that hasn't eaten in weeks, and you're a juicy steak."

I cringed—not because it wasn't quite possibly true, but because hearing my father say it was *wrong*. The word *juicy* in any way, shape, or form—when related to me—sounded icky coming out of his mouth. Knowing lies were usually apparent on my face, I avoided eye contact by walking around the room and collecting empty coffee cups and plates left by the team.

"I think you're exaggerating," I said. "But...so what if he does? Weston is a nice-looking man. It's not like I haven't noticed that."

I snuck a peek at my father's face and found it stern. "Jesus, Sophia... Don't even think about it. That man is beneath you. But in any event, perhaps you could—"

I cut my father off. "Beneath me? What does that even mean? Are there unwritten levels of people I'm not seeing? Perhaps that's why you walked out on my mother. Was she not the same level as you?"

My father rolled his eyes. "Not now, Sophia. I have a flight to catch. We don't have time for yet another argument because your feelings were hurt when your mother and I divorced."

I shook my head and mumbled, not quite under my breath, "Unbelievable..."

Dad took his suit jacket from where it hung on the back of a chair and shrugged into it. "Anyway, as I was saying, the Lockwood boy is interested in you. Perhaps you can use it to our advantage."

"To our advantage? Exactly what are you suggesting?"

"We've had this discussion before. And you're a smart girl, Sophia. You know exactly what I'm saying. We only get one bite at the apple with this bid. It would be helpful to know what the Lockwoods' offer will be so we can bid above it for the minority share."

"Just so I'm clear, you...what? Want me to spread my legs for Weston and then maybe wait until right before he's about to shoot his load and ask him what his bid is?"

"Don't be crude. I'm sure there are other ways you can get a sense of things. Chat him up a little bit."

Over the years, I'd experienced so many disappointments with my father that I'd thought I'd become immune to him letting me down. But apparently that wasn't the case. I shook my head, feeling a new low. "You should go. You don't want to miss your flight."

My father was so arrogant, he didn't seem to notice the disdain in my voice. He walked over as if he hadn't just told me to whore myself out and kissed my forehead. "We'll talk soon."

After he left, I stood in the conference room for a long time. There was absolutely no way my father would ever accept Weston and me having a relationship. William Sterling might be a brilliant businessman, but he was ignorant when it came to the important things like relationships. It wouldn't matter if I told him I'd met the love of my life and was happy. The fact that Weston was a Lockwood and our families had a dumb grudge dating back before I was born was more important to honor than his daughter.

After "lunch" with Weston, I sighed, looking up at the ceiling. "I needed that."

He chuckled. "I guessed that, considering you marched into this room and pretty much grabbed my dick."

I smiled. I had sort of done that. "Sorry. I was just so frustrated. My father is absolutely the most irritating man on the planet."

Weston turned to his side and propped his head on his elbow. He traced soft figure eights with his finger on my stomach. "Don't apologize. I'm happy to reap the benefits of William being a dick. Though, I believe I was the one who was supposed to pick the orifice to make a deposit."

I wrinkled my nose. "*Orifice*? Really?"

He winked. "You're lucky you picked my favorite hole anyway."

"Oh really? I'll have to remember you like sex better than a blow job in the future."

Weston shook his head. "Don't get me wrong, there's nothing better than seeing you down on your knees in front of me. But I fucking love watching your face as you come."

Yet again, that warm feeling flooded my belly even though what he'd said was far from classically romantic. I pressed a soft kiss to his lips. "Well, thank you for letting me use you."

"Anytime." He pushed a lock of hair behind my ear. "You want to talk about it?"

"My orifices?" I joked.

"Whatever went down with your father. But, hey, we can talk about orifices instead. Better yet, roll over and we'll christen a new hole."

I chuckled. But Weston did look interested in what had gotten me angry. So I decided to share what my father had suggested. I rolled onto my side and propped my head on my elbow, mimicking his position.

"My father told me he's noticed you looking at my ass."

Weston's eyebrows jumped. He shook his head. "Shit... How'd the rest of that conversation go?"

"Not well."

He ran his hand up and down, from the curve of my waist to my thigh and back up again. "Sorry about that. I do my best, but it's impossible not to look at you and think about you naked."

I smiled. "That's oddly sweet."

He shrugged, and his eyes stayed glued to my hip as he continued to rub up and down. "It's the truth."

"Well, that's not the worst of it. After he said he'd seen you ogle me, he suggested I use it to my advantage to pump information out of you about your family's bid."

Weston's hand froze, and his eyes jumped to meet mine. "What?"

"You heard me right. My father pretty much told me to seduce you to get information."

Weston got quiet, though the stunned look on his face spoke for him. "What did you say?"

"Honestly, not enough. I think I was just so disappointed, I couldn't come up with an appropriate answer. After he left, I thought of a million things I should've said. Like, I would've loved to see his face after I told him you were probably already waiting for me up in my room since I'd given you a key before I slipped out of bed with you this morning."

I laughed and pointed my thumb at the stack of papers on the desk. "I'm pretty sure I would've had to call 911 if I'd told him you had access to all the work papers I keep in here, not to mention my body. The papers would've probably been a bigger deal, though."

Weston shook his head. "I'm sorry. You deserve better than that."

"Yeah, well, Scarlett has a saying, 'Any time you spend wondering if you deserve better is time wasted. Because if you're wondering, you do.' I've spent too many years questioning whether I deserved the way my father treated my mother and me, so I'm not going to waste anymore time dwelling over it. I always knew the answer."

Weston looked down. "You deserve a lot better from the men in your life—a fuck of a lot better."

CHAPTER 23

Sophia

Weston looked as stressed as I'd felt the last few days.

Our bids were due in less than two weeks, and we both still had so much to do. Though, if I was being honest with myself, it wasn't just the looming deadline that had me on edge. Weston and I hadn't spoken about the logistics of what would happen after the bids were opened, and that had begun weighing on my mind.

Once one family owned the majority of The Countess, the other family would inevitably be pushed out. Weston and I had talked about going to a charity event together Labor Day weekend, but that was two months from now, which seemed like a lifetime. The more immediate question was, what would happen when this contest was over?

One of us wouldn't be involved in the day-to-day operations of the hotel anymore. Did that mean Weston wouldn't be slipping into my room at night? If

I won, would he be holed up at one of his own family's properties across town like he'd been in the months before Grace Copeland died? Or would he be sent back to Vegas where he still owned a house? There was so much up in the air, and the unknown was like a giant shadow following me around.

It didn't help that Weston had seemed to distance himself a little the last few days. Ever since the day my father and I had our blowup, it felt like something had shifted—a crack had formed in the ground of our relationship, and each day it seemed to widen. After the bidding ended, would we need to yell in order to hear each other from the two sides we stood on?

To outsiders, though, we probably looked business-as-usual as we left the construction of the new ballroom.

"It's really coming along great," I said.

Weston nodded. "The mayor and his niece want to come see the room. Louis had been holding them off, but it should be in a presentable state by late next week."

I glanced over at him. "I guess that means *one of us* will get to meet the mayor."

Weston held my gaze. He frowned, but said nothing as he nodded.

Clearly, he had no plan to initiate the discussion we needed to have, and that frustrated the hell out of me. In fact, with each step I took, I felt my anxiety grow. By the time we got into the elevator, I'd started to feel like there wasn't enough air, particularly in the confined car. My choices were to lean over and hyperventilate, or lift the boulder off my chest so I could breathe again. Halfway between the sixth and seventh floor, I decided I couldn't take it. Jamming my finger into the red emergency stop button, I brought the elevator to an abrupt halt.

"What's going to happen next week?" I asked.

At first, Weston looked genuinely confused, but it didn't take him more than a few seconds to catch up. He shook his head and shoved his hands into his pants pockets. "I don't know, Soph."

"Well... What do you *want* to happen?"

"You mean between us?"

I rolled my eyes. "Yes. What else would I be talking about? It's pretty clear from a business standpoint. The lawyer for Easy Feet is going to open two envelopes, and one of us is going to become the majority shareholder. We both know neither of our families will want to manage the property jointly, so the winner will take over running The Countess, and the loser will get some hefty profit checks a few times a year. But where does that leave *us*?"

Weston nodded and pointed to the camera in the corner of the elevator. "Unless you want security to know I'm not ready to stop fucking you, maybe we should have this conversation somewhere else. I have a call in a few minutes. Does six o'clock work?"

"My meeting with legal is at six. Seven?"

He nodded. "I'll order us some dinner and meet you in your suite."

"Okay."

We made small talk through dinner. I was anxious to have a discussion, but figured maybe Weston preferred to wait until we were done so it seemed less like a business meeting and more like a regular couple's date. After we finished, he rolled the room service table out into the hall and walked over to the bar.

"Do you want a glass of wine?"

"Ummm..."

His brows dipped together. "Do you have to go back downstairs?"

I shook my head. "There's nothing that can't wait until morning."

"Are you too full for wine?"

"I'm never too full for wine."

He frowned. "I thought we were past you refraining because I don't drink."

I smiled. "Oh, that's not it. I'm over that. I was just thinking maybe I should keep a clear head for our discussion."

Weston turned back to the bar, took out a bottle of wine, and poured me a glass full to the brim. Passing it to me, he said, "Here. My head is far from clear. This will put us on even ground."

I sipped my wine as we looked at each other. I sat at the end of the couch, and he sat across from me in the chair.

"This is new to me, Soph. You may need to show me how it's done."

"What? Talking about a relationship?"

He shook his head. "Talking about feelings in general. It's been a long time since I even had any, much less discussed them. The ones I did have weren't exactly good, and I did my best to drown them with alcohol."

I set my wine on the table and took one of his hands into mine. "Well, how about this... Let's pretend for a minute that you're not a Lockwood, and I'm not a Sterling. We're just two people who work together, and one of us is going to be laid off in a few days. What do you want from me after that happens?"

Weston stared off for a few minutes. Toward the end, a smile crept onto his face. "I just realized one of us is going to be pissed. *Really pissed.*"

"And the idea of one of us being let down and disappointed made you smile? I think you really are rusty on how these emotional things are supposed to work."

He shrugged. "True. But I smiled because I realized it's been a while since we had a good, angry fuck."

I chuckled. "And what about beyond that? What do you want?"

Weston looked down for a long time. Eventually, he shook his head. "I want it all."

My pulse sped up, but I was afraid to get ahead of myself. "Elaborate," I said. "What does 'I want it all' mean?"

He took my hand and raised it to his mouth, kissing the top of my knuckles. Looking into my eyes, he took a deep breath. "It means I want to start my day the same way I end it every day—in your bed. Or my bed. Whatever. As long as I'm inside of you. You'll tell me all the boring shit you plan to do to fill the hours between me kissing you goodbye and kissing you hello, and I'll listen enough to know when to nod. I want to disagree with you, argue loudly, and then fuck the pissed-off right out of both of us. I want you to go be the badass businesswoman you are during the day, where you're in charge, and then let me be in charge in the bedroom after. I want to watch you from a distance when you buy your morning coffee and daydream about leaving marks all over your beautiful skin. And I want to read boring Shakespeare so I can poke fun at it, just to hear you laugh."

I hadn't blinked the entire time he spoke.

Weston searched my eyes. "How's that? Did I elaborate enough to make my feelings clear?"

"Wow...yeah...clear." I shook my head. "I thought you said you weren't good at this?"

Weston's lips twitched. "I'm not. This is all new to me. But then again, I'm good at everything."

I rolled my eyes. "So full of yourself."

Weston pulled me into his lap. He put one hand on my shoulder and used his thumb to caress my collarbone as he spoke. "Tell me what you want."

I had so many questions. Where would I live? Where would he live? How would we separate business and our personal life when we were essentially competitors? What would our families say? Was it too soon for me to jump into something new? But the one question I knew the answer to was the one he'd just asked.

"You," I said. "I want you."

Weston smiled. "Well, that's easy. You had me from the very start."

The next morning, we both slept in. Well, if you can call sleeping past six o'clock sleeping in. The sound of a cell phone ringing woke us.

I turned and reached over to my nightstand, only to realize it wasn't my phone buzzing. It was Weston's. I gave him a soft nudge. "Hey. That's yours. It's pretty early, so it might be important."

He grumbled something unintelligible and patted over the nightstand without looking. As he found his cell, I could see *Missed Call* on the screen. He peeked one eye open to type in his password.

"Seriously?" I chuckled. "Your code is 6969? How old are you?"

"What's yours? *Uptight* spelled out in numbers?"

I smacked him in the face with my pillow as he hit *Call Back*. But this was what I loved about us. Last night, he'd been sweet and caring. He'd made love to me in a way that made my eyes prickle with tears, and now this morning he was back to his normal, grumpy self. Weston Lockwood was a walking dichotomy, and I enjoyed the friction just as much as I enjoyed the smooth.

"This better be important," he barked into the phone.

He listened for a moment and then sat up in bed. "*Fuck*. I'm on my way."

The phone was barely swiped off, and he was climbing out of bed.

"What happened?" I asked. "What's going on?"

"There's a flood." He grabbed his pants from the floor and yanked them on. "In the damn construction area—on the *one night* we didn't have a crew working around the clock because the wood floors were being finished."

"Oh, shit." I climbed out of bed and scrambled for my clothes. Weston was already tugging on his shirt by the time I located anything of mine.

He walked over and kissed the top of my head. "Take your time. I'll run up and start damage control."

"Okay, thanks."

Fifteen minutes later, I joined Weston in the ballroom. Sam Bolton was already there, and it looked like he'd come straight from bed, too. All of the overhead lights were off, and both men were using their phone flashlights. I could see their faces but not really the extent of the damage—though the sloshing sound the water made as I walked gave me a hint that things weren't good.

"Hey," I said. "What happened?"

Sam shook his head and pointed to the ceiling. "Water main busted. It must've happened right after we left based on the amount of water all over the place. Floor refinishers put the topcoat of sealant on last night, which needed to dry for at least twelve hours, so the place had been empty since five o'clock. Can't step on the floors while they're wet. So we locked the door and told security to skip checking in on their normal rounds."

"I thought we replaced the rusty pipes."

"We did. Not sure what happened, but you can be damn sure I'll be getting to the bottom of it. Had to be a poorly done soldering job or something. Bob Maxwell, the owner of the plumbing company, is already on his way over."

"How bad is it?" I asked.

"Besides the plumbing work, a lot of the electric got wet, so that's going to need to be changed out. The floors hadn't been sealed yet, so most likely all that wood is going to warp and will need to come up. Not to mention, new sheetrock and insulation."

I blew out a loud breath. "Damn... We were barely going to make it for the first event scheduled as it was. And the mayor and his niece are coming to see her venue next Monday."

Sam Bolton rubbed the back of his neck. "I'm so sorry. I've worked with this plumbing contractor for more than twenty years and never had a problem. Obviously I have insurance to cover everything, and we'll do our best to get things back on track. But I'm afraid Sophia's right. This is going to throw us off our completion date. I don't know by how much yet, but we'll do our very best."

Weston had been pretty quiet until now. He put his hands on his hips and spoke to Sam. "I'm going to call Ken Sullivan and ask him to come over and take a look at things."

Sam opened his mouth to speak, but I beat him to it. "Ken Sullivan from Tri-State Contracting? Why?"

"Because I want to know what happened here, and I need some assurance that someone around here knows what they're doing."

"Weston..." Sam said. "I realize you're upset, but I can assure you I know what I'm doing. I've been at this for forty years, and I've worked with the Sterling family for almost as long."

"Exactly my point. You haven't worked with the Lockwood family. I don't know how things usually run for you firsthand, so I'm going to bring in my own team to make sure whatever is going on here won't happen again."

Sam puffed his cheeks and blew out an audible breath. "Fine."

Rather than argue with Weston in front of Sam, I waited until we were out in the hall alone.

"I think you're overreacting," I said as the door closed behind us.

"A pipe should not burst like that unless it freezes. If it was my contractor who caused this mess, you'd be the first one questioning whether he was incompetent."

I put my hands on my hips. "By questioning my contractor's competency, you're also questioning *my* competency in hiring people."

"Don't get bent out of shape over this, Sophia. It's business."

"Whatever..." I waved a dismissive hand at him.

Weston tilted his head toward the elevator bank down the hall. "I'm going to get coffee and then run to my room for a quick shower. Do you want me to pick you up something?"

I shook my head. "I'll get my own."

He shrugged. "Suit yourself."

The day only got worse after that.

As expected, my father didn't take the news about the flood very well. He basically called me incompetent, as if *I'd* installed the pipe incorrectly and not a contractor that he, himself, had been using for decades. Then while I was upstairs with Sam and the plumber, I tripped over a tool on the floor and my iPhone went flying from my hands. It slammed into a pile of debris that had fallen from the ceiling and now no longer turned on. After that, the legal team learned of a new lawsuit just filed against the hotel, which we needed to somehow value in the next day or two in order to factor that into our bid price. And to top it all off, Liam had left two messages on my office phone. So when Weston let himself into my office at four o'clock, I was in no mood.

"If you're coming to tell me how incompetent I am again, just turn around and let yourself back out."

Weston walked to my desk and extended an envelope. "Actually, I was coming to give you this."

Inside were two tickets. "Drunk Shakespeare? What is this?"

"It's a show here in the City. A bunch of actors get together. One of them downs at least five shots of whiskey, and then they attempt to act out Shakespeare."

I laughed. "Are you serious?"

"Yep. Figured it might be the only play the two of us would both enjoy."

I caught the date on the tickets. The play was almost a month and a half from now. My anger was quickly replaced with that warm feeling once again. I looked up at him. "When did you buy these?"

"A few days ago. They were just delivered by messenger, so I figured I'd use them as a white flag."

"You bought us tickets to an event a few months away before we'd even had a discussion about our future?"

"You're the only one who needed that discussion to make things formal, Soph."

I stood, walked around my desk, and wrapped my hands around his neck. "Why don't you go lock the door..."

Weston flashed a cocky smile. "Already did on my way in, sweetheart."

I tucked my blouse into my skirt and turned my back to Weston. "That works better than Xanax," I said over my shoulder. "Zip me, please."

He zipped my skirt and pushed my hair to the side to kiss my neck. "Happy to be of service. What's on your agenda for the rest of the afternoon?"

I turned and smoothed down my clothes. "We have that conference call with Elizabeth, the hotel's attorney, in a little while about the new lawsuit. I'd planned on running to the store to get a new cell. I dropped it earlier, and now it won't turn on." I looked at my watch. "But I don't think I'm going to have time. I don't want to miss the start of the call, and there's usually a line at Verizon."

"You want to take mine? I'm just going back to my office to go through reports. That way if you're still at the store, you can dial in for the call."

"You sure you don't mind?"

Weston held out his phone to me. "No problem. You already know my top-secret code."

The gesture felt monumental. It was something a *couple* did for one another. Things we keep in our phones can be very personal—not that I was planning on scrolling through his and searching for anything. But it meant Weston had nothing to hide. Even more than that, it meant he *trusted me*. And that spoke volumes.

I took the phone and kissed him. "Thank you. I'll tell you what, as a token of my appreciation, tonight we can do a live reenactment of your code."

CHAPTER 24

Sophia

It was a good thing I borrowed Weston's phone.

I'd been standing around the Verizon store, playing with a bunch of phones I had no interest in buying for the last forty minutes, waiting for my name to be called. I had to dial in for the conference call with the hotel's attorney in five minutes. So I rummaged through my purse to find the paper with the telephone number. As luck would have it, one minute before the call was to begin, my name was called.

I held out my broken iPhone to the sales clerk. "Hi. My phone isn't working. I dropped it, and it won't turn back on. I have AppleCare on it, so if I could either get this one fixed right away or get a new one, that would be great."

"Sure. No problem. Is your account under the email address you used to sign in for your appointment?"

"It is."

"Okay. Let me have someone take a look at your phone, and then I can let you know your options."

I looked down at the time on Weston's cell phone. I needed to dial in for my call. "Do you know how long that will take? I have to jump on a phone call for work."

"About fifteen minutes."

I nodded. "Okay, great. If I'm still on my call when you're ready for me, could you possibly take the next customer and come back to me?"

"Sure. No problem."

What I thought would be a fifteen-minute phone call turned out to be nearly an hour. After I finally hung up, the sales rep was already on at least his third customer, so I had to wait for him to finish up. As I paced back and forth, Weston's phone buzzed in my hand. Out of habit, I looked down to see who it was. The screen illuminated and showed a preview of an incoming text from someone named Eli that started: *Yo, dude, did you fall off the face of the planet?*

It made me smile because I was pretty sure most of my friends would feel the same way about me lately. I didn't want to invade his privacy, so I didn't swipe to open the rest of the message. But as I went to push the button on the side to turn off the screen, a second message popped up. This one was an email preview:

Did you get what we need from the Sterling girl?

I froze.

What was that about?

Certain I must've read it wrong the first time, I read the message preview again, more slowly. It had come from Oil40@gmail.com

Did you get what we need from the Sterling girl?

My heart started to race, and I felt a little nauseous, though I tried to remain calm. There had to be a logical explanation for a message like that.

Maybe the email was from Sam Bolton... They'd gotten an estimate for the flood work and wanted both of our approvals to proceed.

Though that would be pretty fast.

And Oil40? Why would Sam's email be something about oil?

I shook my head. *I'm being ridiculous.* This message could be any number of contractors Weston was working with. Why did my mind automatically go to the worst place and think something ominous was going on?

Maybe Weston had been getting bids for something and told the contractor he needed my sign-off? We'd been so busy lately that he probably hadn't even mentioned it to me. That was it. That definitely had to be it.

Yet...

Did you get what we need from the Sterling girl?

The Sterling girl...

It was definitely not the right way for a contractor to refer to a person he wanted to do business with. But I suppose there are plenty of old-school idiots out there who still refer to a woman as a *girl*.

That was not Weston's fault.

This contractor, whoever he was, was obviously a jerk.

In fact, I should probably open the email and take a look at the sender so I could be aware of exactly who referred to women in such a derogatory manner.

But... Weston had given me his phone because he trusted me, and opening his email would be a violation of that trust.

Though I'd already read the preview, so the damage had been done. Seeing the sender wouldn't be anymore of an intrusion on his privacy than I'd already accidentally committed.

Not really, anyway.

Right?

I stared down at the cell phone with my finger ready to swipe open the preview. Yet I couldn't bring myself to do it. It felt wrong, no matter how many different ways I tried to justify things in my mind.

So when the sales rep walked over to talk to me, I slipped Weston's phone into my purse and tried to put thoughts of what I'd been about to do out of my mind. It turned out my phone wasn't repairable, so the rep brought me a new one and offered to transfer all the information from my old phone. He said it would take another ten minutes, and he'd be back soon.

Unfortunately, that gave me more time to stand around and overanalyze.

Why did I feel so unsettled after one little preview of an email?

That wasn't too hard to figure out.

Because I have trust issues. Just about every man I'd put my faith in had let me down. So, not surprisingly, my imagination wanted to think the worst.

Weston didn't really have feelings for me.

He'd been using me to get something.

Did you get what we need from the Sterling girl?

God, the message sounded like something my father would say.

Get what we need from the Lockwood boy.

But there were so many ways to interpret that sentence. It could mean anything. But the bottom line was, if I opened his email, I'd be violating Weston's trust. In some ways, I'd be no better than Liam. Because without trust, there was no relationship.

Miraculously, I managed to keep Weston's cell phone in my purse while I finished up at the Verizon store. Outside on the street, the fresh air made me feel a tiny bit better. During the two-block walk back to The Countess, it dawned on me that Weston was going to see the email at some point after I handed him back his phone. If he was waiting to talk to me about something that had come up—whatever that email exchange referred to—he'd probably bring it up soon enough anyway. I likely wouldn't have to wait long to feed my curiosity.

In an hour or two, I'd be laughing at how silly I'd been for stressing over some email from a sixty-year-old plumbing contractor or something like that. Weston would tell me he had an estimate to go over that needed my sign-off, and that would be that.

Yeah, that was what would happen.

I'd probably get a good laugh at myself, too.

Though as I walked back into The Countess, I definitely felt more anxious than amused.

"So... Do we have any open issues we need to discuss?" I asked.

I'd just finished up for the day and walked over to his office. It was almost ten o'clock at night, and Weston had had his cell phone back for hours now. Yet he still hadn't mentioned anything he needed my sign-off on.

He shook his head. "Not that I can think of."

Maybe he needed a little reminder, because he forgot... "What about any repair work or estimates we both need to sign-off on? I brought you one from the Wi-Fi company that wants to upgrade our service a few hours ago. Do you have anything for me?"

Weston seemed to give it some thought. "Nope. The only thing I have outstanding is the revised timeline the Boltons owe us. Other than that, I think we're all good."

My stomach felt hollow. Could he have forgotten the email?

"Well, I'm going to head upstairs. I have a lot of *emails* that came in today that I still need to respond to. How about you? You buried under, too?"

Weston shrugged. "Nope. Actually, I'm all caught up." He smirked. "Guess I'm a lot more efficient than you."

I forced a smile. I wasn't ready to walk away from his office yet, because I was still clinging to hope he'd remember something. But I also couldn't think of anything else to say. So I stood there awkwardly. At least I felt awkward.

Eventually, Weston said, "I'll meet you upstairs in a little while. I need to finish a few things."

I felt deflated. "Okay."

Back in my room, I was disappointed in myself. Why hadn't I just asked him about the email? Reading one line of a message preview on his phone had been entirely accidental. He couldn't be mad about that. Yet instead of putting myself out of my misery, I'd allowed my dark thoughts to fester.

In my heart, I knew the real issue had nothing to do with me having done anything wrong. I wasn't nervous about telling Weston I'd read a message on his phone. I was nervous about him saying it wasn't what I thought, and me not believing him. My trust issues ran deep, and I hated that I assumed the worst. So instead, I hid my fears and attempted to cling to hope that the situation would resolve itself.

He's probably going to see that email and mention something to me when he gets up here. I'm making a mountain out of a molehill.

Rather than wear away the carpet with my pacing, I decided to take a bath. I filled the tub with warm water and tossed in some bath salts. Slipping in, I closed my eyes, took a deep breath, and blew out a big exhale.

I'm on the beach in Hawaii. The sun is warm on my body, and the sound of the waves gently crashing against the shore is lulling me to sleep.

But... Where's Weston? Why didn't he come with me?

Because he's a lying bastard who I don't talk to anymore. That's why.

I took another deep, cleansing breath and tried to change my focus.

This time, I went to a happy place I'd had in London, which had nothing to do with Weston—a small park that overlooked the river, a few blocks from where I'd lived. Unfortunately, when I imagined myself sitting on a swing, taking in the peaceful view, I noticed a couple lying on a blanket in my periphery.

Liam and my cousin.

I turned to run the other way, and my father loomed over me.

He tsked. "*I told you so.*"

I sighed and opened my eyes. Maybe I should try some music, something I could sing along to. Reaching over to where I'd left my phone, I called up my Spotify app and dug out a playlist of oldies I figured I'd know most of the words to. After about six or seven songs, I finally felt my shoulders relax a little. Until Billy Joel's "Honesty" came on. He crooned about how lonely the word was and how hard it was to find truth, and whatever tension I'd managed to soak away seeped right back in. Frustrated, I got out of the tub and turned off the music before the song finished.

After I dried off, I wrapped myself in one of the hotel's comfy robes and slathered on some face and body cream. I headed down the hall to the bedroom, and jumped when I found Weston inside, taking off his shoes.

"Holy shit." My hand covered my heart. "You scared me to death. I didn't hear you come in."

Weston tossed his second shoe aside and stood. He smirked. "That's because you were busy belting out some bad old songs. You're lucky you're gorgeous and smart, because you can't sing for shit."

I cinched my robe closed tighter. "Singing helps me relax."

Weston walked over and placed his hands on my shoulders. "I know something that'll help you relax that doesn't entail neighboring guests thinking we're murdering cats in here."

He was teasing, but I found it hard to force a smile, and he noticed.

Weston slipped two fingers under my chin and tilted it up so our eyes met. "You okay?"

I looked away. "I just have a lot on my mind."

"Yeah, I get it. We're getting down to the wire now. I'll tell you what, I'm going to take a quick shower, and then I'll come back and rub your shoulders with that cream you like so much." He leaned down to look at me.

I wanted to trust him in the worst way, so I searched for any sign of insincerity. But I found nothing.

"Why don't you take off that robe and climb under the covers and get ready for me?" he said. "I'll only be a few minutes."

I forced a smile and nodded.

He gently kissed my lips before disappearing into the bathroom. A few minutes later, I was still standing in the same place when I heard the shower turn on. What was I going to do? He had no idea what was on my mind, so he was likely going to come out of the bathroom, rub my shoulders, and think that was foreplay. There was no way I could let that happen the way I felt. I had to have a conversation with him.

My head spun as I went round and round, weighing my options on how to approach the subject without sounding accusatory. I was so lost in thought that the sound I heard coming from the bathroom didn't register right away. Weston was playing Journey's "Don't Stop Believin'," one of the songs I'd sung along with toward the end of my bath. I patted my robe pocket and realized I must've left my phone next to the tub, and he'd decided to flip on my playlist. A few seconds later, a deep voice joined Steve Perry for the chorus. Weston could not only carry a tune, but his voice was kind of sexy. Even with all the horrible things I was thinking, I had to smile at his sense of humor. He was mimicking me to tease.

God, I *really, really* liked him and wanted everything to be one big misunderstanding on my part. I felt desperate to be put out of the misery of not knowing.

I walked over to what had become my side of the bed. But my eyes caught on something silver toward the foot of it—right next to where Weston had just sat.

My heart started to palpitate.

Weston's phone.

I had another chance.

I could take a quick look, and this could all be over.

I wouldn't even have to bring it up.

Weston would never know I'd doubted him.

In less than thirty seconds, I could be out of my misery and know he'd done nothing wrong.

Or...

Or...

I couldn't bring myself to think about the alternative.

But I had to know for sure.

There was no letting the opportunity pass this time.

My heart raced as I grabbed the cell from the foot of the bed. I'd started to type in Weston's code when the music in the bathroom stopped.

Shit.

He was done in the shower.

It would only take a minute or two to dry off.

I had to hurry.

My hands shook as I typed in the last two digits and the phone unlocked. I opened his email app and scanned through messages. Two pages down, I opened a random email to see what time it had come in and realized it had arrived before the one I was looking for. I must've missed it in my haste. So I scrolled back up and read the first line of every single message, until I'd returned to the one sent before the email in question.

Nothing.

No sign of that email that had come in earlier.

Glancing up at the still-closed bathroom door, I felt like a ticking bomb was about to go off in my chest. Weston would be out any second.

Where the hell was that damn email?

Oh! Shit.

Deleted!

I needed to check his deleted email.

Quickly finding the folder, I tapped to open, and my heart stopped. The message was right at the top. It was the only one he'd taken the time to delete this afternoon.

Glancing at the bathroom door one more time, I took a deep breath and opened the email.

To: Weston.Lockwood@LockwoodHospitality.com

From: Oil44@gmail.com

Did you get the information from the Sterling girl yet?

You need to step up here, Weston. Show me the value you can still bring to this family. We need their bid amount.

The bottom of the email had a signature block:

Oliver I. Lockwood

CEO, Lockwood Hospitality Group

Underneath, was a response:

To: Oil44@gmail.com

From: Weston.Lockwood@LockwoodHospitality.com

I have it. Just waiting until she's done to see if anything changes.

I felt like I might throw up. Though that was not exactly what I did when the bathroom door opened.

CHAPTER 25

Weston

"This robe is damn comfy," I walked out of the bathroom rubbing one of the arms. "No wonder you put it on all the time. I thought you were just being modest. Do you think—"

Whack. Something hit my head. *Hard*.

I reached up and felt wetness, right above my left eyebrow.

Confused, I expected an intruder or something. But instead, what I found when I looked up was one very pissed-off woman.

"What *the fuck*, Sophia? Did you just throw something at me?"

Her face was bright red. "You piece of shit!"

My cell sat a few feet away on the floor. There was a crack down the middle of the screen. "Was that my phone?" I looked at my fingers. The wetness was blood. "I'm freaking bleeding!"

"*Good*!"

"Have you lost your mind? You just cracked my head open with my phone!"

"Apparently, I have—for ever having gotten involved with you in any way. Get out, Weston. Get out *now*!"

"What's going on? What the hell did I do?"

"What did you do? I'll tell you what the hell you did. You were *born*!"

"Soph, I don't know what crawled up your ass. But whatever you think I did, you don't throw a damn phone at my head."

She marched over to the end table and picked up a bedside lamp. "You're right. This will hurt more. Now get out or it'll be the next thing to hit your head."

I held up my hands. "Just tell me what I did—or what the hell you think I did, and I'll go."

She stared at me and spoke through gritted teeth. "*Did you get what we need from the Sterling girl?*"

My face wrinkled up. "What? What are you talking about?"

"Does that not ring a bell? How about *I have it. Just waiting until she's done to see if anything changes.*"

Maybe it was the head injury, but even that took a few seconds to sink in. But when it did, it hit me harder than the phone had. I closed my eyes.

Shit.

Shit.

Shit.

Shit.

She'd read my emails.

I shook my head. "I can explain."

"Get. The. Fuck. Out."

I took a step toward her. "Soph, listen—"

"Don't take another step!" She went quiet for a long moment. I watched as tears filled her eyes, though she did her best to fight them back. Her voice shook when she finally spoke again. "Just leave. I don't want to hear anything you have to say."

When her bottom lip trembled, I felt it in my heart. "I'll go. But we need to talk, Soph. It's not what you think."

A fat tear rolled down her cheek, but she held my gaze steady. "Can you look me in the eyes and tell me that email is about something besides you using me to steal information on our bid?"

I swallowed. "No. But—"

She held up her hands. "Please just go, Weston."

I looked down. "I'll go. But this isn't over. We need to talk when you're calm."

Not wanting to disrespect her anymore than I already had, I walked to the door. Giving her the space she needed was the very least I could do. So I left quietly, without another word.

Out in the hallway, an older woman stepped out of her room a few doors over. Seeing me, she pulled her cardigan closed and turned her head. It wasn't until then that I realized I was still wearing only the hotel bathrobe. I'd also left my room key inside, not to mention my now-broken cell phone. Glancing briefly back at Sophia's suite, I decided knocking was not an option. I'd just have to suck it up and walk down to the lobby like this to get a new room key. And the cell phone...well, that was the least of my worries now. The only thing that mattered was getting Sophia to listen to me.

Though I wasn't sure even that would fix what I'd destroyed.

The next day, I dragged my ass out of bed at seven, though I hadn't slept a wink. I pulled on a pair of pants and shirt, brushed my teeth, and splashed some water on my face. The Band-Aid I'd stuck on my head last night was darkened with dried blood now, so I changed it to a fresh one. That was the extent of the grooming I could muster. *Fuck shaving. Fuck showering.*

I'd spent the last eight or nine hours going over what I was going to say to Sophia. If I told her the truth, she wasn't going to like a lot of it. But lying and keeping things from her was what had gotten me into this mess, and if I was ever going to regain her trust, I had to start coming clean right now. Even if the truth hurt.

Downstairs in the lobby, I bought two large coffees and went directly to Sophia's office. Her door was shut, so I headed to her team's conference room.

I knocked and pulled open the door. "Is Sophia here?"

Charles shook his head. "Rough night?"

"Huh?"

He pointed at the Band-Aid on my forehead.

"Oh," I said. "Something like that. Is she here?"

"Nope. Try her cell. Though she should be boarding right now. So you might not catch her for a few hours."

"Boarding? Where's she going?"

"To West Palm. To see her grandfather."

Fuck.

She'd had a trip planned for later this week, the day before the bids were due, but not today. "Do you know why she went?"

Charles pursed his lips. "I'm assuming to discuss business. And I'm sure I've already given you more information than the Sterlings would want me to. So if you have any other questions, you should direct them to Sophia."

Deflated, I walked to my office. I needed to get in touch with her, though I'd have to get her number from someone since I didn't have it committed to memory, and I still didn't have my cell. Opening my office door, I found a pile of stuff on my desk. At the top of the stack of folded clothes I'd left in her suite last night was my cracked cell phone.

My shoulders slumped. Sophia's message was loud and clear. *She's done with me.*

The rest of the day, I went through the motions. I dealt with the fallout from the flooding in the ballroom construction, reviewed a few last-minute appraisal reports that had come in, met with my legal team, and stopped by the cell phone store to get my screen repaired. Luckily that seemed to be the only damage, which was surprising, considering it had hit my skull hard enough to crack. I'd called Sophia four times, but each time I was sent to voice mail. The things I needed to say to her weren't things that could be said over the phone, much less in messages. So each time I hung up.

By six in the evening, I was starting to go stir crazy, so I decided to take a walk outside. The first bar I passed caught my attention, but I kept going, not slowing down. The second one was on the same block. I hesitated slightly, but nevertheless walked on by. By the third bar in as many blocks, I started to feel the damn things calling my name. So when I slowed to a crawl, I forced myself to call an Uber rather than even attempt to walk the couple of blocks back to The Countess.

Lucky for me, New York was flooded with as many Ubers as it had cabs these days, so my car pulled up within two minutes.

"The Countess hotel?" the driver said, looking in the rearview mirror. He was probably thinking *what a lazy fuck* since it was so close.

"Yeah...actually, no—scratch that. Can you take me to 409 Bowery, instead?"

The guy made a face. "You'll have to do that in the app."

I grumbled and dug into my pocket. Peeling a hundred from my billfold, I tossed it over the front seat. "Just drive. We good?"

The guy scooped up the hundred and stuffed it in his pocket. "You got it."

"Well, well, look what the cat dragged in. It's almost time for *Jeopardy!*. Did you at least bring me scratch-offs if you're going to interrupt my show?"

It was the first time I could remember showing up empty-handed. And it wasn't that I hadn't remembered.

"Sorry," I told him. "I didn't want to stop. The deli I usually go to down the block sells beer."

Mr. Thorne picked up the remote and flicked off the TV. "Take a seat, son."

He said nothing more, instead waiting for me to tell him what was going on. I knew he'd sit patiently until I sorted out my head, so I blew out a deep breath and raked a hand through my hair. "I don't know where to start."

"Then start at the beginning."

I dropped my head into my hands. "I fucked up."

"That's okay. We all make mistakes. Every day is an opportunity for a new chance at sobriety."

I shook my head. "No, it's not that. I didn't drink anything. When I realized I was heading in that direction, I grabbed a ride and came straight here."

"Well, that's good. That's what a sponsor is for. I'm glad you felt like you could come to me. So tell me what's going on, then."

I blew out a jagged breath. "You know the woman I've mentioned a few times—the one you met the other day at The Countess?"

He nodded. "Sure. Sophia. The woman who wants to kick you in the balls half the time and is way too beautiful for your ugly ass?"

I cracked a sad smile. "Yeah. That's her."

"What about her?"

"We're together now. Or, at least we were."

"Okay...what happened to change things?"

"I betrayed her trust."

"You cheated on her?"

"No. Well, not in the way you're thinking anyway."

"Then how?"

"It's a long story."

"I guess you're lucky you have a captive audience. You do know my legs don't work, and I can't get up and leave no matter how boring your sorry-ass tale of woe is, right?"

I sighed. "Yeah."

Even though Mr. Thorne already knew the worst of me, I was embarrassed to admit what I'd done. At least most of the shitty stuff I'd pulled over the years could be blamed on the alcohol.

"Go on," he encouraged. "Trust me, whatever it is, I've done worse, son. I'm not going to think any less of you."

"Okay." I took a deep breath, readying to start at the beginning. "Well, I told you our families don't get along. Our grandfathers fought over a woman named Grace more than fifty years ago. Grace died a few months ago, leaving forty-nine percent of the hotel each to my and Sophia's grandfather's."

Mr. Thorne grumbled. "Only thing my ex ever gave me was divorce papers."

I smiled. "Anyway, my grandfather loathes Sophia's grandfather. And you know what a bad place I've been in with him ever since my last screwup."

He nodded. "I do."

I inhaled deeply. "Well, my grandfather called me right after I'd gotten off the plane Sophia had been on with me. I mentioned who I'd just sat next to, and he laid into me about getting distracted by a skirt." I shook my head. "He told me to turn around and get back on the next return flight, said I wasn't the man for the job because women and booze were my weaknesses. I told him he was wrong, but he said he'd send my father instead. Then he hung up on me. I'd just exited security, so I figured I'd get some fresh air and decide what to do next. Ten minutes later, Grandfather called back and said he'd changed his mind and had a new strategy. Since I was a womanizer, he wanted me to seduce Sophia and get the Sterlings' bid from her."

Mr. Throne's eyes were dark with disappointment. "And you agreed to do that?"

I closed my eyes and hung my head, nodding. "I didn't think beyond getting him to let me stay so I could prove I'm not a total loser. I would've agreed to anything. After I sobered up, I realized I didn't have much left in my life except for my job. I'd lost Caroline, and most of my friends were partyers, and I had to take myself out of that environment." I scoffed. "You're pretty much the only friend I've got."

He shook his head. "Of all the things we've talked about over the years, that last part has to be the saddest. But we'll come back to that. Let's keep our focus on the girl. So you told your grandfather you'd do it, and then what?"

I shrugged. "Then...I fell in love with her."

"So you started things with the intention of seducing this woman, and that changed?"

"That's the thing. Even though I told my grandfather I'd play his game, I never really did. Sophia and I have had this odd love-hate relationship since high school. So when I was giving her a hard time and things got heated, it wasn't part of playing her. It was real. It was always freaking real. Nothing I ever said or did with Sophia had to do with my grandfather." I raked my fingers through my hair, tugging at the strands. "But every time he asks if I'm going to be able to come through with their bid information, I assure him I will."

"But you never intended to get that information out of Sophia?"

I shook my head. "I was planning on making up a number a little under mine and rolling the dice. If my work coming up with the number was right, we'd win the bid anyway, and no one would be the wiser."

"Did you tell Sophia that?"

"She never gave me the chance to."

"And now you think she isn't going to believe the truth when you finally lay it out for her."

"I'm certain she won't. The entire thing sounds like bullshit—even when I just told you the story."

Mr. Thorne nodded. "I hate to say it. But you're right."

"Great." My shoulders slumped. "I came here thinking you'd tell me something different."

"Considering I'm your only friend, I'd say it's my job to tell it like it is. You don't need me blowing smoke up your ass. You need a friend to vent to, to work through your problems with, and help you figure out how to solve them. And most of all, you need someone to remind you that drinking is only going to make shit worse."

I looked up at him. "I know. I guess I just wanted to pretend there's an easy way out of this mess for a little while."

"I know, son. When something good happens, our first instinct is to drink to celebrate. When something bad happens, we're ready to drink to forget. And when nothing happens, we drink to make it happen. That's why we're alcoholics. But we can't drown our problems. Because our sorrows are Olympic swimmers."

I forced a smile. "Thanks."

"Anytime. That's what best friends are for. Just don't expect me to braid your hair. By the way, I've been meaning to mention that you could use a damn haircut."

I wound up staying at Mr. Thorne's for most of the night. We never did come up with an easy way out of the mess I'd gotten myself into. But it wasn't for lack of trying. Unfortunately, there just wasn't an easy way out of this one. I hoped there was a way out at all.

CHAPTER 26

Sophia

Knock. Knock. Knock.

It was almost midnight. Unless housekeeping was knocking on my office door, which I sincerely doubted, there was only one person it could be at this hour.

I kept quiet, hoping he'd think I'd left my light on and go away. The last thing I needed was a showdown with Weston. I felt drained, physically and emotionally exhausted, after spending the last two days with my grandfather and father. Tonight, when I'd snuck back into The Countess, all I'd wanted to do was crawl into bed. But my grandfather had asked me to send him a bunch of information, and since I was on shaky ground after what I'd told him, I wanted to show him I was a hundred-percent committed. So I'd come right up to my office, before even going to my room. I'd been relieved to find Weston's office light off when I'd passed by a few minutes ago.

Knock. Knock. Knock.

I held my breath the second time.

"Soph, I know you're in there. I've been watching the hotel's security cameras on my phone since you left, waiting for you to come back. I saw you walk in a little while ago."

"Just go away, Weston."

Not surprisingly, he didn't listen. Instead, he cracked open my office door. But rather than swing it wide, he stopped with it slightly ajar. "I'm coming in. Please don't throw anything. I just want two minutes."

I grimaced. As much as I hated him at the moment, a tiny part of me felt bad that I'd thrown his cell and injured him. I'd never been violent toward another person.

The door slowly creaked open until Weston was fully visible. The way he looked caused an involuntary ache in my chest. His hair was disheveled, and it looked like he hadn't shaved in a few days. He wore a wrinkly dress shirt, slacks that I was pretty sure he'd slept in, and a large Band-Aid covered his forehead above his left eyebrow.

I sighed. My mood had shifted yesterday from angry to sad. I no longer wanted to throw a cell phone; instead, I'd cried myself to sleep last night. I never even cried when Liam and I split up, and we'd been together for a long time. Though I wasn't about to give Weston the satisfaction of knowing how hurt I was. It was bad enough I'd fallen for his con. My pride couldn't take him also seeing how pathetic and sad it had left me. So I tried my best to channel mean and bitter, though I lacked the energy for it. I just wanted this game over so I could move on.

"What do you want, Weston? I'm exhausted from traveling and need to finish some work before I go to bed."

He stepped inside and quietly clicked the door closed behind him. "I'm so sorry, Soph."

"Okay. Great. Thank you. Are we done now?"

Weston's puppy dog eyes feigned hurt pretty damn well. If I didn't know what a stellar actor he was, I might've believed he was as upset as I was.

"I know it doesn't look good from what you read. But I swear, I never took any information from you, and I was never planning on giving anything to my family. You have to believe me."

"No. I actually don't. What I have to do is learn from the mistakes I've made. And believing anything that came out of your mouth was mistake number one. Trust me, I won't be doing that again."

He took a few steps closer. "My grandfather didn't trust me here when I told him you were running the show for the Sterlings. Based on my track record the last few years, he knew women and alcohol were my downfall. He wanted my father to take over. The only way he'd let me stay was if I agreed to try to get information from you."

"My father told me to do the same thing. I believe his exact words were to use my '*feminine wiles*' to pump information out of you. But you already know that, don't you? And do you know *why* you already know that? Because I told you about it."

Weston closed his eyes. "I know."

I felt the familiar burn in my throat, the precursor to tears. Swallowing hard, I said, "And I was dumb enough to leave you alone in my suite with all my files and my laptop. You must've had a good laugh as you rummaged through my things. I was the easiest mark ever."

"No, it wasn't like that. I never once looked through your stuff. I swear."

My head spun with all the dumb things I'd done around this man. "Jesus. We had sex without a condom. Do I need to get tested for STDs right away? Did you lie about that, too?"

Weston shut his eyes. "No. I'm clean. I would never do that."

God, I really had been an idiot. I'd placed my trust in my *sworn enemy*—trusted him over the judgment of my own family, and in the process jeopardized my career.

"What can I do, Soph?" Weston pleaded. "What can I do to prove to you that I'm telling the truth? We can call my grandfather on speakerphone, and I'll ask him if I ever gave him any information. Anything. Just tell me."

I shook my head. "If you'll do anything for me, then go away, Weston."

Our eyes met, and his were filled with tears. God, I was such an idiot. Even after everything that had happened, I *still* wanted to believe him. I wanted to pretend I'd never seen the email and go back to the way things were. I'd really fallen hard.

Eventually, he nodded. "Okay."

He turned around and opened the door, but I thought of one thing I needed him to do for me. So I called after him.

"Hey, I told my family I'd accidentally left some of my work papers in an area you had access to. I was too embarrassed to tell my father and my grandfather that access was in my bedroom where I'd given you more than just insight into our bid. So if you want to do something for me, at least keep up that charade. The last thing the men in my family need to know is that I let my emotions get in the way of business."

Weston winced. "I get it."

After he walked out, I sat staring at my closed office door. It felt symbolic. The way we'd left things the other night had been so unfinished. We'd obviously needed to have a final conversation. Now that it was over, I should feel some closure. Though, closure meant accepting what had happened and walking away from the closed door. My heart didn't want to walk away. So instead, I'd have to put a double lock on that door to make sure it didn't accidentally creak open again.

CHAPTER 27

Weston

Two days later, I waited impatiently to see if Sophia would show up.

We had a meeting scheduled with Elizabeth Barton, the hotel's attorney, to discuss some last-minute contract-renewal issues. I'd expected to get a call that the meeting was canceled, or at least moved to a conference call instead of being in person. I'd arrived a half hour before our scheduled appointment, just in case Sophia showed. But with every minute that ticked by, I lost a little more hope that she would.

At nine on the nose, a flash of red appeared in the doorway. The entrance to the lobby was a wall of glass, so I watched as Sophia hesitated with her hand on the door. She took a deep breath, raised her chin, and squared her shoulders, and I swear I fucking fell even harder for her.

All along, I'd thought our arguing made her so irresistible to me. Her anger was like my flint, and I was the little boy who liked to play with matches. But in this moment, I realized it wasn't her anger I'd been attracted to at all—it was her strength. When she walked into a room, her beauty was undeniable. When she smiled, it made my knees weak. But when she straightened her spine and her eyes glinted with determination, she wasn't the flint to my spark. She *was* the fire. An undeniably beautiful wildfire.

Gorgeous.

Simply perfect.

My heart pounded in my chest as she walked to the front desk and said something. Though she was only five feet away, and the reception area was otherwise quiet, I couldn't hear a single word. The blood rushing in my ears was way too loud.

Ever since our conversation the other night, I'd been practicing what I would say to her if I got another chance. I'd planned to give her more details—lay all my cards on the table and convince her I'd never planned to betray her. But truly, none of that mattered anymore. Whether I'd planned to go through with stealing information from her or not was almost irrelevant. The fact that I'd agreed to do it and never told her about it was betrayal enough. What I needed to focus on now wasn't what I'd done wrong, but how I felt about her and what I was going to do to make things right.

With a new plan of action, I got up and walked over to the receptionist, where Sophia was still standing.

"Oh, hi," the woman said. "I was just telling Ms. Sterling that Ms. Barton is running a few minutes behind. She had an overseas conference call before your meeting, and it started late."

Sophia stood a little taller, completely ignoring me next to her. "Do you know how long she's going to be?" she asked. "I have another meeting after this."

I would've bet my bank account there was no meeting after this.

"She shouldn't be more than ten or fifteen minutes," the receptionist said. "Can I get you a cup of coffee or tea while you wait?"

Sophia sighed. "No. Thank you."

She looked to me, and I waved my hand. "I'm good."

"Okay. Well, why don't you both have a seat, and I'll let you know as soon as she's off her call."

"Actually." I took one step closer. "Would you happen to have an empty conference room?"

"Umm...sure. The one you'll be meeting in is available. Did you need to make a call or something?"

I shook my head. "No. Ms. Sterling and I have some business to discuss. Do you think we could make use of that room before Ms. Barton is available?"

The receptionist smiled. "Sure. No problem." She stood. "Why don't you follow me, and I'll let Elizabeth know where you'll be when she's done."

Sophia seemed momentarily confused, so I took advantage, knowing once she regained her footing she wouldn't voluntarily walk into a room with me. I put my hand low on her back and held out my other for her to walk first.

"After you..."

Her jaw clenched, but she wasn't about to make a scene. That wasn't Sophia's style, at least not in the lobby in front of the receptionist. Though I had no doubt she'd ream me a new asshole once the conference room door clicked shut. So I'd have to keep her off her game, by jumping in before she had a chance.

We followed the receptionist into a long conference room. I was glad it wasn't one of those fishbowl rooms that corporate America loved these days, where everything that went on inside was visible to anyone passing by.

"Are you sure I can't get you coffees?" the receptionist asked from the door after we were both inside.

"No, thank you," Sophia said.

"I'm good." I smiled and motioned to the door. "If you don't mind, I'm going to shut this."

"Oh. Sure. Yeah. I'll do that for you." She grabbed the door handle and gently closed it behind her.

"Weston—" Sophia jumped right in.

But I cut her off. "I need thirty seconds. If you want, I'll go wait in the lobby after that." I had no idea how much time we had, or if we'd get a chance to talk again before we wrapped things up at The Countess, so I needed to say what I needed to say—and fast.

Sophia's lips flattened to a grim line. She didn't acknowledge granting me the thirty seconds, but I figured her not talking might be as good as I was going to get. So I paced back and forth, looking down at the floor, trying to choose the right words.

My ribs felt like a weight was sitting on them, squeezing the air from my lungs. And I knew exactly what that weight was. I had this moment to get everything off my chest.

Now or never.

Don't be a chickenshit all your life.

So I took a deep breath and looked across the table, waiting for Sophia to look up. Eventually, the awkward silence tricked her into meeting my gaze, and I went for it.

Fuck it.

Go big or go home.

"I love you, Sophia. I don't know when it started or if it even matters anymore. But I need you to know it."

At first, I saw hope bloom in her eyes. They widened with surprise, and the slightest hint of a smile formed at the corners of her mouth. But just as quickly as that hope had blossomed, it wilted.

And I watched as she remembered.

Remembered how I'd fucked her over.

Remembered how she's supposed to hate me.

Remembered how nothing I say should be trusted.

In the span of less than ten seconds, that slightest upturn at the corners of her mouth melted into a giant downturn, and her wide eyes narrowed with suspicion.

"You have no idea what love is."

I shook my head. "You're wrong. I might not know a lot of things—like how to have some balls when dealing with my family, or how to tell my grandfather *no* when he tells me to do something morally reprehensible, or even how to be in a relationship, because fuck knows I've never had a real-life role model of what a normal one is supposed to look like. But I absolutely, positively know that I'm in love with you. You know how?"

She didn't answer. But she also didn't tell me to stop.

So I kept going.

"I know I love you because for the five years since Caroline died, I have *never* wanted to be a better man. I've never once looked in the mirror and given a shit whether I liked what I saw. But every morning since you got on that plane and made me move out of that window seat, I've stared at myself, wondering what I could do today to be a better person—a better man who deserves a woman like you.

"I know I love you because my family would disown me for falling in love with you. And that doesn't scare me half as much as you leaving this room without believing that my heart belongs to you more than it's ever belonged to anyone.

"I know I love you because for my entire life I felt like I had no purpose except to be spare parts for my sister...until you.

"I know I love you because..." I shook my head and dragged a hand through my hair. "Because *you are the finest, loveliest, tenderest, and most beautiful person I have ever known—and even that is an understatement.*"

Sophia's lips parted, and tears welled in her eyes. I didn't have to tell her I'd borrowed that one from F. Scott Fitzgerald instead of Shakespeare. A month ago, I'd searched for quotes to taunt her about her ex, but lately I'd started to enjoy reading them. So many reminded me of her, like that one.

I cleared my throat. "Soph, I fucked up. It's not the way you think, but I realize it doesn't matter if I intended to give my grandfather any information. I should have told you about it or not led him to believe I was playing his game. I didn't have to violate your trust to lose it. Even the smallest lie can create the biggest damage."

She sniffled. "I feel like an idiot for wanting to believe you." She shook her head and looked down. "I just can't, Weston. I can't."

"Soph, no. Don't say that. Look at me."

She kept shaking her head. When a tear leaked from her eye, she looked up at me and whispered, "Countess."

My forehead wrinkled. Then I remembered I'd made her pick a safe word in case things got to be too much. She'd never said it until now. It felt like my heart was breaking in two.

Sophia walked to the conference room door. I went to reach for her, but she put her hand up, stopping me.

"Please don't. I need to use the restroom." Her voice was so soft and filled with emotion that it sliced through me. "Don't follow me. Please let me be. You said what you wanted to say. I listened. I really did. And I want to be left alone now."

I dropped my head and nodded. "Go. I don't want to make you feel worse."

Sophia didn't come back for ten long minutes. When she did, I could tell she'd been crying. I felt like an idiot for making her upset right before a business meting. We were both quiet as we waited at the conference table. I stole glances at her while she avoided eye contact. When Elizabeth Barton eventually walked in, Sophia finally met my eyes.

I knew it was causing her pain to sit across the table from me, so I stood as Elizabeth took her seat. I'd gotten what I came for, and the rest of it didn't matter. None of it mattered. The very least I could do was make Sophia feel a little lighter by not having to look at me.

I buttoned my jacket and cleared my throat. "Sorry, Elizabeth, but something's come up, and I need to run."

The attorney looked surprised. "I'm sorry. Should we reschedule?"

I looked over at Sophia. "No. You two go ahead. I'll catch up with you at some point, if you have time."

Elizabeth rightly looked confused. "Oh...okay. Well, why don't you book a time on your way out with the receptionist and we'll talk later."

I gave a noncommittal nod. "Sure."

Over the next forty-eight hours, I visited Mr. Thorne four times. It was either that or drink a bottle of vodka. I ignored phone calls from my grandfather and never did catch up with Elizabeth Barton to get the information I needed from her. Just about the only responsibility I didn't blow off was dealing with the Boltons. The estimates and revised construction plans had come in, and I worked with Travis on cutting some things that would mean we'd still have a shot of finishing everything on time for the first event planned next month. It wasn't that I gave a shit about the construction anymore than anything else, but Sophia was vulnerable, and I didn't want her to spend any time with a man who had an interest in her. I might've fallen in love, but I was still a selfish prick.

Sophia and I passed each other in the halls. She did her best to avoid eye contact, while I did my best not to fall to my knees and beg for her forgiveness. The hours ticked by as the deadline to turn in our bids neared. In less than twenty-four hours, everything would be over. One of us would bring our family victory, while the other would never live down the loss. But most importantly, Sophia and I would no longer have any reason for contact. One of us would most certainly be asked to vacate the premises as a guest, and we'd go back to what we'd been for the last twelve years—people who saw each other occasionally at an event and stayed on the other side of the room.

The night before the day the bids were due, I couldn't sleep. I'd emailed my final valuation for the hotel to my grandfather, along with my recommendation for the bid. He'd emailed back asking if I was certain the bid was higher than the Sterlings'. I'd told him it was, though I had no fucking clue.

At four thirty in the morning, I couldn't lie in bed anymore, so I decided to go for a run. I usually ran three miles, but today I ran until my legs burned, and then I ran all the way back, relishing the agony each pounding step caused in my body.

The lobby coffee shop had already opened, so I grabbed a bottle of water and went and sat in a quiet corner where Sophia and I had sat before. A big painting of Grace Copeland hung nearby, and for the first time I took a good look at it.

"That was done from a snapshot taken on her fiftieth birthday," a familiar voice said.

I looked over to find Louis, the hotel manager, admiring the painting with me. He pointed to the chair next to me. "Mind if I take a seat?"

"Not at all. Help yourself."

We continued to look at the painting in silence, until eventually I asked, "You were with her from the very beginning, right?"

Louis nodded. "Almost. I worked the front desk when this place was a rundown jalopy. The years after she bought out Mr. Sterling and your grandfather were touch-and-go. There were weeks she couldn't make payroll, but we were all so dedicated to Grace that we figured out how to survive."

I looked back at the painting again. Grace Copeland had been a beautiful woman. "How come she never married after the broken engagement with old man Sterling? It couldn't have been for a lack of opportunity."

Louis shook his head. "There were definitely plenty of suitors interested in Grace. And she dated a bit. But I think her broken heart never really mended. She learned to live with it in pieces, and occasionally she gave out a sliver or two, but she felt strongly that you only committed to a person when they had your full heart."

I looked back at Louis. "You're married, right?"

He smiled. "Forty-three years. Some mornings I can't wait to get out of the house to get a little break from my Agnes. She tends to talk a lot, and mostly about other people's business. But every night, I can't wait to get home to her."

"So do you think it's true?"

His brows furrowed. "What's that?"

"Do you believe if someone takes your heart, you won't be able to love the same way after that?"

Louis thought for a moment. "I think some people get inside our hearts and stay, even long after they physically leave."

My phone rang at ten after nine. The number wasn't familiar, but I had a feeling I knew who it was.

"Hello?"

"Mr. Lockwood?"

"Yes."

"This is Otto Potter."

I leaned back into my chair. "I figured I might be hearing from you."

"Well, I just wanted to make sure that what I received on your bid form was correct."

I took a deep breath and blew it out. "It is. What's written there is my bid on behalf of the Lockwood family."

"And you're aware that this isn't a round-robin-type bidding process. It's a one shot, best bid offer."

I swallowed. "I am."

"Alright, then. We'll be back in touch soon."

After I hung up, I closed my eyes, expecting panic to set in. Surprisingly, it didn't. Instead, I felt eerily calm. Maybe for the first time in a long time—or maybe for the first time ever.

CHAPTER 28

Sophia

"Well, congratulations again, Sophia." Elizabeth Barton extended her hand as we stood from the conference room table.

"Thank you." I managed to force out an acceptable smile.

Seven days had passed since I'd received the call that I'd won the bid for my family, yet it still felt like I'd lost the war. My father had flown in to take me out to dinner to celebrate *without Spencer*, and my grandfather had offered me a position overseeing our family's entire west coast hotel operation, the largest region we had. Everything was falling into place, yet I'd never felt so empty inside. The reason for that was obvious.

"Will you be staying on to manage The Countess?" Elizabeth asked.

"I'm not sure yet. There's a position open on the west coast, but I haven't made up my mind where I'll land."

She nodded. "Well, I'll keep in touch until you tell me otherwise."

"Thank you."

Elizabeth extended a hand to Otto Potter. "It was nice meeting you, Otto. I wish you the best of luck with Easy Feet."

"Considering the check you just handed me, I think Easy Feet will be walking on Easy Street for a while."

She smiled. "Are you heading back uptown? Want to share a cab?"

Otto shook his head. "Actually, I'm going to hang around here for a bit."

The two shook, and then it was just Otto and me left. He smiled warmly. "I was hoping I could talk to you for a moment, if you have time."

I extended a hand back to our seats. "Sure. I have plenty of time."

After we settled in, Otto took a piece of paper from his pocket and unfolded it. He slid it across the table to my side. "The terms of the bidding were confidential. But I figured now that the papers are all signed, and you're the majority shareholder of The Countess, there's no harm in sharing the bid I received from the Lockwoods."

I picked up the paper and skimmed it. It was the same offer form I'd signed to submit my family's bid, only this one had $1.00 filled in the spot where the bid amount was to go. My eyes scanned down to the bottom to check the signature. Sure enough, none other than Weston Lockwood had signed it.

I shook my head and looked up at Otto. "I don't understand."

He shrugged. "Neither did I. So I called Weston to make sure there wasn't a mistake. He confirmed that this was indeed his family's bid."

"But...that means he wanted to lose?"

Otto took the paper back and folded it up. Sticking it in his pocket, he said, "I think it's more like he wanted to make sure someone else won."

My heart raced as I stood in front of the door. The last few weeks had been hell. Every step I'd taken had felt like walking over a long bridge. Today was supposed to be the day I finally crossed to the other side. But instead, I stood right back at the place I'd started.

This morning, my plan had been to sign the legal paperwork for The Countess to make things official and then try to relax and figure out what was next for me. I'd told my grandfather I'd get back to him about the west coast job by tomorrow, so I had some big decisions to make. I'd assumed I'd be in a better mental place after today's formalities. But I was more confused than ever now, and I needed to hear things straight from the horse's mouth.

So I raised my hand and took a deep breath as I knocked on Weston's hotel room door. It had been eight days since I saw him in that conference room. His office had been dark and shut, and he was nowhere to be found in the hotel. If I didn't know better, I'd have thought he left. But I did know better, because I'd monitored the hotel's reservation system to see if he'd checked out. As of last night, he hadn't.

On a jagged exhale, I forced my knuckles to connect with his door. My heart pounded as I waited for it to open, and my head felt almost as if I had a cold—full of foggy thoughts I couldn't clear. I had so many questions. After a minute or two and no response, I knocked again, this time louder. While I waited, the elevator down the hall dinged, and the doors slid open. A bellman pushed a full luggage cart out and walked in my direction. He tipped his hat.

"Afternoon, Ms. Sterling."

"Call me, Sophia, please."

"Alright." He slid a key into a room two doors down and proceeded to take the bags inside. When he was done, he pointed at the door I stood in front of.

"Are you looking for Mr. Lockwood?"

"I am. Yes."

He shook his head. "I think he might've checked out a little while ago. Saw him with his luggage at the front desk when I came in, about nine o'clock."

It felt like my heart stopped. "Oh. Okay."

Since there was no point in standing here, I debated going downstairs to the front desk and confirming what the bellman had said. But I wasn't sure I could hold back the tears once I did. So instead, I walked to the elevator and hit the button for my own floor. At least it was afternoon, so technically I wouldn't be drinking in the morning.

It took all of my effort to put one foot in front of the other and exit the car, but when I did, my sluggish steps faltered.

I blinked a few times. "Weston?"

He sat leaning against the wall next to my hotel room door with his eyes cast down, his luggage parked next to him. Seeing me, he stood.

My heart sped up. "What—what are you doing?"

Weston looked even more awful than the last time I'd seen him. Dark circles framed his glassy red eyes, and his naturally tanned skin had turned sallow. He'd grown what was almost a full beard, but it wasn't groomed and neat. It just looked like he hadn't bothered to shave. Even so, he was still stunningly handsome.

"Could we talk?"

I'd just gone looking for him, yet my self-protective mechanism had me hesitating.

He noticed and frowned. "Please..."

"Sure." I nodded. The camera in the corner of the hallway caught my eye. "Let's go inside."

As I opened the door, my nerves grew frazzled. I needed a drink in the worst way, and that made me think of something. I turned back and looked into Weston's bloodshot eyes.

"Have you been...drinking?"

He shook his head. "No. Just not sleeping well."

Nodding, I set my laptop and purse on the coffee table and took a seat on one end of the couch, adjacent to the chair, where I assumed Weston would sit. But he didn't take the hint. Instead, he sat down on the couch right next to me.

After a minute, he reached out and took my hand. "I miss you." His voice broke. "I've missed you so fucking much."

I tasted the familiar salt in my throat, but there were no more tears left.

Before I could figure out how to respond, he continued. "I'm so sorry I hurt you. I'm so sorry I made you doubt what you mean to me."

I shook my head and stared down at our hands. "I'm afraid, Weston. I'm afraid to believe you."

"I know. But please give me a second chance to show you I can be the man you deserve. I fucked up. It won't happen again. I promise you, Soph."

I stayed quiet for a long time, sorting through the mess of tangled feelings and doubts. When I was finally able to focus a bit, I looked up at him.

"Why did you bid one dollar?"

I could tell he hadn't expected me to know what he'd done.

"My family didn't deserve to take care of this hotel—not with what my grandfather did to yours all those years ago, and not with what he thought I should be doing to you. Things needed to be made right, once and for all."

"That's very noble of you. But what if your grandfather finds out what you did?"

Weston looked into my eyes. "He already knows. I flew to see him the day after I turned in our bid and they informed you that you'd won. I told him in person."

My eyes widened. "How did that go?"

The corner of Weston's lip twitched. "Not too well."

"Did he fire you?"

He shook his head. "He didn't have to. I'd already quit."

"God, Weston. Why would you do that? To prove your loyalty to me?"

"It was more than that. I needed to do it for myself, Soph. It's been a long time coming. This was just the last straw. I realized my family had a lot to do with my struggle with alcoholism. I drank because I didn't like myself. And that started with how they made me feel. I spent most of my life trying to prove to my parents and grandfather that I'm more than just spare parts. I finally realized the only person I need to prove that to is myself."

I didn't know what to say. "It sounds like you've done a lot of soul searching over the last week."

"I have."

"What will you do now? I mean, now that you're not employed by the Lockwoods anymore?"

He shrugged and gave a faint smirk. "I'm not sure. Got any positions open over at Sterling Hospitality?"

I looked him in the eyes. He'd hurt me badly, that was for sure. But it hurt way more being apart from him. Would I get burned if I gave him a second chance? Quite possibly. Nothing in life was certain. Well, except for the fact that I'd be miserable if I didn't take the risk and give things another chance with this man. Weston had jumped off a cliff. Maybe if I did, too, together we could learn to fly.

"Actually..." I took a deep breath and stood at the imaginary edge. "There is a position at this hotel I think you'd be perfect for."

Weston lifted a brow. "Oh yeah? What's that?"

"Well, it's a position underneath me."

His eyes flickered with hope. "Underneath you? I could deal with that."

"And it has long hours."

His lip curled at one corner, just the slightest bit. "That's not a problem. I have plenty of stamina."

I raised a finger and tapped it to my bottom lip, as if contemplating. "Actually, I'm not sure you're right for the position. There are a few other candidates I need to consider first. Can I get back to you?"

"A few other candidates...for underneath you?"

I lost the battle to contain my smirk. "That's right."

The spark in Weston's eyes lit to a fire. Taking me completely by surprise, he leaned forward, pressed his shoulder into my chest, and lifted me up off the couch fireman style. In one stealth move I was in the air, flipped to my back, and suddenly landed on the couch with a thud.

Weston followed, hovering over me. "I think you're right," he said. "A position under you might not be the right spot for me. You got anything available on top? I like control too much and think I'd be a much better fit in that department."

I laughed. "Nope. Sorry. All filled up."

Weston growled. "I'll fill you up."

God, I missed him. I cupped his cheek. "You do seem like you'd do a good job. Let me give it some thought. Maybe I can figure out the right place for you after all."

"I know the right place, sweetheart." He brushed a lock of hair from my face. "Inside of you. That's where I belong. How do I apply for *that* job?"

I smiled. "I'm pretty sure you already have that job, Mr. Lockwood. You've been inside of me for a long time. I was just too afraid to admit it."

Weston looked deep into my eyes. "Yeah?"

I nodded. "Yeah."

"I love you, Soph. I'll never let you down again."

I smiled. "I love you too, you pain in my ass."

Weston brushed his lips with mine.

My heart felt full, yet there was still something I needed to know. "What would your real bid have been?"

"For The Countess?"

I nodded.

"I valued the hotel at just under a hundred million. So my bid would have been two million for the minority share. Why?"

I grinned. "My bid was two point one. I would've won anyway."

Weston chuckled. "Is that important to you?"

"Hell, yeah. I would've beaten you fair and square. Now I can lord it over you, rather than have you think you *let me* win."

He smiled. "You're going to lord it over me?"

"Just every chance I get."

"You know, I'm in grovel mode now. Eventually it'll irritate me if you rub that in my face. I don't like to lose. But it's fine. There's no one in this world I'd rather fight with or make up with. I see a lot of fighting and fucking in our future."

I rolled my eyes. "How romantic."

"That's me. Mr. Romantic. You're one lucky girl."

EPILOGUE

Weston - 18 months later

"Come in!"

My office door opened, and a face I hadn't expected to see smiled at me.

Louis Canter glanced around the room. "Well, look at you roughing it."

My office furniture consisted of a folding table, metal chair, and three milk crates I'd used as makeshift file cabinets. A lone light bulb hung overhead from a long, orange extension cord. Making my office presentable wasn't high on my to-do list.

I got up and walked around my desk to greet him. Clasping hands, I teased, "What, are you slumming today? You know the only view of the park we get at this hotel is the one across the street where crack deals go down."

He chuckled. "The construction in the lobby looks good. It reminds me a lot of the early days when I started at The Countess."

"Somehow I don't think Grace had to pay off bums to stop urinating in the entrance way."

"Maybe not. But the energy feels the same. There's a buzz when you walk in that front door—contractors trying to finish up the last of things, new employees running around to get everything in tip-top shape for when the first guests arrive. It feels like something special is about to happen."

I smiled. I'd thought it was just me who felt it. Six weeks after the Sterling family had taken over at The Countess, I'd been on my way to visit Mr. Thorne when I noticed a *For Sale* sign in the window of a boarded-up hotel. The real estate agent happened to be inside, so I stopped in. While she talked on her cell phone, I looked around. The place had been a disaster of cobwebs and neglect. But the sign over what had once been the lobby's reception desk caught my eye. *Hotel Caroline.* At that moment, I knew my life was about to change.

The building had been shuttered for five years. Later I'd come to find out the hotel had closed one week to the day after my sister passed away. I'd never been much of a believer in fate, but I liked to think my sister was looking down on me that day, giving me a sign that it was time to get my shit together and grow some balls. This wasn't the best neighborhood right now, but it was up and coming—what I could afford—and I had faith in the area. More importantly, I had faith in myself. Finally.

One month after walking into Hotel Caroline, a day that happened to be my thirtieth birthday, I handed a check for almost five-million dollars over in exchange for the deed to a hot mess of a hotel. It was the first time I'd touched a dime of the trust fund my grandfather had created as my compensation for being a body of spare parts for my sister.

As a courtesy, that afternoon I'd called my grandfather and father to tell them I'd gone out on my own. Neither had really gotten over what I'd pulled with The Countess. But letting them know felt like the right thing to do.

Neither wished me luck. They also didn't try to tell me I'd made a mistake. Honestly, they didn't give two shits. Not to mention, neither remembered it was my birthday. *Good riddance. Don't let the door hit you on the ass on the way out.*

Later that night, I went to see Sophia and celebrated being free exactly the way I'd wanted to—a good fight with my girl. She'd been a little upset that I hadn't mentioned *any* of my plans to her until after it was too late. I'd bought a rundown hotel and basically excommunicated myself from my family without saying a word.

To this day, I'm not sure exactly why I did that. Maybe I was afraid she would try to talk me out of it, or maybe it was just something I needed to do on my own. Either way, she wasn't happy about being kept in the dark. Though she'd forgiven me by the time I gave her three orgasms and untied her.

"So what brings you down here, Louis?" I asked. "Everything still set for tonight at The Countess?"

"Everything is perfect. The maintenance crew started putting things together the minute Sophia left for the airport yesterday. It'll be all set up by the time you arrive tonight."

"Great. Thank you."

Louis had a small, brown paper bag in his hand. He extended it to me. "Thought you might like this. I found it in one of the boxes we pulled from storage."

My brows drew together. "What is it?"

"A Christmas gift I gave Grace in 1961. I'd forgotten all about it. But take a look. I thought it might be pretty damn fitting for the occasion tonight."

Inside the paper bag, a glass ornament was wrapped in old newspapers. At first, I didn't get the significance, but when I turned it around and saw what was painted on the other side, I looked up. "Holy shit."

Louis smiled. "Life's a giant circle, isn't it? Sometimes we think we've reached the end and closed the loop, only to realize we've arrived back at the beginning again. Good luck tonight, son."

Sophia

I watched from the airport escalator with a smile as Weston scanned the crowd, looking for me. Even if he hadn't been the tallest person in most rooms, he'd stick out above the rest. There was something so magnetic about him. Sure, he was tall, dark, and handsome—that went without saying. But that wasn't what set him apart. It was the way he carried himself—feet planted wide, chin held high, a glimmer of mischief in his eyes that matched the cocky grin that always seemed to threaten at the corners of his lips. He stood in baggage claim, holding a bunch of flowers, and I was certain the hearts of a few women in the vicinity were going pitter-patter at the scene.

Halfway down, he spotted me, and his ever-threatening grin burst into a full smile. We'd been together more than a year and a half now, and it was almost a year since we'd taken the leap and moved in together, yet his sexy smile could still melt my panties. He strode through the arrival area toward the escalator, his eyes never leaving mine.

"What are you doing here?" I asked, smiling as I stepped off.

Weston took my suitcase, snaked his arm around my waist, and pulled me to him. "I was anxious to see you."

He kissed me as if I'd been gone a month, though I'd just left to visit my grandfather yesterday morning. "Well, this was a nice surprise. Thank you for picking me up."

Outside the airport, I yanked my coat closed. "I'm definitely not in Florida anymore."

"Yeah. Supposed to get snow tomorrow."

"Oooooh. I'd love that. I hope it sticks around for Christmas so we can have a white one."

"Sweetheart, if it snows tomorrow and it's still around in two weeks, it's gonna be a dirty, gray Christmas."

I pouted. "Don't ruin my dream just because you're Scrooge."

"I'm not Scrooge."

"Oh good. So then can we finally decorate the apartment this weekend?"

"Yeah, sure."

I knew the holidays were a tough time of the year for Weston, because decorating reminded him of Caroline. But I wanted to do more than we'd done last year, which was not much.

On the drive into the City, I filled Weston in on my trip. He gave me an update on Hotel Caroline, which was set to open just after the new year. Since he seemed to be in a good mood, I thought I'd broach another conversation I wanted to have.

"So...my grandmother is going to be eighty next month. My grandfather is throwing her a surprise party down in Florida."

Weston glanced at me. "Oh yeah? That's nice."

"I thought maybe we could go down for the party."

"*We*?"

"Yes, we."

"You want me to come to a party filled with Sterlings."

I nodded. "I do."

"What do you think your grandfather would have to say about that?"

"I mentioned it to him. He's...coming around." That was true. Well, sort of. At least this time he hadn't said *over my dead body* when I'd mentioned him getting to know the man I lived with. I took that as progress.

Weston tapped his fingers on the steering wheel. "I'll go if you want me to."

My eyes widened. "*You will*?"

"It's important to you, right?"

"Yeah. I know my grandfather would love you if he would just get to know you."

Weston shook his head. "Why don't we shoot for tolerating my presence, so you're not disappointed, babe."

I smiled. "Okay."

After we got through the tunnel, Weston turned right instead of left. "Aren't we going home?"

"I need to stop at The Countess."

"What for?"

"Uhh... I had a package shipped there by accident. I ordered from your Prime account, and the last address you shipped to was there, and I didn't notice."

I yawned. "I'm tired. Is it important? I can just bring it home tomorrow after work."

"Yeah. It's important."

"What is it?"

He was quiet for a minute. "None of your business. That's what it is."

I grinned. "It's my Christmas present, isn't it?"

We pulled up down the block from The Countess, and Weston parallel parked. He unbuckled and started to get out.

"I'll just wait here," I said.

"No."

"What do you mean no? Why can't I wait here?"

Weston raked a hand through his hair. "Because the package is in your office, and I don't have the key."

I reached for my purse, which I'd set on the floor. "Oh. I'll give you my keys."

Weston huffed. "Just come with me."

"But I'm tired."

"It won't take more than a minute."

I huffed. "Fine. But sometimes you're annoying. You know that?"

He grumbled something as he exited the car, yet jogged around to open my door. When he took my hand to help me out, I noticed his palm was sweaty.

"I didn't think your car had a heated steering wheel."

"It doesn't."

"So why are your hands so sweaty?"

Weston made a face and tugged me to start walking. At the entrance to The Countess, he waved off the doorman and swung the door open for me. His mood had shifted from happy to grumpy really fast.

Inside, I walked four or five steps and then stopped. I blinked a few times, confused. "What...what is this?"

"What does it look like?"

"It looks like the biggest Christmas tree I've ever seen."

Weston guided me closer. We stood a few feet in front of an enormous balsam fir, and I looked up. It towered over me, positioned between the two curved staircases that led to the second floor. It almost met the ceiling on the second story. It had to be thirty-feet high and made the entire lobby smell like Christmas.

"Do you like it?" he asked.

I shook my head. "I love it. It's huge!"

Weston winked and leaned in to me. "I've heard that before."

I laughed. "Seriously, I can't believe you did this."

Len from maintenance walked over. He had an extension cord in one hand and a plug to something in the other. He looked to Weston. "You ready?"

Weston nodded. "As I'll ever be."

Len connected the cords, and the entire tree lit up in white lights. I couldn't even take a guess how many thousands had to be strung on it. A few seconds later, the tree started to twinkle. It looked absolutely magical. And I'd been so mesmerized by it all that I hadn't noticed Weston moved. But when I did, the world seemed to stop.

Everything except the man down on one knee seemed to fade away.

I covered my mouth with my hands, and my eyes immediately began to water. "Oh my God, Weston! And I didn't want to get out of the car!"

He chuckled. "That was obviously unplanned, but pretty damn fitting, don't you think? We had to argue right before I came in to do this. We wouldn't be us if everything was smiles and roses."

I shook my head. "You're right. We wouldn't."

Weston took a deep breath, and I watched as his chest rose and fell. He took my hand, and I finally understood why his palms were sweaty. They still were. My cocky man was *nervous*. I lifted my other hand to my chest and covered my racing heart. *He's not the only one.*

Weston cleared his throat. "Sophia Rose Sterling, before I met you, I had no purpose. It didn't take long after you stormed into my life to realize the reason I'd been lost was because you hadn't found me yet. My purpose in life is to love you. Deep down, I knew that from the first day we stepped foot into this place. But it didn't make sense. It took me a while to figure out that love doesn't have to make sense; it only has to make us happy. And you do—you make me happier than I've ever been, Soph. I want to spend the rest of my life fighting with you just so we can make up. And I want the rest of my life to start today. So, will you please do me the honor of marrying me, because *'I would not wish any companion in the world but you'?"*

Tears streamed down my cheeks. I don't know why, but I got down on my knees and pressed my forehead to his. "How can I say no, when you finally quoted Shakespeare right? Yes! Yes! I'll marry you."

Weston slipped the most gorgeous, cushion-cut diamond onto my finger. The thousands of lights illuminating the tree above us dimmed in comparison to its sparkle.

In true Weston style, he reached around my neck and squeezed hard, bringing my lips to crash against his. "Good. Now shut up and give me that mouth."

He kissed me in the middle of the lobby, in front of the big Christmas tree, long and hard. When we finally came up for air, I heard people clapping. It took a few seconds for it to register that they were applauding for us. People had been watching the proposal. My eyes came into focus as I looked around.

Oh my God! Mr. Thorne is here.

And...is that... I blinked a few times. "Is that...?"

Weston smiled. "Scarlett. It is. I flew her in last night to ask her permission to propose. I figured I wouldn't have much luck with your father, and you value her opinion more anyway."

We were still both kneeling on the floor, so Weston helped me up. Scarlett and Mr. Thorne congratulated us, as well as a ton of the staff.

I looked up at Weston, still in disbelief. "I can't believe you did all this. Do you remember the story I told you about the last time a tree was in this lobby?"

"I do," he said. "The three of them used to decorate a big tree together, right here in this very spot. Grace always hoped our grandfathers would come around some day, and they could all be friends and do it again. That never happened, so she never put another tree in here. That's why I did this. Our grandfathers are too stubborn to come around, but I think Grace Copeland would be happy that the Sterlings and the Lockwoods have finally made friends again."

I smiled. "She would be. I'm sure of it."

Weston reached into his coat pocket. "Oh, I almost forgot. I had the lights hung so it would look nice for you, but we're going to decorate it together. Just like they used to. There're a couple of dozen crates of ornaments stashed behind the tree. But I have the first one for you to hang."

"You do?"

He unwrapped a glass ball from a wad of newspaper and handed it to me.

"Louis gave Grace this as a gift one year. He found it in storage yesterday. If I'd had any doubt that proposing to you in front of this tree was the right decision, this ornament solidified that it was meant to be."

I looked down at the Christmas ball, which was personalized like many ornaments still are today. Painted in silver were three stick figures holding hands, the two on the ends a bit bigger than the middle one, and below that, names were painted.

Sterling–Copeland–Lockwood
Forever

"That's us, with Grace Copeland bringing us together, Soph."

"Oh my God! You're right!"

Weston leaned down and brushed his lips with mine. "Of course I am. I'm always right."

I hung the ornament on the tree and wrapped my arms around his neck. "You know. I don't like the ring you picked out, and I think you could have used a bit more creativity in your proposal. Oh, and the tree...it's pretty lame."

Weston's eyes widened. "I hope you're joking."

"I'm not." I tried to hide my smirk, but failed. "Perhaps we should fight about it later when we get home."

My fiancé's eyes darkened. "Why wait that long? Meet me in the laundry room in five minutes..."

ACKNOWLEDGEMENTS

To you—the *readers*. Thank you for allowing me to be part of your reading escape. Life seems to be turned upside down lately, and I'm so grateful to let you escape for a short while. I hope you've enjoyed Weston and Sophia's enemies to lovers story, and you'll come back again to see who you might meet next!

To Penelope – The last few years have been one big, crazy adventure, and there is no one I'd rather take the ride with.

To Cheri – Thank you for always being there for me, and always keeping the secret of my age. ;) Books brought us together, but friendship made us forever.

To Julie – Thank you for your friendship and wisdom.

To Luna – So much change in a year, and I've enjoyed watching every bit of it. Thank you for your friendship.

To my amazing Facebook reader group, Vi's Violets – 17,000 smart women who love to talk books? There is no greater gift. Thank you for being part of this crazy journey.

To Sommer – This one is my favorite. I know I've said that before. But this time it really is...until you top yourself next time! Thank you for yet another amazing cover.

To my agent and friend, Kimberly Brower – Thank you for being there always. Every year brings a unique opportunity from you. I can't wait to see what you dream up next!

To Jessica, Elaine and Julie – Thank you for smoothing out all the rough edges and making me shine!

To Eda – Thank you for all of your help and feedback!

To all of the bloggers – Thank you for inspiring others to take a chance on me. Without you, there would be no them.

Much love

Vi

OTHER BOOKS BY VI KEELAND

Inappropriate
All Grown Up
We Shouldn't
The Naked Truth
Sex, Not Love
Beautiful Mistake
Egomaniac
Bossman
The Baller
Left Behind (A Young Adult Novel)
Beat
Throb
Worth the Fight
Worth the Chance
Worth Forgiving
Belong to You
Made for You
First Thing I See
Cocky Bastard (Co-written with Penelope Ward)
Playboy Pilot (Co-written with Penelope Ward)
Mister Moneybags (Co-written with Penelope Ward)
British Bedmate (Co-written with Penelope Ward) Park
Avenue Player (Co-written with Penelope Ward)
Stuck-Up Suit (Co-written with Penelope Ward)
Rebel Heir (Co-written with Penelope Ward)
Rebel Heart (Co-written with Penelope Ward)
Hate Notes (Co-written with Penelope Ward) Dirty
Letters (Co-written with Penelope Ward)
My Favorite Souvenir (Co-written with Penelope Ward)

ABOUT VI KEELAND

Vi Keeland is a #1 *New York Times*, #1 *Wall Street Journal*, and *USA Today* Bestselling author. With millions of books sold, her titles have appeared in over a hundred Bestseller lists and are currently translated in twenty-five languages. She resides in New York with her husband and their three children where she is living out her own happily ever after with the boy she met at age six.

Printed in the USA
CPSIA information can be obtained
at www.ICGtesting.com
LVHW030808291023
762326LV00004B/119